hourglass

Myra McEntire

EGMONT
USA

New York

EGMONT

We bring stories to life

First published by Egmont USA, 2011
443 Park Avenue South, Suite 806
New York, NY 10016

1 3 5 7 9 8 6 4 2

www.egmontusa.com
www.myramcentire.com

Library of Congress Cataloging-in-Publication Data
McEntire, Myra.
Hourglass / Myra McEntire.
p. cm.
Summary: Seventeen-year-old Emerson uses her power to manipulate
time to help Michael, a consultant hired by her brother, to prevent a
murder that happened six months ago while simultaneously navigating
their undeniable attraction to one another.
ISBN 978-1-60684-144-0 (hardcover) — ISBN 978-1-60684-254-6 (e-book)
[1. Psychic ability—Fiction. 2. Space and time—Fiction. 3. Murder—Fiction.
4. Brothers and sisters—Fiction. 5. Orphans—Fiction. 6. Science fiction.
7. Mystery and detective stories.] I. Title.
PZ7.M47845424Hou 2011
[Fic]—dc22
2010043618

Printed in the United States of America

CPSIA tracking label information:
Printed in April 2011 at Berryville Graphics, Berryville, Virginia

To Ethan,

For being my best friend and helping me throw strikes.

And to Andrew and Charlie,

Never be afraid to chase your dreams, because they

really can come true.

What lies behind you and what lies in front of you, pales in comparison to what lies inside of you.

—Ralph Waldo Emerson

Chapter 1

*M*y small Southern hometown is beautiful in the haunting way an aging debutante is beautiful. The bones are exquisite, but the skin could use a lift. You could say my brother, the architect, is Ivy Springs's plastic surgeon.

I shuffled through a relentless late-summer downpour toward one of his renovation projects . . . our home. I couldn't care less about the weather. I was in no hurry. My brother might know what to do with feng shui and flying buttresses and other architectural things, but with me? He had no clue.

Before I'd escaped to take out my frustrations on a treadmill, Thomas and I had argued about my upcoming senior year. I didn't think attending school was necessary. He, being a traditionalist, disagreed.

I reached our building only to find a wide-eyed Southern belle wearing a Civil War–era dress blocking the front door. A silk parasol and a full hoopskirt completed her ensemble. I wore something like it to a costume party once, but hers was an original. Frustration was back, and now it was in my way.

In the form of freaking Scarlett O'Hara.

Sighing, I stuck my hand through her stomach to turn the knob, meeting no resistance. I rolled my eyes as she gasped, fluttered her eyelashes, and disappeared in a puff of air.

"You know, Scarlett, Rhett didn't give a damn, and frankly, I don't either."

A loud crack of thunder sounded as the wind slammed the door shut behind me. I trudged up the stairs and made my grand entrance into our loft—actually a "warehouse to loft apartment conversion"—with my long hair plastered to my face and my pink raincoat dripping water. I found my brother at the kitchen table, a set of massive floor plans spread out in front of him.

"Emerson." Thomas looked up to greet me, folding the plans in half and then unfolding them again. His hopeful smile was the twin of my own—three years' worth of first-rate orthodontia—except I wasn't smiling back today. "I'm glad you're home."

That made one of us.

"I thought I might have to hitch a ride on the ark." Not mentioning my encounter downstairs with Miss O'Hara, I shook the rain from my coat, causing him to wince as a puddle formed on the floor beneath me. He probably had an umbrella stashed somewhere that color coordinated with his outfit. Thomas the Boy

Scout, perpetually prepared. That part of our family's gene pool missed me altogether.

We shared the same blond hair and moss-green eyes, but Thomas inherited our father's square jawline while my face was heart-shaped like our mother's. He was also blessed with Daddy's height. I got shorted in that department. In a major way.

Thomas smoothed out his floor plans a few more times than necessary, hedging. "I'm sorry about our . . . disagreement earlier."

"It's fine. It's not like I have another option." I looked at the floor instead of at him. "I can either go back to school or let a truancy officer haul me to juvy."

"Em . . . we could try new medication. Maybe it would make going back easier?"

"No new meds." Actually, no meds at all. Not that he knew that. The guilt of keeping such a secret almost forced a confession from me. It was on the tip of my tongue, so I opened the fridge to grab a bottle of water and hide my face. "I'll be fine."

"At least you have Lily."

Lily was the only childhood friend I had who still talked to me, and possibly the only good thing about coming back from the boarding school where I'd spent my sophomore and junior years. The official line was that my scholarship for senior year had been cut due to "dwindling alumni donations," but I wondered if maybe they'd just run out of charity for girls with dead parents who occasionally hallucinated and made their classmates uncomfortable. I had money for incidentals from the small trust fund my parents left, but not enough to cover my last year of school. Thomas offered to pay for my senior year so I could stay in Sedona, but I declined. Often and loudly. I would live with him because he was my legal guardian, but I wouldn't accept his money outright.

Back to Tennessee it was. Surely I could survive anything for a year, even public high school.

"I had something else to talk to you about." Thomas flattened the plans again. I kept expecting the ink to rub off the paper. "We . . . We have a new contact. A consultant who says he can help."

Every few months or so Thomas heard a rumor about someone who could help me. So far, they had all been freaks or flakes. I slammed my water bottle down on the counter, crossed my arms over my chest, and leveled a glare at him. "Another one?"

"It's different this time."

"It was different *last* time."

Thomas tried again. "This guy—"

"Has a third eye you can visibly see?"

"Emerson."

"I don't have a lot of faith in your contacts," I countered, crossing my arms more tightly, as if I could protect myself from the onslaught of unwanted "help." "I swear, you must get their names from the popup ads on the paranormal sites you search all the time."

"I only did that . . . twice." He tried not to grin. He failed.

"Where did you find this one?" It was hard to stay mad when he was trying so hard to help. "Fresh from rehab?"

"He works for a place called the Hourglass. The founder was part of the parapsychology department at Bennett University in Memphis."

"The department that was shut down because no one would fund it? Stupendous."

"How did you know about that?" Thomas asked in surprise.

I gave him a look that loosely translated as: I'm a teenager. I know how to work a search engine.

"The Hourglass is a very reputable place, I promise. My contact—"

"Okay, okay . . . if I say I'll meet him, can we stop talking about it?" I asked, holding up my hands in mock surrender. Thomas knew he would win. He always did.

"Thanks, Em. I only do it because I love you." His expression turned serious. "I really do."

"I know." He really did. And regardless of any disagreement, I loved him, too. Eager to avoid any displays of emotion, I looked around for my sister-in-law. "Where's the wife?"

Thomas and Dru were a renovation dream team—interlocking pieces of a puzzle—their skills complementing each other perfectly. I once watched Dru take a sledgehammer to a wall to help speed up work on a job site. When she finished, her manicure was still intact.

"At the restaurant with the new chef. He wanted her opinion on which wines to serve tonight."

"She would know." Her taste was impeccable. Thomas's cell phone started chirping. Seeing my chance at escape, I threw my empty water bottle into the recycling bin. "Getting late. Need a shower."

As the door swung shut behind me, I inhaled the scent of new paint. Dru had recently refinished the walls in the front room with a deep red Venetian plaster. Cozy leather couches with silk-covered pillows in sepia tones complemented hardwood floors. One wall was nothing but plate-glass windows; another was lined with bookshelves holding leather tomes and ragged paperbacks. I ran my fingers across their spines, itching to grab one and settle in. Not tonight. Thomas and Dru had renovated the old phone company into a chichi restaurant that they actually decided to keep and operate instead of selling to an investor. The big opening was in a few hours. My attendance had been requested, sort of as a reintroduction to town society.

My brother had a gift for making broken things shine. I was pretty sure he was hoping that tonight his magic would work on me.

Losing our parents four years ago threw us together, even though Thomas and I hadn't been close when I was growing up. I was a surprise baby, and there were almost two decades between us. He hadn't exactly been ready to raise his younger sister, and I'd done my best to keep my particular brand of crazy out of his life. Receiving that scholarship had been an answer to a prayer. I wanted to get away from my hometown, all its memories, and

Thomas's renovation sites. I didn't like the position I was in, now that my scholarship had evaporated.

Mainly because of "my problem."

"Hello."

The unfamiliar voice threw me off balance. I spun around to see a man standing by the wall of windows, looking unreasonably at home and completely out of place at the same time. Exceptionally handsome, tall, and slim, he was dressed in a black suit. A lock of hair the color of wheat fell over one eyebrow but didn't mask the elegant features of his face. Slipping a silver pocket watch attached to his vest into his pants pocket, he clasped his hands behind his back.

"Can I help you?" I tried to keep the sound of apprehension from my voice but couldn't. He hadn't been there a second ago.

"My name is Jack." He made no attempt to move toward me but stood still, his bright blue eyes assessing me. I shivered. He was giving my goose bumps a field day. I sure hoped this wasn't the new contact Thomas was talking about. He was a little creeptastic for my taste.

"Are you here to see my brother?"

"No, I don't know your brother." A slight smile lifted the corners of his mouth, causing my heart to skip a beat. "Actually, I'm here to see you, Emerson."

The pocket watch and the suit could be from another generation. His hairstyle didn't fall into any specific era. Maybe this guy was one of my hallucinations, but if so . . .

How did he know my name?

Chapter 2

Thomas!" I yelled, before anxiety choked off my air supply.

I turned my head toward the sound of a chair clattering to the floor in the kitchen. It seemed to go on forever. When I looked back at the windows, Jack was gone. Thomas flew into the room, skidding to a stop beside me.

"Why, why, why?" I asked, slumping back against the side of the bookcase, hitting my head against it with each question. "Why do you have to keep renovating buildings? Why can't you just put up a new one?"

Thomas's mouth dropped open in shock. "It happened? Here?"

He was asking about my problem with those who were . . . no longer living.

Not dead, exactly. I hadn't quite figured out *what* the things I saw were; I knew only that I'd never heard a ghost story that involved the ghosts popping like balloons and dissolving if someone touched them. I'd started seeing them when I was thirteen, just before my parents died. Thomas had been renovating an old glass company, turning it into office spaces.

My first time on the job site I'd had a lovely conversation with an older man wearing a hard hat. He smelled of tobacco and sweat. His nose sat slightly off center, the veins decorating the bulbous end indicating he liked his brewski. He was pleasant enough, even offered to share his dinner. I declined, but he insisted I have a taste of the icebox pie his wife had included in his well-used lunch pail.

That was when things got tricky. As he tried to place the food in my hand, I realized he wasn't solid. He came to the same conclusion, dropping the pie and pail, screaming like a woman who forgot to take her panties off the clothesline before the preacher came to call. Then he disappeared. Poof.

Welcome to insanity. He was followed by a long string of people—dead people—who showed up in the strangest of places and disappeared only when I touched them. From my restroom stall at Denny's to the dressing room at Macy's, I never got used to it.

"I can't believe I let you talk me into living here. I should have known nowhere this old was safe. And this guy knew my name."

That had *never* happened before.

Thomas visibly tensed. "He knew your name?"

I nodded, closing my eyes. Jack had also said he was here to see me. Thomas didn't need to know that part.

"Em, I thought it stopped."

My boarding school had been in Sedona, Arizona. Pioneers didn't roll up on the town until the turn of the century, so it wasn't real hard to tell the difference between an ancient Yavapai potter and, say, my gym teacher.

I had thought things were better, but now I wasn't so sure. Unless their clothing was obviously from a different time period, I couldn't always tell if people were part of the here and now or that window from the past. I had become a historical fashion guru, not because I loved clothes but because being able to identify attire from different decades was helpful. Women were easier to nail down, but with the exception of the butterfly collars and blue tuxedos of the 1970s, classic menswear spanned generations and posed a bigger problem.

I avoided any theme parks or museums where the employees dressed true to period. Complete nightmare. I also spent a lot of time trying not to touch people. Unless they happened to be wearing a hoopskirt. And they were standing in my way.

"It did stop. I thought it did," I said.

At least until I flushed my meds.

My brother had walked a hard road with me. Keeping the grief locked away inside—both from losing my parents and the insanity of seeing people who weren't really there—hadn't been a good mental health choice. Hospitalization followed by a strong cocktail of medications to stop the "hallucinations" worked for a while. But last winter, tired of living in a zombielike fog, I took the plunge and weaned myself from the pharmaceuticals without telling anyone.

Even Thomas.

The visions slowly returned. Em the Zombie Girl was gone, but Em the Potentially Psychotic Girl wasn't working out so well either. Now I was back to wondering if the people I spoke to on the street were real.

"I'm sorry, Em."

I looked up at Thomas. "You have no reason to apologize."

"I am the one who bought the building." His eyebrows were puckered so close together it looked like a caterpillar was inching across his forehead.

"Well, hells bells, by all means change your occupation to coddle your freakish little sister." I pushed myself away from the bookcase. "Like I haven't caused enough trouble in your life already."

"Don't say that. You're still going to come to the restaurant opening, aren't you?" Thomas asked, anxiety evident in his expression. "Bring Lily."

Since my feelings of guilt were already on the surface, it didn't take much for Thomas to swing the decision to his advantage.

"We'll be there."

To avoid any more accidental freakiness, I went to Lily's to get ready.

Most of the people I had grown up with avoided me like a cold sore. It all stemmed from the one key public event that got me committed. Long story short, I had a loud argument with a guy in the cafeteria at school about how rude he was to take my seat when I'd only left it to get a fork. I then proceeded to threaten to poke him with said fork.

No one else saw him.

In case the straight-up screaming argument with thin air wasn't enough to convince the lunch crowd I'd gone over the edge, the hysterical laughing that followed did. It turned to blubbering when Lily wrapped her arm around my waist and hurried me to the bathroom.

Lily'd been my best friend since the day we met in third grade. She's always accepted me for who I am, whatever that involves. I do the same for her. I wasn't exaggerating when I told Thomas she was the only reason going back to school in Ivy Springs would be okay.

Lily and her grandmother lived in the apartment above their restaurant. Using the back entrance, I let myself in. I found her in the middle of her living room, stretching her long legs into a Pilates pose. It looked painful. I preferred to run—put in the earbuds and go, keeping my eyes focused on the ground and try-ing not to run through anybody—or to spar. I needed to find the nearest karate studio. Earning my brown belt before I left Arizona made me hungry to train for my black. And as a side benefit, ass kicking can be very relaxing.

"Hey, did you decide what you were wearing tonight?" I asked when she twisted her body in my direction.

"Don't be mad."

"If you aren't going, it's too late. I'm already mad."

"Please?" She dropped to her knees and held her hands together like an orphan begging for more porridge. "I got called in to a night shoot. Some cavern wants stills for their Web site."

Lily works a camera as easily as some people work a toaster. Her talent had snagged her a summer job as an assistant to one of the Appalachians' most successful nature photographers. "Tell me you know I wouldn't bail if I thought I could get out of it and keep my job."

I rolled my eyes. "I know you wouldn't bail if you thought you could get out of it and keep your job."

"Thank you, thank you." Lily scooted across the room on her knees to wrap her arms around me in a hug. "Oh, look at that, I'm practically your height now."

Laughing, I gave her a shove in the direction of her exercise mat and went to her room to put my stuff down, laying the dress my sister-in-law had coerced me into wearing on Lily's bed along with shoes, purse, and jewelry. Dru had given me very specific instructions about how to put it all together. Sometimes she made me feel like I wasn't capable of dressing myself. I am; it's just that I've always been a minimalist. And accessories confuse me.

While Lily finished her contortions, I took a shower, then used her computer to do a quick Internet search on the Hourglass.

I liked to be prepared when it came to my brother and his parade of physicians, therapists, and witch doctors, but aside from an assortment of shopping results and one particularly embarrassing link to a strip club, I got nothing. I didn't have time to look extensively because I knew Thomas would kill me if I wasn't on time.

Dru really did have exquisite taste. The black velvet dress had a ruched waist, three-quarter length fitted sleeves, and a short skirt that swung like a bell when I walked. Assuming I would be able to walk once I put on my shoes. They were killer. I don't mean they looked good, even though they did. I mean, they were really high and pointy, and although I'm not clumsy, they were potentially lethal both to me and anyone in my general vicinity.

Lily came into the room fresh from her workout—or not so fresh if you were standing downwind—just as I blotted my dark red lipstick.

"You look dramatic and mysterious," she said, sucking in her cheeks and fluttering her lashes, much like Scarlett had earlier this afternoon. "I like to see you live up to your potential."

"Wow, that's high praise coming from you."

She crossed her eyes and started messing with my hair.

A classic beauty with skin the color of caramel, Lily's the kind of girl who causes men to run into street signs and trip over chairs because they're too busy looking at her to walk. If she didn't have a wicked sense of humor and more loyalty than a Saint Bernard, I would probably hate her on principle alone. I felt for the necklace

Dru had sent with the dress, sure I'd put it on, while Lily pulled and twisted pieces of hair around my face.

"The necklace is still on the dresser," Lily said, not taking her eyes away from me. "Your earrings are in the bag on the bed."

I smacked her hands away. "How do you always know where to find things? And are you sure you can't go? You could meet the boy of your dreams."

"There's not a boy alive like the one in my dreams," she muttered, glancing toward the dresser before reaching out to fiddle with another wayward strand of hair. "All the rest are too much trouble."

"Well, if he *were* alive, he wouldn't be able to get past the smell. Hit the showers." I smacked her playfully on the backside. "I don't want to absorb your stink."

She laughed and left the room in an exaggerated runway walk, but stuck her head back around the doorframe to flash her killer smile. "You really do look gorgeous. Try not to hurt your-self in those shoes."

I turned to assess the finished product in the mirror. After spraying myself with my favorite perfume, a light lilac scent with a hint of vanilla, I scooped up my wrap and purse. I was almost out the door when I remembered my umbrella. It didn't color coordinate. Maybe they wouldn't let me in.

Chapter 3

*N*o such luck.

When I entered the Phone Company, I got two thumbs up from Dru and an obnoxious catcall from my brother. After explaining that I was flying solo, I politely said hello to all the "important people" as Thomas introduced me, the images of their faces erased by the glare from more sequins, beading, and diamonds than should ever be allowed on a human who isn't walking the red carpet. As soon as I could get away, I hid behind the jazz trio, practically under the spiral staircase near the bar, sipping on some kind of sparkling fruit juice and trying to blend into the wall. Watching the show.

And I had slipped out of the killer shoes.

I'd always leaned toward the shy side but was never unsocial until I started seeing visions of people from the past. It's a really strange existence, not knowing if the person you're talking to is physically there or not. Not knowing if you're one hallucination away from a psychotic break. Once I began having visions on a regular basis, I would watch to see if someone wasn't getting any attention, which was a big clue that that person might not actually be there. Of course, I usually ended up feeling sorry for those people and talked to them anyway. Although I made sure no one was watching.

Just in case.

A long time ago I'd decided against popping the people I saw like balloons. Sticking my hand out into what looked like a person, only to meet thin air . . . it had to freak them out as much as it did me. I tried to leave the visions alone, unless I had to walk through them.

At least things had been normal so far tonight. I was beginning to relax when I saw a young guy standing by the back patio doors at the other end of the room. His broad shoulders showed off a very well-cut black tux, which looked amazing on him but was unfortunate for me. Sizing him up, I ran through the usual checklist of details that helped me determine if someone was alive or not. First was clothing style. Black tie was way harder for me than street clothes. It was called classic for a reason, and he was as classic as they came.

His black hair was on the longish side—no help there either. Casually sexy, but no definitive style. I focused on his face. Clean shaven, but I'd bet his five o'clock shadow was heavy. Wickedly arched eyebrows accented long-lidded dark eyes. Olive skin suggested Mediterranean ancestors, and his defined cheekbones were congruous with the angles of his face. The exception was his very full mouth. His lips disturbed me.

I really hoped he was alive.

I gave myself a mental shake. What was I doing? Lips weren't on my checklist. And when it came to guys—drop-dead gorgeous or not—I never got caught staring. But if the slow grin spreading across his face was any indication, I just had. Shoving my feet back into the killer heels, I searched the room for Thomas and Dru but couldn't see them. I looked back at Tuxedo Guy. He was walking straight toward me.

Time to go. I reached out to leave my glass on the edge of the piano, then watched, shocked, as it went right through and crashed to the ground, a thousand little glistening diamonds on the ceramic tile.

My brother materialized immediately. "Are you okay?"

"No. Unless you see the jazz trio?" Please, please . . .

"Don't see them."

"Then no, definitely not okay." The phantom musicians kept playing. I hadn't attempted to come into physical contact with any of them—probably the only reason they didn't fade away.

They. Three at once? And a *piano*? I'd never seen a whole *scene* before. I couldn't breathe. "I need air. I need air!"

"Excuse us." Thomas smiled at the real live people nearby, the gracious host aiding his slightly hysterical sister. He guided me across the wide room to the French doors that led outside. It was a horrifying journey. I tried to pretend I didn't see all the eyes following us. We exited onto the patio, empty due to the chill in the air from the earlier rain.

I took a deep breath, willing the adrenaline rush coursing through my system to slow down. "How many old buildings do you plan on renovating for public consumption? Just so I can prepare myself."

At least I didn't live in Europe. Whole centuries of long dead people walked around over there. In the U.S., I only had to deal with a few generations of those who could be confused for living in the present time. When Thomas and Dru had tried to plan a day trip to the annual Cherokee Indian Fair in North Carolina, I had flat refused. No historical reenactments. Ever.

"I can't believe it's this bad," Thomas said, patting my arm in an attempt to extend comfort. I just shook my head. Now wasn't the time to come clean about the meds.

Especially since the guy in the tux was walking through the open double doors.

"Do you see him?" I whispered, covering my eyes with my hands and peeking out between my trembling fingers, shaken by the thought of another vision so soon after the jazz trio.

"Do I see who?"

"Him." I motioned for Thomas to look over his shoulder. If Tuxedo Guy wasn't a living, breathing human being from this century, I was going to beg to be recommitted.

"Yes, I see him," Thomas answered, the words ripe with relief. "That's Michael."

"Who's Michael?"

"He's the new consultant I was telling you about."

Chapter 4

*T*uxedo Guy looked even better the closer he got to us—tall, wide shoulders, smooth skin, those lips. I couldn't believe he worked for a place called the Hourglass. Fifty-year-old bespectacled men with paunches should work for the Hourglass. Not a prince too gorgeous to be walking around with the peasants. He couldn't be much older than me. Maybe he was an intern. Maybe Thomas got him on the cheap because he played in the minor leagues instead of with the big boys.

"Were you going to tell me he was here?" I said under my breath to Thomas, my emotions raging in the space between anger and horror.

"I was going to let him observe you first."

"Like some kind of specimen?" I hissed. "Where's my glass jar?"

I was ready to launch into a tirade but stopped when I realized

Tuxedo Guy stood two feet away, eyeing me as if I might suddenly burst into flames.

"Michael Weaver, meet my sister, Emerson Cole." Thomas's hand on my back pushed me slightly forward, the motion suggesting he thought Michael and I should shake.

Michael looked from Thomas to me and tentatively held out his hand. I shuddered, turning away to hide my face in my brother's shoulder. Even if Thomas's acknowledging his presence proved he was currently alive, I didn't want to touch Michael. When I looked back at him, he'd slipped his hand into his pocket.

The door to the patio opened once again, and this time it was Dru. I assumed Thomas hadn't given her the latest news about my hallucinations, with all the preparations for the opening they'd done that day. I didn't want her fussing over me.

"I'm sorry I'm so clumsy." I waved her away as she started to hover, the motion helping to hide the shaking of my hand. "Everything is fine, go back inside."

Dru has the kind of blue eyes most people describe as icy, which I really don't understand, because ice is clear. Right now they exuded worry.

"You're not clumsy; that's why I'm concerned," she said, ignoring my protests and placing her hand on my forehead before moving it to my cheek. "Are you sick? Are you feeling faint? Do you need food? Do you need to sit?"

"Couldn't be better. Really," I lied through my perfect teeth. What I needed was a way to escape the jazz trio I could still hear and the gorgeous consultant standing beside me. I really wished he were a little less male model, a little more tax auditor. I felt distracted enough already.

"In that case, Thomas, I hate to pull you away, but Brad from the bank wanted to talk to you regarding that property on Main." She raised her well-groomed eyebrows, so I knew it must be a lucrative deal. "I can stay here."

Thomas's pained expression exposed his inner battle. I let him off the hook. "Go. You too, Dru. Make money."

"No, I'll stay with you, sweetie. I want to make sure you're okay." Dru tucked her arm around my waist to give me a quick squeeze.

"No. Really. Go. I'm fine," I insisted.

"Will you stay with her?" Thomas asked Michael, his voice as serious as if he were negotiating my dowry. Or a real estate deal. "I don't want to leave her alone."

I shot Thomas an evil look. He was so going to pay for that later.

"Absolutely," Michael answered.

I jumped at his voice, the sound putting every cell in my body on alert. It was mellow, husky. I'd bet he could sing. After I assured Thomas and Dru again that I was fine, I watched the only familiar people in the building walk away and wished desperately to be any-where else in the world . . . except maybe Colonial Williamsburg.

I exhaled deeply, looked up at Michael, and offered a smile. When he returned it, my breath caught in my throat.

Buttered biscuits and honey.

"You're not what I expected," I said, hating the way my voice broke slightly in the middle of the sentence.

"I've heard that before," he said, scoring major points by pretending not to notice.

"I'm glad you're close to my age." Please be close to my age. "Makes me feel like we're on an even playing field."

"I didn't realize we were playing a game." His dark eyes narrowed slightly. He was probably already wondering if he was getting paid enough to deal with me. "Should I call you Em or Emerson?"

I frowned. I didn't recall anyone calling me Em in his presence.

"Emerson will be fine for now. Are you Michael or Mike? Or Mikey?"

"Do I *look* like a Mikey?" he asked.

"Um . . . no."

"Michael will be fine. For now," he said, pressing his lips together. Not in a prudish way. In a very sexy, trying-to-hide-his-smile way.

He reached out to run his hand over the wrought-iron fence that lined the patio, and then turned to face me, shaking the rain from his fingers. "Your brother has a gift. I've never seen someone put so much effort into recapturing the beauty of a place. Did he renovate all of these buildings?"

The patio displayed a bird's-eye view of the award-winning

restoration prominently featured in the town square. Warm light shone behind many of the second- and third-story loft windows, home mostly to young professionals and empty nesters, with the occasional family thrown in for balance. Replicas of antique gas lanterns lit streets lined by quaint businesses, antique shops, coffeehouses, and galleries. Window boxes and planters spilled out brightly colored seasonal flowers. Even though it currently ranked in the top ten of America's best small towns, it was too easy to imagine it as it had been a century ago, which was proving to be a problem for me.

No way was that horse-drawn carriage real.

The beginning notes of Rodgers and Hart's "Bewitched" floated through the rain-scented air, mixing with the smell of the purple sweet peas climbing the iron fence. I looked away from the overactive town square and refocused on Michael.

"Yes, Thomas had a hand in every single renovation. His vision is very specific." And expensive . . . yet somehow always profitable.

"How's your vision?" Sneaky. His tone was light, but I could sense the deeper question behind the words. I wondered what Thomas had told him about me.

I reached out to wrap my fingers around the iron bars, avoiding the damp sweet peas. "Why are you here, Michael Weaver?"

"To help you." The concern on his face was a welcome difference. He looked like he wanted to know what my problem was. I almost wanted to tell him.

Almost.

Instead, I let out a derisive laugh. Leaning away from the fence, I held on with one arm and swung back and forth slightly, like I'd done on the poles that held up my swing set when I was a little girl. "'To help you.' That line is so tired."

"How many times have you heard it?"

"Let's see, there were the two sisters who claimed they could see into my past and my future. Apparently I'm a descendant of Mata Hari, who is somehow next in line for the Finnish throne."

"There's not a—"

"*I know.*"

"Ouch." A sympathetic crease formed between his eyebrows.

"I made Thomas give me the refund on that one—*and* his credit card—so I could go for some shopping therapy. I tried really hard to bankrupt him." I grinned at the semihappy memory, and Michael smiled with me. It almost made me forget what I was saying. "Um . . . then there was the shaman who thought I needed to be exorcised. That one was fabulous; he claimed he could do it with pickle juice and ashes."

Michael shook his head in disbelief. "Where does your brother find these people? He's clearly a shrewd businessman—why would he hire such obvious frauds?"

"Desperation? My boarding school was in Sedona. No shortage of 'spiritual healers' there. I guess the news that a concerned brother was throwing around a surplus of cash to help his loopy sister spread pretty fast. And none of the people using traditional methods could help me. They all wanted to drug me into a vegetative state or commit me." I let go of the iron bar and bit down hard on my bottom lip, stopping short of telling him they succeeded, angry with myself for being so honest. If he was a fake like all the others, maybe he would feel guilty and go away before inflicting any damage.

"I'm sorry," Michael said. No pity, just empathy. His expression was easy to read, or he was a really good actor. He reminded me of old Hollywood, very Cary Grant–ish, except for the slightly shaggy hair.

"So what's different about you?" I asked, growing weary of the conversation. Already anticipating the disappointment. "What kind of promises are you going to make?"

"None that I can't keep." The set of his jaw was resolute, his voice full of certainty.

"What are your qualifications? Did you climb a mountain and meet with a guru?" I asked, baiting him. Wanting a reaction. "Did you have an out-of-body experience, and now people speak to you through mirrors and mud puddles?"

"Listen, I can understand why you don't have a lot of faith"— he kept his voice low and even, but I suspected a hint of temper— "but what if I *can* help you? Why wouldn't you let me?"

"What if I don't think anything's wrong with me?" Not anything I expected him to be able to fix, anyway.

"I didn't say there was."

"Offering to help me implies I'm in distress. I'm not currently."

"What about ten minutes ago when you tried to put your drink on a piano that wasn't there?"

"That wasn't distress. That was . . ." I sucked wind.

He saw the piano.

Chapter 5

I punched him in the stomach. Hello six-pack. Even with the protective layer of muscle, he let out a rush of air and bent over, wrapping his arms around his middle.

"I'm sorry, I'm sorry," I apologized, shaking the feeling back into my tingling hand. The streetlights seemed to flicker, and I wondered fleetingly if we were in for another storm. "I needed to make sure you were really here."

"And there wasn't a better way to do it?" Michael groaned. He was lucky I aimed high. I'd considered kicking him, but remembered my lethal shoes at the last moment.

"Stress reaction." I shrugged and stepped out of my high-heeled weapons before I had the urge to do any more damage, appreciating the feel of the cool concrete beneath my feet.

Michael straightened, looking down at me and sizing me up.

I couldn't tell if he liked what he saw. Was surprised to find that it mattered.

"Why were you worried about whether or not I was real? You wouldn't shake my hand a few minutes ago, even though your brother saw me."

"It's been a different kind of day. My world's been turned upside down and sideways."

"Probably for the best anyway." He gave me a grin that made me wonder what he wasn't saying. "So tell me, what's been so different about today?"

"I've never seen a full jazz trio before, for one thing. It threw me off. The rules must be changing."

"What are the rules?"

"I see people from the past." The bells in the clock tower on the town square loudly chimed the hour, but I kept my voice low. "They're like a film projection, no substance, and when I try to touch them, they disappear. I've sure as heck never seen three at once accompanied by a piano." Or a horse-drawn carriage.

"At least they sounded good. That bass was smooth." He inclined his head toward the building, where the music spilled from the open windows. "Still is."

"You don't seem to be impressed. No one's ever been able to see or hear what I do. What's your story?" I asked, although it was clear. He was as screwed up as I was.

"Let's just say my mom thought I had a lot of imaginary friends."

I tilted my chin up to get a better look at him. "So it's been happening since you were little?"

Michael nodded. "You?"

"Four years." The bells stopped after ten chimes, and the air felt eerily quiet. Time for a subject change. Distract and divert. "I really am sorry I hit you."

"You're forgiven." He winked. "I think I can handle a tiny little thing like you."

I bit my tongue. So we would work on the male chauvinism.

"If you help me, how does it work? Do we have . . . sessions or something? What are you going to do to me?" Oops. Scary, scary light in his eyes. I cleared my throat. I would need to watch my phrasing. "I mean, *for* me."

The light didn't fade as he answered. "I'd like to start by hearing your story."

"Simple enough." As if reliving every terrifying moment was easy. As if I wanted to make myself vulnerable to a total stranger. I rubbed the knot of tension forming at the base of my neck.

"Emerson." I loved the way he said my name. Or maybe I just liked watching his lips move. "I know this is hard for you, but I want you to be honest with me. You can trust me."

He obviously had not heard the rule that you *never* trust anyone who says "you can trust me."

"We'll see how things go. When do we start?" I asked.

"How does tomorrow sound?"

Too soon.

The next morning I dressed in my favorite jeans and a black fitted T-shirt, slipping on my black Converse sneakers for comfort and courage. They always made me feel ballsy. Twisting my hair into an updo, I pulled out some of the pieces the sun had made blonder than the others. I took a little more care with my makeup than usual, playing up my clear complexion. All for breakfast with Michael.

Hmm.

I walked through downtown slowly, enjoying the peace. The humidity hadn't kicked in yet, and after yesterday's rain I could almost smell the crisp air of the approaching autumn. I was a sucker for falling leaves, hayrides, scarecrows, and especially Halloween. When your everyday life was as spooky as mine, Halloween really was all about ridiculous amounts of candy and the Great Pumpkin—as long as I stayed home to answer the door. None of my visions had ever rung the doorbell, so I was generally pretty safe with Charlie Brown on the television and a contraband stash of Twizzlers in my hands.

Michael and I were meeting at Murphy's Law, the combo coffeehouse/café/bookstore owned by Lily's grandmother. Not only is the woman a saint, but she makes killer Cuban espresso and apple empanadas that taste so good they'd make a nun cuss. There was only one downside to the location.

When I'd suggested Murphy's Law the night before, I'd been too flustered to consider that Lily could be present during the meeting. I was saved from having to develop a plausible story to tell her when I ran into her on the sidewalk, heading away from the building. She had her camera bag slung over her shoulder.

"Lily! How did the shoot go?"

She faced me but continued walking backward. "Pretty well. Except for the bats the boss failed to mention. That and the film crew. At least I was only hit on by one production assistant this time."

"Wow, just one guy? You must be losing it." Lily's boss sometimes worked in conjunction with documentary filmmakers. She claimed most of them displayed more entitlement issues than the whole of the English monarchy. And most of them thought they were entitled to her.

"Losing it? We can only hope." She reached into her camera bag, fumbling around before pulling out a huge blueberry muffin wrapped in a napkin and taking a bite.

"Are you in a hurry?" I asked, trying to be nonchalant. I tilted my head toward her camera bag. "Another shoot?"

"Clean up from last night, maybe a little Photo-Chop." She stopped walking and looked at me. Her eyes widened along with her mouth, and she treated me to a glimpse of chewed-up bread. "Look at you, all sexy first thing in the morning. Where are you going? How did the party go?"

I mentally debated telling her about Michael. There was no way I really could without giving her the whole story, and Lily was mostly in the dark about my . . . visions.

"Nowhere really. And you didn't miss a thing." Except a jazz trio, some broken glass, and the most gorgeous guy who ever drew a breath. "Go. We'll talk later."

Lily raised the hand that was holding the muffin to look at her watch. She hated being late, but I could see the desire to interrogate me in her expression. I hoped manners would beat out curiosity.

"You'd better," she said over her shoulder as she ducked down the side street that led to the photography studio.

Close one.

Pausing in front of the coffeehouse, I placed my palm to my stomach, trying to quiet the butterflies fluttering inside. I couldn't decide if I was anxious because of the upcoming discussion or whom I was about to see. I pushed through the front door, setting the bell attached to the doorframe jingling, breathing deeply to inhale the rich scent of brewing coffee. And to calm my nerves.

Michael sat near the back, reading a paper in something that looked like Spanish. After I ordered I joined him, tucking my backpack under the table and pulling out a chair. He had a day's worth of stubble and was dressed almost exactly like me in a black T-shirt with a well-worn pair of jeans. I took a moment to appreciate the snug fit of both. The boy's muscles had muscles.

"Are you really reading that, or are you just trying to show off?" I asked, lowering myself into the seat.

He looked over the paper, opened his mouth, and a torrent of foreign words flew out.

"Okay, sorry, just asking. Wait, how many of those were curse words?"

Michael laughed, flashing white, even teeth. It was a good sound, comfortable, like he did it a lot. I wished I could laugh like that. His smile distracted me just as much as it had the night before.

"What language was that?"

"Italian."

"How did you learn Italian?"

"My grandmother." Michael put the paper down and leaned across the table toward me, unexpectedly intense. "What do you want?"

"I already ordered an espresso," I answered, reflexively leaning back.

"No, I mean what do you want from life?"

"Good morning to you, too. Isn't it a little early for philosophy?" I pushed a stray strand of hair back from my face and shifted in my chair.

"Why does the question make you uncomfortable?"

"I don't go around discussing my deepest desires with strangers." The waitress brought my drink and empanada to the table. When she walked away, I continued. "Technically, you might not be a stranger, but still, I just met you yesterday."

"I'm not so strange." Another distracting flash of white teeth. "Let's start with something simpler than what you want from life. What do you want from today?"

I wrapped my hands around the cup I held to blow on the

contents, feeling the steam rise to my face. Maybe he would think I was just . . . warm . . . instead of blushing.

Michael looked at me as if he had all the time in the world to listen, so genuine he threw me off balance. The butterflies in my stomach stirred. I wasn't ready to be completely honest with him. Maybe I never would be. I wasn't a very good liar. But avoidance?

At avoidance I was a master.

"Why don't you tell me about yourself? I'm sure I would be more comfortable with this whole situation if I knew more about you." There. He couldn't argue with that. And I really did want to know more about him. A lot more.

Michael placed his hands on the table. His fingers were long, his nails squared off but a little longer on his right hand, making me wonder if he played the guitar. He wore a silver ring on his left thumb.

"I have a sister; her name is Anna Sophia. My mom is in real estate, high-end historical homes, very successful—a lot like Thomas. She's also my hero. My dad has been out of the picture since I was eight or so." He gave me a small smile. I wondered about the rest of the story. "I grew up outside Atlanta, and I've been working for the Hourglass for almost a year."

Since my Internet research returned void, I knew nothing about the Hourglass, but the mental image in my brain involved Marlon Brando in the back room of an Italian restaurant surrounded by cigar smoke and heavily armed men named Paulie and Vito. I needed a clearer picture. Or at least a less frightening one.

"What does the Hourglass do, exactly?" I asked.

"Consulting jobs, mentoring."

"How did you find them? Or did they find you?"

"They found me. I was assigned a mentor, who helped me learn about my ability. When I came here for college last year, I started doing small consulting jobs. Talking to kids who needed a friend, gathering information, stuff like that. Then things changed. When my mentor died"—he paused, taking a deep breath—"I asked for more responsibility. I wanted to give back what I had been given."

Michael's eyes and the set of his mouth expressed pain and something else, maybe anger. I could only guess how much emotion was swirling underneath the surface.

"I'm sorry about your friend."

"Life is about gains and losses," he said, the pain winning out over the anger in his eyes. "You know that firsthand."

Except my life was too heavy on the losses. "What kind of job am I? Consulting or mentoring?"

"Part of what I do is talk to people who are struggling to accept themselves. I listen." He shrugged.

"Like you're listening to me."

"You're different."

"I am?"

"Yep." He grinned, and the butterflies in my stomach were sucked up into a hurricane. "I'd listen to you anyway."

I stuck my face in my tiny cup again. After I took another sip of coffee I asked, "So you're already in college?"

"I'm getting ready to start my sophomore year. What about you?"

"Thomas's plans are to enroll me at Ivy Springs High School for my senior year. I only have a semester left because I've done summer school the past two years. Really, I just want to take my G.E.D. and get it over with. But Thomas won't let me." I laughed, but there was no joy in it. The last thing I wanted to do was go back to the scene of my public mental collapse. "I wish he would. I need a break."

"My guess is that if anyone deserves a break, it's you," Michael said, his voice full of understanding. "Maybe you can find another alternative for school that you and Thomas can agree on."

"Maybe." But doubtful. "Anyway, I'll try to get myself straightened out as soon as possible. So you can move on to keggers, football games, and sorority girls."

"I don't drink, I prefer professional baseball, and sorority girls aren't really my type."

I bet they wished they were.

"And Emerson," Michael said, resting his forearms on the table and looking into my eyes. "Just to be clear. There's nothing wrong with you."

Uncomfortable with the sentiment and his proximity, I looked away. "Thanks for the vote of confidence. But I disagree. No offense."

I heard him sigh. "I know you have more questions. Why don't you go ahead and ask them?"

Stalling, I twisted my napkin between my fingers under the table. Michael could see the same things I could, but he wasn't freaked out. He came across as calm, comforting. Talking to him almost made the tightness in my chest go away. I wanted to trust him. I wanted to ask him questions. I wanted to know why it was different for him than it was for me, because it obviously was.

"What was it like the first time you saw a vision from the past?" I asked in a low voice.

"My mom found a deal on a house in the Peachtree District of Atlanta. Civil War era."

I thought of yesterday's experience with Scarlett and couldn't suppress my groan. Right after I started seeing things, I was forced to go on a field trip to one of the unfortunate Civil War reenactments we're so given to here in the South. I'd had no idea who was dead or alive. I didn't come out of my room for a week afterward.

"The things we see . . . what are they?" I met his eyes. "I mean, I have no idea why, but I never really thought of them as ghosts. But I don't know what they are. Do you?"

Michael leaned closer. "I call them time ripples, rips for short. Almost like time stamps left by those who make a deep impression on the world while they're alive. That's the basic definition."

"Isn't that the same thing as a ghost?"

"It's a little more complicated than that."

"How?"

"It's kind of hard to explain," Michael answered, frowning and drumming his fingers on the tabletop. "It involves theoretical physics, but I'd be glad to—"

I held up one hand. "No, thanks. I'll just believe you. For now."

I thought about his definition. The man I saw yesterday came immediately to mind. I was sure he'd made impressions in his own way. "Time ripples. At least that explains why I see people from the past. It makes sense, as if crazy ever could make sense. Sorry."

"Don't apologize." He frowned again. "I don't want you to edit anything you say."

"You won't have to worry about that." I gave him a bleak look. "Most of what comes out is complete truth. My edit button is broken."

"Good." Michael leaned back in his chair, crossing his arms over his chest and stretching out his long legs underneath the table. His black biker boots were huge next to my small sneakers. "I'm a big fan of the truth. I hate it when people hide things."

I knew all about hiding things.

"How many people know the truth about you?" I asked.

"My family, the Hourglass." He cleared his throat and twisted the ring on his thumb. "A few good friends. A select few."

I wondered if the select few included a girlfriend. I wanted to ask, but figured I should probably keep things professional. "Was it hard? Telling them about the things we see?"

"Not really. Some of them have special qualities of their own."

"The same as us?" I liked grouping myself in his category. It was disturbing to realize how much I wanted to be the only one in it besides him.

"No."

"So there are other people who have . . . special . . . things they can do?"

"More than you would think," he answered, his gaze steady on my face.

"Hmm." I rolled that around in my brain while concentrating on my empanada. Michael gave me the space I needed, returning to his newspaper.

The moment I started seeing things . . . ripples . . . I turned into a freak show. Then I became a freak show with no parents. When kids are orphaned—it happens—they might go under for a while, but they recover. I didn't. I didn't even resurface for air until I'd spent quality time in a private hospital with intensive therapy and nuclear-powered drugs.

Now Michael sat across from me, as normal as next Tuesday, claiming he was like me. Claiming that there were other "special" people out there. The idea that others existed with abilities, people I could possibly form relationships with—the thought both overwhelmed and comforted me. I could already think of one I wouldn't mind forming a relationship with—and he was sneaking looks at me from behind his paper. I could almost believe he was checking me out.

But he was probably just waiting for me to go kooks and wanted to make sure he saw it coming.

"Okay," I broke the silence. "What do I need to do?"

"It all goes back to my original question." He folded his newspaper in half and placed it on the table. "What do you want?"

"I want to be normal, but I know that's not possible."

"Normal is overrated." His grin was delicious.

"Well . . ." I faltered, distracted by his mouth again. "If normal isn't an option, I guess I just want to be able to understand as much as I can about the way I am."

"The way we are," he corrected. "How about dinner tonight? You can take the rest of the day to think up more questions for me."

Dinner. Tonight. Oh my. Yes. "I'll get us a reservation at the Phone Company. I have an in. Seven?"

"It's a date," he said, smiling as he stood to leave. As quickly as his smile appeared, it faded away. "Um, not a date, exactly. The Hourglass doesn't look too fondly on its employees mixing business with . . . pleasure."

I smiled back as he walked away, but all the lovely butterflies in my stomach landed one by one in a cold, dead heap.

Of course they didn't.

Chapter 6

On my way home I stopped by the Phone Company to make reservations. Thomas decided since everyone kept calling it the Phone Company, regardless of any name he tried to attach to it, he'd stick with it. He used the old logo and decorated with recycled hardware from the building. Very quaint, lots of shiny dark wood and polished metal. Nice, if you liked that kind of thing.

Apparently, a lot of people did, because without my connections I couldn't have gotten us a table. I wasn't shy about using them either, practically forcing the hostess to write my name at the very top of the reservation list. No way would I miss out on this date . . . dinner. I almost let a nervous giggle escape, but I swallowed it. The hostess looked up at me from the corner of her eye. I knew I was just providing more fuel for the town gossip fire. Fire it up.

Reservations in place, I walked across the square to the loft, willing myself to keep my eyes to the ground and go with the flow. I almost made it, but as I stepped up from the asphalt street onto the concrete sidewalk, I stepped *through* a 1970s hippie chick with love beads. She popped and disappeared in a tiny gust of air, just like ripples—at least I had a name for them now—always had.

I considered closing my eyes and feeling my way up to the loft, but I didn't want to cause myself any unnecessary injuries before dinner. Silence greeted me when I opened the front door, and I was grateful for the chance to decompress and be alone.

Dru had decorated my room right before I came back to town, and it reflected my personality down to the last detail. Deep brown walls, a few shades lighter than my espresso from breakfast. White furniture with clean lines was accented by upholstery in soft corals that made the room come alive, and thoughtfully placed photos in frames made it feel like home. A leather chair and ottoman sat between two corner windows. Well-framed prints by John William Waterhouse lined the wall behind my bed. My favorite, *The Lady of Shalott*, resting in the exact center. A large mirror hung over a dresser topped with a small lamp.

Dru walked in without knocking, startling me.

"I'm sorry, Em. I didn't know you were home." She put a fluffy tangerine-colored throw that still had the tags attached on the edge of my bed before backing toward the door. "I saw this today and thought it would be nice to cover up with. I'll leave you alone."

"Stay. You know, you don't have to keep buying me things." I said the words softly as I sat down on my bed and pulled the throw into my lap. I wanted her to know she didn't have to try so hard. "But I love it. Thank you."

She blushed, her porcelain skin glowing even more than usual, pleased that I was pleased. I owed a lot to Dru. Not only had she accepted me into her life as a surrogate daughter when still newly married to Thomas; she'd gone out of her way to make sure I felt loved when I had to come back home. She made me feel like leaving school didn't mean I was a failure—constantly reminding me that it wasn't my fault my scholarship had been cut.

"So," she said, dropping into the leather chair in the corner, "will you tell me about Michael? He's not exactly like the others, is he?"

I tried for about a half a second to keep my opinion to myself.

"I can't stop thinking about his mouth." Time to get my edit button repaired. I hadn't meant to be *that* honest. I felt my eyes get huge and my face go hot, and I hoped frantically that Dru hadn't heard me clearly.

She had.

"*What?* Emerson Cole, I have never heard you say anything like that in your entire life!"

I bit my lip, but the giggles escaped anyway. It felt completely normal, unlike me. Dru joined in.

"Well"—she wiped her eyes on her shirtsleeve—"your brother might not be, but I'm glad to hear it. You've dealt with a lot in the past few years," she said, her voice growing serious. "More than most people deal with in a lifetime."

As much as I didn't want to talk about the past, it kept coming up today. Time to work in some more avoidance. I kicked off my shoes and pulled my knees up to my chest, wrapping my arms around my legs. "Michael and I are going to have dinner later."

"It's not a date, is it?"

I rolled my eyes. "I wish. He was careful to make the point that the Hourglass doesn't allow employee/client *privileges*."

It was Dru's turn for an eye roll. "I know all about that. Thomas clarified it with Michael several times before he hired him. But still . . . I saw Michael looking at you last night."

"I dropped a glass and almost hyperventilated in the middle of your party. Everyone was looking at me."

"No, before that."

I'd seen it, too.

Maybe he was just happy to find someone else like him, or maybe the whole opposites-attract thing was baloney. I wouldn't know. I'd been so busy hiding out the past few years I'd never been out on a normal date. Group dates, sure, which were their own particular brand of hell if I didn't know everyone, but never a regular date and certainly never a blind date. Yeesh. Anyway, whether I wanted it to be or not, tonight wasn't a date.

"Tonight isn't a date." I said it out loud, reminding myself. "It's a business dinner—he's getting paid to take me out. Thomas hired him. It's not like Michael turned up and asked for an introduction."

Dru didn't meet my eyes. "What are you going to wear?"

I could practically see her fingers twitching, desperate to help me clothe myself. "How about I leave it up to you?"

Two minutes later she handed me another pair of killer heels and a dress in a shimmery copper color. "This. It'll make the green in your eyes stand out. I'm going to make a call. I want to make sure you two get the perfect table. And we got a wine shipment, so I'll be there tonight. But I swear I'll act like I don't know you. Now scoot!"

It was a testament to how much I loved her that I let her boss me around that way.

When I was at boarding school I would have killed for a bathroom like the one I had now. Heaven. All the times I crammed myself into one of the tiny shower stalls with their dinky plastic curtains or waited for an empty sink so I could brush my teeth simply floated away, completely forgotten. I luxuriated in the spray of the shower heads—three of them, and all adjustable. They felt amazing once I'd figured out how to aim them so that I wouldn't drown. I resisted the urge to linger. As seductive as the shower was, it couldn't compete with the evening I was anticipating.

Or rather, the company I was going to keep.

I walked into my bedroom in my towel and submitted before she asked, sitting down in front of Dru. She was armed with her makeup bag and various hair-styling instruments. It was all art to her, from applying makeup to dressing people to decorating buildings. She had the aesthetic thing nailed. I knew firsthand that she excelled at taking care of people.

When she finished, I put on the dress and looked in the mirror. My eyes did look greener than usual. My hair felt like silk flowing over my bare shoulders. Dru dusted my collarbone and upper chest with some sort of luminous-looking powder that smelled like spun sugar, and between it and the metallic dress I felt really shiny. She had done my makeup in soft iridescent colors that also made me feel very . . . shiny. Like one of those reflective Christmas globes.

"Are you sure about this?" I asked.

"Trust me." She apparently never heard the trust-me rule either. At my doubtful look Dru said, "No, I'm serious. The lighting in the Phone Company is very soft, lots of candlelight. You'll glow."

"Aliens glow."

"Not like that. Here." She turned on the small lamp on my dresser and turned off the overhead light, pulling my now straight curtain of blonde hair back from my face. I looked in the mirror again. An exotic stranger stared back at me.

"He's going to think I tried too hard."

"He's going to be too busy looking at you to think much of anything."

And that didn't make me nervous at all.

Chapter 7

I arrived at the restaurant early to wait for him, thinking I'd be more comfortable if I were seated first. The maître d' led me to an intimate little table for two, tucked into a cozy alcove and illuminated by two brushed metal sconces. I felt like some kind of seductress and considered switching tables, but that changed when I caught a glimpse of Michael walking toward me.

His crisp white shirt complemented his olive skin perfectly. Khaki slacks rode low on his hips and accentuated his muscular build. In the soft light he looked like some kind of dark angel, his eyes almost as black as his hair. They met mine before flickering over my face and neckline. I felt uncomfortable until he let out a low whistle. Then I felt uncomfortable in a whole different kind of way.

"Hey." The word came out on a wispy breath of air. I sounded like I was trying to imitate Marilyn Monroe.

Michael didn't answer, only smiled and took his seat. I caught the scent of his cologne: light, crisp, and citrusy. Tempting me to move closer.

I started to bite my lower lip, thought about the gloss Dru had so artfully applied, and stopped myself. "How was your afternoon?"

"Productive," he answered, pulling his napkin into his lap. "Yours?"

"The same."

"I talked to Thomas about taking one of the lofts in your building. My roommate from last year transferred, and I'd rather live alone than play the live-in lottery."

I was really glad I didn't have anything in my mouth, because I'm certain I would have choked on it. Iced tea streaming out of my nose—not pretty.

"A loft? In my building? Wow, really? Wow." I cleared my throat. "So you're planning on sticking around for a while."

"As long as it takes." Michael's eyes searched my face, lingering on my mouth a fraction of a second too long. Again, I fought the urge to bite my lip.

Tried really hard not to think about biting one of his.

"So," he asked, leaning closer to me from across the table, "did you come up with some more questions for me?"

Time to get down to business. My list was in the front pocket of my purse, but I doubted I'd have to refer to it. Feeling fidgety, I reached out to play with a tiny pink rosebud in a vase on the table. "Well, I was thinking about what happened last night. What I see is getting stronger. I mean—a jazz trio? Fully equipped with a grand piano? Did it gradually get worse for you?"

He was silent for a moment before answering. "I can't explain what you saw yesterday. Rips that come with scenery are new to me, too. I wouldn't worry. My guess is that it has something to do with our ability growing stronger as we age."

"Your guess? That's comforting." I laughed in disbelief. "Are you serious? I'm not supposed to worry when you can't even give me a decent answer to my first question?"

Michael focused somewhere over my left shoulder. His voice was firm when he spoke. "I'll get the answer. Don't worry."

"Okay," I said, doubt almost crowding out curiosity in my mind. "Have any of the rips ever known anything about you?"

"What do you mean?" His gaze returned to my face.

"Like your name, or . . ." I trailed off. Maybe I should keep that specific incident to myself. I pictured the list of questions in my mind. "Um, when you know you're seeing a rip—how do you approach it?"

"Very slowly." Michael grinned, breaking the tension.

I was still fiddling with the rosebud in the vase. Sidetracked by his smile, I stopped paying attention and tipped it over, spilling water onto the table.

Good thing I wasn't on a date. I might've been embarrassed.

We reached to pick up the vase at the same time, and our fingertips touched. A current of energy pulsed through his hand to mine. My skin felt too small, stretched too tight, as if searching out more exposure to his. I heard several pings, and the table went dark.

Something was very, very off.

I slowly raised my eyes to meet Michael's. The muscles in his face tensed; his expression was completely unreadable. Confused, maybe scared, I pulled away. I could still feel the way electricity had flowed through his fingers to mine, all the way to the roots of my hair. The remaining lights returned to normal.

I could've sworn I was twitching. Michael tucked his hand under the table and stared down at his menu.

"Um . . . what was that?" I asked, my voice wispy air again as I watched the water from the vase soak into the white tablecloth.

"It's kind of complicated."

So it really happened. "Did we cause it?"

He nodded, his face poker straight.

"Have you ever experienced that before?"

"Not exactly."

The waitress arrived to take our orders. The interruption did nothing to resolve the tension. I just wanted her to go away so I could touch him again. Instead, I held my menu up in front of my flaming face, willing my body back to normalcy. Michael ordered the special, and without even looking to see what it was, I did the same.

"I'll have that right out," the waitress said, taking our menus. She eyed the sconces above the table, her hot pink lips pursed. "And I'll bring y'all a candle . . . it's dark over here, isn't it?"

Neither of us answered, and she walked away. I felt exposed without my menu to hide behind.

"Are we going to talk about what just happened?" I asked.

"Would you believe me if I told you it's better to leave it alone for now?"

"Is there another option?"

"Probably not." He lifted the corners of his mouth in a smile, but his eyes didn't get the memo. "Maybe you could go ahead and ask me your other questions."

"How about 'what the hell was that?'"

His expression practically hung out a shingle announcing the topic was off-limits.

"Fine." I tried to catch one of the thoughts racing through my mind so I'd have something to say. I couldn't, so I retrieved my list and laid it on the table in front of me. "How do you tell the difference between real people and time ripples?"

"You mean besides punching them in the stomach?"

I blushed, not because I'd hit him, but because I was thinking about his abs. "Besides that."

"There's the way they disappear into solid objects." He tapped his lips. "Also, I . . . um . . . I've been seeing rips for so long now I have a way of sensing them."

I could see how that would be helpful.

"How do you make them go away?" I asked, referring to my list again. "I mean, not forever, but when you see them—if they're in your path?"

"I try to ignore them. Since I recognize what they are now, they're easier to avoid, but if I need them gone for some reason, I touch them. Not that there's really anything to touch. How about you?"

I nodded, unable to stop myself from staring at his fingers. Unable to stop thinking about how badly I wanted him to touch me again.

Dinner arrived, saving me from my own mind. I tucked my list back into my purse. Once I smelled the food I regained my appetite; it was some kind of glazed salmon and grilled asparagus. Michael took a few bites before pushing his plate to the side. Propping his elbows on the table, lacing his fingers together church and steeple style, he said, "Dealing with the ripples will get easier. Hasn't it already? Since you first started seeing them?"

Easier? "I guess."

"How did it start for you?"

I hedged a little, chasing a wayward asparagus stalk with my fork. "How much do you know about me?"

"Thomas told me part of your story—you started seeing things just before your parents died. His renovation sites seem to trigger it."

"Anything else?"

Michael took a deep drink of iced tea before speaking, appearing to choose his words carefully. "He mentioned that you had a pretty rough road."

I stared at my plate, too self-conscious to look at him. "Did he tell you I was hospitalized for a while?"

"He did. But he didn't tell me why. I asked him to leave it up to you." His voice was quiet, comforting.

"It was for depression. Mostly." Keeping my eyes down, I picked up what was left of my dinner roll and began to tear it into small pieces. "I started seeing rips. Not too long after that, my mom and dad . . . died. I kind of went over the edge. It wasn't pretty. I was committed and medicated. Heavily medicated. Everything went away. Not just what I could see—the rips—but my personality, my desires, all of it. I was like a shell."

Less than a shell.

"It was good for a while, being empty. I didn't hurt anymore. But as time went on, it was like I could hear myself from far away, begging for permission to come back." I tore the small pieces of dinner roll into smaller pieces. "Once I was released from the hospital and away at school, I found a counselor, Alicia. It helped to be able to talk to someone, tell her everything."

Almost everything, anyway.

"I stopped taking the meds last Christmas." I couldn't believe I was telling him so much, but the words kept spilling out. Something about his eyes and the way he seemed to look right into me without judgment made me talk. "Thomas and Dru don't know.

I don't want them to worry about me, and they will if they know I've gone 'all natural.'"

"Unless you're trying to make a pile of bread crumbs to find your way home, you should probably give that roll a break." Michael's voice barely hid his concern. My heart stumbled a little, but the tenderness in his voice kept me from falling.

I dropped the remains of the bread, crossed my arms over my chest, and continued. "As the chemicals left my system, I started seeing things again. It only happened a couple of times last semester. I saw a rip at my friend Lily's place earlier this summer. Then yesterday I saw a Southern belle in a hoopskirt and a guy in my living room, and then last night, there was the . . ."

"Jazz trio, yeah." He twisted the silver ring on his thumb. "Are you glad you aren't taking the medication anymore?"

"I hated it. I never felt like I was in control, although crazy people don't generally get to claim self-control as a personality trait."

"Stop." Michael's voice wasn't loud, but the word was a command. "You are not crazy. What you see is real, Emerson. It's valid; you're valid. What you went through was horrible—losing your parents."

Losing my mind.

"All I'm saying is . . . please don't be so hard on yourself." He reached as if he were going to touch my hand but pulled back. "Cut yourself some slack."

His words sent a wave of relief through me. Not just what he said, but the way he said it, as if he wouldn't accept any other alternative. Some of the anxiety broke loose and flowed away, and the release was sweet. Tears filled my eyes.

"Oh, damn. I'm not a crier, I swear. I never cry. I *hate* to cry." I wiped my eyes on my napkin before any of the tears fell. He flagged down the waitress and asked for the bill, giving me some time to regain my composure.

"It's on the house," she said brightly, her eyes flicking briefly to me before giving Michael a tentative smile.

"Thanks." He smiled back. When she walked away, he dropped a twenty on the table.

Nice tipper. Always a good character trait.

After a few seconds I looked up at him. "Thank you." He nodded. I knew he understood I wasn't thanking him for dinner.

"You want to get out of here, go to your place?"

Chapter 8

*I*t took a few seconds before I remembered to blink.

He didn't bother hiding his grin. "So you can show me the lofts?"

"Oh, right, yes, lofts. Good. Lofts. You ready to go?" I stood, knowing my cheeks sported a ridiculous shade of red.

We walked through the restaurant to the bar area, and his hand accidentally brushed the small of my back, the heat so focused where he touched me that the rest of my body felt chilled. I looked up at him from the corner of my eye. He put his hand in his pocket.

Behind the bar, Dru counted bottles of red wine while the bartender loaded them into a teakwood rack. "Dru? Michael wants to see the lofts. Can I use the master?"

"Sure." She pulled a set of keys from her pocket and removed one from the ring, giving it to me. Her gaze darted back and forth between the two of us as her face registered surprise, or maybe concern.

I was sure she noticed her flawless makeup application was smudged.

We walked through the town square in silence. My emotions were ridiculously close to the surface, as if my insides were flipped to the outside, but the feeling of vulnerability didn't scare me. As I showed him the two lofts, the energy still hummed between us, keeping all my senses on overdrive. Even though the mood was intense, I was experiencing an unknown. For the first time in a long time, I felt . . . safe.

We stepped into the hall, and I locked the door to the last loft before turning to face him.

"I like both spaces. Thomas and Dru can put me wherever they want." Michael rocked back on his heels. He stared into my eyes for a few seconds, those seconds stretching into what felt like hours as he reached out until his fingertips were an inch from mine.

"Are you sure?" I asked in a low whisper.

"It's not going to go away," he whispered back. "Might as well get used to it."

Bracing myself for the jolt of energy, I gave him my hand.

It was better than I remembered.

I was grateful that the hallway lights were more ambient than bright. I didn't know where to look when they flickered.

Michael seemed to be fighting some sort of internal battle, his face full of indecision. I started to tremble. The jolt settled into a low hum; even so, with all the sparks we were throwing off, we could possibly light the Southern Hemisphere.

"I'm sorry," he said, his voice low, full of regret. His hand felt warm and solid in mine.

"For what? It's definitely different, but I'm fine." Basically. Getting a full-body buzz with a guy I'd just met was as weird as seeing dead people. But much more enjoyable.

"Not the . . . touching thing. The ripple thing. I'm sorry you've had to deal with all of it by yourself."

"Thanks, but alone is kind of how I work." Carefully extracting my hand, I stepped back slowly to make sure my knees were working and that my legs would hold me up.

"Just remember I'm here to help." Michael dropped his hand down by his side. "I plan on sticking around until you tell me to leave."

Or until my brother stopped paying him.

"Well, I should probably"—I gestured toward my door—"go. Good night."

"Good night."

I watched him walk away and held on to the doorknob, trying to keep myself upright, feeling the connection between us stretch down the hall and all the way out the front door.

I used the master key to get into the loft, laying it on the cold marble counter in the kitchen.

Intending only to take a quick shower to wash the powder from my arms and chest, the warm spray and the quiet seduced me. My skin was pink and pruned by the time I emerged and slipped on my pajamas. I pulled back the down comforter and ran my hand over the snow-white sheets, appreciating the concept of high thread counts.

The family pictures on my bedside table caught my eye. One was of Thomas and Dru—tan and smiling—and the other was of me. Mine was hollow, empty. It was from some vacation taken in an attempt to distract me after my parents died. From Disney to the Bahamas, none of them had.

Another was of my parents, from their last Christmas. I picked up the heavy silver frame and looked into the familiar faces I would never see again, unless my parents appeared to me as rips. I didn't know if I feared that or desired it.

Tonight's conversation about my past had opened a wound. The wide hole my parents' deaths left had been sutured by time, but talking with Michael loosened the threads. Seeing the picture tore them open.

I'd never been as honest with anyone as I'd been with Michael. He made me feel safe, like I could be real—shattered and fragmented and wholly imperfect—even though he was the polar opposite. Intact, complete, fully perfect.

And totally off-limits.

I looked back at the picture, tracing the outline of my mother's face, thinking that if she were still alive I would go to her room, curl up on her bed, ask her for advice.

Instead, I lay down, turning off the bedside lamp and holding the picture close to my heart.

Just before I drifted off, I sensed someone, but I was too close to sleep to tell if it was a dream or reality. I couldn't think of any reason why a long-dead man from the past would be worried about me.

But Jack appeared to be sitting on the foot of my bed, a look of intense concern on his face.

I blinked, and he was gone.

Chapter 9

I woke up the next morning feeling raw, like my usual armor was missing. My comfortable layer of protective sarcasm had slipped. I needed it back to be able to deal with everything I'd learned. More sparring with Thomas was just the ticket. He always brought out my A game. Between a good argument with him and my Chucks, I should be able to get my life back on track.

He sat at the table in the kitchen with his silk tie thrown over his shoulder, comfortably eating the same breakfast he'd eaten every morning since I could remember: Fruity Pebbles. The smell of sugar and fruit flavoring permeated the air around him, food coloring and preservatives beginning the embalming process where he sat. That seemed like a good enough place to start.

"It's so encouraging to see an entrepreneur such as yourself starting the day with a healthy breakfast." I walked behind him, intending to flip his tie into his bowl. "The economic future of our little town hinges on whether or not your blood sugar drops before your morning snack of Ho Hos and a Yoo-hoo."

Thomas snaked a hand up and grabbed my wrist before I could get to his tie. "Good morning, little sister. I hope we aren't grumpy because we didn't get a good-night kiss?"

I ran my free hand through his perfectly groomed blond hair just to piss him off. "How do you know whether or not I got a good-night kiss?"

"Excellent security in these buildings. Security guards, security systems, security cameras." He pulled me around to face him. "That way I won't have to worry about anything inappropriate happening. Since it is strictly a professional relationship."

"You were spying on us? Are you trying to start a fight?" I asked, jerking my arm away. The bowl of Fruity Pebbles hovered dangerously close to becoming an accessory. "What does it matter if we run off to Vegas and get married—all you want him to do is help me be 'normal,' right?"

"Michael and I have an agreement. No employee/client relationships. He has a job to do, and I expect him to do it. I'm not kidding, Em."

My upper lip trembled, and I had an irrational desire to cry. What was my problem? I considered unloading my frustration on Thomas, but he was saved when Dru came running into the kitchen from their bedroom, waving something in her hand and screaming.

My brother jumped up from his chair, cereal forgotten as he scooped Dru into his arms. With all the laughing and crying, I couldn't understand a word they were saying.

"Put me down, Thomas!" Giving him a smacking kiss, she wiggled until he placed her feet tenderly on the ground. I finally realized what she held in her hand.

A pregnancy test.

Several emotions passed through me as the truth hit. Gratitude, because I knew they had wanted this for a very long time. Joy, because I knew my family was expanding in the best possible way. And finally, my familiar nemesis, anxiety, because where would I live once the baby was born?

Dru must have read the concern on my face, because she pulled me into a tight hug.

"Don't worry! We've been holding out on renting the third loft for this very reason—in case we needed to expand. After all this time, we didn't want to set ourselves up to be disappointed, but we couldn't help it. Auntie Em isn't going anywhere. Unless you want to."

"No! No, I want to stay." It was true. "As long as you'll have me."

"We want you here with us. All three of us." Thomas reached out for my hand and gave it a quick squeeze. I hadn't seen him this happy in a long time. The way that he looked at Dru made me feel the need to disappear.

"I think I'm going to head out for a run, give you two some time to, um, talk about nursery colors. Congratulations. You're going to be amazing parents." I hurried to my bedroom, tears close to the surface, threatening my badass reputation. I quickly changed into a sports bra and running shorts, grabbing a hair elastic and carrying my shoes and iPod to put on outside. Dru and Thomas were nowhere to be seen as I walked through the living room. The closed door to their bedroom suggested they were celebrating the way I thought they would.

Good thing I ran distance.

I cranked the volume, letting classic alternative rock numb my brain. I didn't want to think about anything but running and breathing. The late-summer day was perfect, leaves just tinged with color, stirring in the slight breeze. I couldn't wait until they blazed red and gold and the shop fronts were decorated with fat orange pumpkins and spicy-smelling mums.

I wondered if Michael would still be around then.

People were out en masse, walking dogs, pushing babies in strollers, enjoying runs of their own. I cruised along the sidewalk toward Riverbend Park, settling into a moderate pace as I followed the path some genius developer I was related to put in place a couple of years ago to appeal to local families and tourists.

Thomas and Dru brought so much to our town. They met when he left a prestigious architectural firm and started his own business, his main goal to renovate downtown Ivy Springs. She was new to the design business and consulted on his first job. It began as a professional relationship, but it didn't take long for that to change. They'd been married for six months when my parents died.

I fiercely loved both of them, and I knew they felt the same way about me. The guilt of not being completely honest with them about the medication situation ate away at me. But I really didn't want them to worry, and now that a baby was on the way . . . well. They had other things to think about, even though Thomas had apparently appointed himself as the boss of my love life. Maybe now he'd be so consumed with picking out names and setting up a college fund that he'd leave me alone. Kicking my pace into high gear, I kept my eyes to the ground to avoid any surprises and settled into my rhythm.

Until I slammed into a solid wall of muscle, hitting it so hard my teeth rattled. Clenching my fists in front of my face and jumping back into a wide stance, I faced my would-be attacker.

Michael.

My scream died in my throat, and I jerked my earbuds from my ears. "What the—you can't scare people like that!"

Michael's mouth formed an O of surprise, and then he doubled over, laughing so hard he gasped for breath. Staring down angrily at him, I couldn't help but admire the muscle tone in his tanned arms and legs. When he looked up at me, his gaze turned appreciative. Wishing I'd thrown on a T-shirt instead of just a sports bra, I crossed my arms over my chest, hoping it made me look pouty instead of self-conscious.

Michael tried to arrange his face into a serious expression, going through several before finally settling on one. "I'm sorry. Jumping out at you was not a smart move."

"It's fine." It really wasn't.

"I just didn't expect you to go all ninja on me." Michael lost the battle and gave himself over to laughter again. I found myself wishing I'd managed to land at least one solid kick before I figured out who he was. I glared at him for another moment then resumed my run.

It took him a few seconds, but soon I could hear him pacing me. It had to be hard for him since his legs were so much longer than mine, but I didn't care. He deserved to suffer. We ran in silence for a while until I snuck a sideways look at him. He was still laughing. I stopped so fast he ran right past me.

Spinning around, he clasped one hand over his mouth. He would have been wise to put the other hand over his eyes because they were giving everything away.

"Michael, knock it off."

He reached out, hooked his arm around my neck, and pulled me to his side. I waited for him to give me a noogie and tried not to be intrigued by the full-body tingle.

"I apologize," he said, but I heard the smile in his voice. "I really do. You're just so damn cute."

"And so damn sweaty," I said, looking up at him sideways.

Maybe it was our close proximity, or that he had his arm around me and we were both sweating and breathing hard. All I knew was that even though I was hotter than hell, the second our eyes met my whole body convulsed in one giant chill. Our gaze stayed locked for an endless moment before he released me and gently pushed me away.

"Truce?" Michael asked hesitantly, holding out one hand.

I struggled to catch my breath, willing my gooseflesh to disappear. When I finally regained control, I gave him a sweet smile and reached out to shake.

Then I flipped him over my shoulder.

As he lay on the ground panting, I walked to stand over him, looking down, my smile still in place. "So I'll see you later?"

He blinked once. I took that as a yes.

Chapter 10

When I got back to the loft, Dru and Thomas were gone. I felt great. The sass was back. It's amazing what flipping a grown man over her shoulder does for a girl.

After a shower, I borrowed Dru's laptop, taking it to the cushy chair in my room to settle in, enjoying the rich scent of the buttery leather. I got cozy—good thing—since I searched for an hour before I found what I was looking for. Just when I was about to give up, I came across a blurb in the *Bennett Review* about a scholarship funded by the founder of the Hourglass, Liam Ballard. I searched his name.

Jackpot.

I uncurled myself from the corner of the chair, placing the computer on my ottoman and leaning over so I could better focus on the screen. When I clicked on the first article, a huge picture of a completely devastated building popped up below the caption: No Answers in Laboratory Fire.

The story questioned the death of Liam Ballard, a scientist who was killed when his private lab was destroyed by a fire. No traces of any combustible materials were found, nor were any accelerants. The building had just passed a fire inspection. His home and several outbuildings, also located on the property, were not damaged. No one else was injured.

My skin prickled as I continued reading. After a lengthy investigation by authorities, the case was closed due to lack of evidence. There was no logical explanation for the fire.

A knock sounded at the front door, and I practically jumped out of my skin.

I exited to the search results page and hurried to answer, stopping for a quick check in the mirror. Opening the door, I found Michael, looking sheepish and holding a bouquet of fragrant zinnias.

"An apology," he said, holding out the flowers. "You *will* explain how you did that. Soon."

I reached out to take the flowers, and our fingers touched. Electricity sizzled, and I pulled away quickly.

"Maybe I will, maybe I won't." I gave him a look, before spinning on my heel and walking toward the kitchen. I was glad he couldn't see my face—I knew I was blushing. Since my back was to him anyway, I stuck my nose in the bouquet and inhaled the sweet fragrance, creating a scent memory.

I'd never gotten flowers from a boy before.

"This place is amazing," he said. Directly behind me, his footsteps echoed off the hardwood floor.

"Thanks. Dru is an excellent decorator. She loves to have a project. And now she and Thomas have a new one." I made a hand motion indicating a bun in the oven before taking a crystal vase from a shelf and placing it in the sink to fill it with water, grateful I could concentrate on a task.

"Tell them I said congratulations." He leaned back against the counter beside the sink, watching me. "That's amazing news, especially for two people who seem to be as in love as they are."

"They're lucky they found each other," I said, looking up at him.

"Yes, they are." Focused on each other, the only sound in the room was the water flowing from the running faucet.

I broke the stare, shifting my attention back to the vase before it overflowed. "I'm supposed to tell you that you can take loft number two. But it doesn't come cheap. I hope helping little old me pays well."

"For you, I'd work pro bono."

"For me?" I bit my lip, turning off the water before looking up at him again.

"You're special."

"That all depends on your definition of special."

His answering smile was slow and deliberate. I stared at his mouth for a few brief seconds before giving myself a mental pinch and shoving the flowers haphazardly into the vase. "Thanks again. Zinnias are my favorite," I said, after clearing my throat.

Twice.

"I'm glad you like them," he said, his smile growing softer. "They made me think of you."

More staring at his mouth.

Geez a lou.

I scooped up the flowers, and he followed me to my room, taking a seat in my recently vacated chair. I'd just finished clearing a space on my dresser when he spoke my name.

"Emerson?"

"Yes," I answered absentmindedly, concentrating on arranging the fragrant blossoms so that the taller ones were in the back.

"Why were you doing a search on Liam Ballard?"

The tone of his voice sent chills up my spine. I stopped fiddling and answered cautiously, watching him through the mirror. "Because he's the founder of the Hourglass?"

Maybe I caused some kind of brain damage when I flipped him over my shoulder. His expression changed, moving from concern to anger in the split second the word *Hourglass* was uttered.

"Michael?" I turned around. He was just as frightening face-to-face as he was in the reflection, his brown eyes almost black, his full lips flattened into a thin line. "What—"

He interrupted me. "How did you find Liam's name?"

"It came up in an article about the Hourglass and Bennett alum—"

"What else did you find when you searched him?" The question sounded more like an accusation, his tone stone cold. I didn't know this Michael.

I didn't like this Michael.

"That he"—I paused, forcing my voice to stay level—"that he died in a fire."

He stood and crossed the room in a few long strides. I took an uncertain step back, my spine bumping uncomfortably against the dresser.

Speaking each word distinctly, he leaned over and looked into my eyes. "You need to mind your own business."

I swallowed the baseball-sized lump in my throat. "Why does that sound like a threat?"

"It's a warning," he said, placing his hands on the dresser. His forearms bumped against my shoulders. I was glad I was wearing a T-shirt instead of a tank top. I didn't think his bare skin touching mine would be helpful in a situation like this. "Forget Liam Ballard."

"Why?" I asked breathlessly, feeling caged in, trapped by his stare as much as his arms.

"Just do," he answered, authoritative and dismissive, his voice as hard as steel. "I'll handle the Hourglass. Trust me."

"Sorry, boss," I said, making the jump from scared to angry. "I don't generally believe people who have to tell me to trust them."

"You need to this time."

Michael held still, his face close to mine. Gold flecks mixed with the dark brown of his eyes. His skin was flawless, smooth, with just a hint of stubble I wouldn't have noticed if he weren't a whisper away. It could have been a lovely position, if I wasn't so mad I was vibrating.

"Emerson?" The question sounded more like a plea.

"Fine," I snapped, making my decision. "Now *back up*."

He pulled away from me, his eyes searching my face. I wondered if he could see my pulse pounding in my throat. I could feel it. I needed to think, and when he was close to me, thinking was impossible.

"Please don't misunderstand . . . I'm only trying to . . ." With his fingertips still on the edge of the dresser, he closed his eyes, struggling with his words.

Seeing an escape, I ducked under his arm. There were some advantages to being short. "Trying to what? Scare me? Piss me off?"

"I didn't mean to do either of those things." He pushed away from the dresser to face me. "I'm so—"

"Stop." I cut him off before he could say anything else. "Whether you meant to or not, you did. And now you should probably go."

I didn't want to hear an apology. I just wanted him out.

Our eyes met again, and unspoken words hung in the

atmosphere. His face was a strange mix of emotions—the set of his mouth angry, his expression regretful.

"Was there something else?" I asked, and then held my breath. He shook his head and left my bedroom without saying another word.

The front door to the loft opened and closed before I exhaled.

Chapter 11

Michael moved in the next day.

I could hear him shuffling things around next door. The walls of the building were well insulated, but the weather was crisp and sunny, and we had both opened our windows. The loft Dru gave him shared a bedroom wall with mine.

Magnificent. I could already imagine trying to sleep knowing he was practically lying beside me. Even though he'd made me furious yesterday, I couldn't deny that the attraction still existed.

I was an idiot.

The sound of John Lee Hooker and his guitar floated from Michael's room through my window. So much in common—I loved the blues, too. I sat on my bed to listen to the music, watching the shifting shadows cast on my floor by the leaves from the oak outside my window. It was a beautiful afternoon, perfect for hanging out at the lake and grabbing the last bit of warmth before the weather turned cold. If you were a normal teenager. Since I'd left normal behind a lifetime ago, I stayed at home, trapped with my thoughts.

Even though I promised Michael to mind my own business, I was tempted to resume my Internet search on the Hourglass. Liam Ballard died under mysterious circumstances, and Michael didn't want me asking questions. Why? What was he hiding?

I looked at Dru's laptop, still on the ottoman, mocking me. Would I break my promise if I touched the power button and looked at what popped up on the screen?

I reached toward the computer, and Jack appeared in front of me. I almost yelped in surprise, but the open window and the thought of Michael possibly hearing stopped me. Since I was alone, and lonely, I figured a conversation with a dead guy wouldn't be a horrible way to pass the afternoon.

"Hello." His voice still sounded smooth, cultured.

"What's up?"

"What's . . . up?" Jack asked.

"Never mind," I said as I walked to the window to slide it shut. I leaned back and rested my bottom against the sill. "I meant, how are you?"

"Better than you appear to be."

"Yes," I sighed deeply, "but don't feel too good about it. Better than me is not a hard thing to accomplish."

"Oh, I don't believe that at all." Jack folded his hands together behind his back. "Don't sell yourself short."

"Is that supposed to be some kind of joke?" I asked. I held out my arms and looked from my feet to the tips of my fingers.

He pulled his head back in dismay before he erupted into warm, contagious laughter. I couldn't stop myself from laughing with him.

"Your size makes you seem delicate, like a spiderweb. But the wise fly knows that delicate can also be strong."

I was suddenly very aware that even if he wasn't *alive*, he was a man, and he was in my bedroom. And he'd just paid me the best compliment I'd ever received.

"So"—I paused and made a conscious effort to lower the pitch of my voice—"is there a reason for your visit?"

Jack shrugged. "I wanted to take advantage of human companionship while I had it, unless, of course, you find my presence intrusive?"

Weighing his words, I tried to decide if it did feel intrusive. If he were alive, he would probably fall into the creepy-stalker category. Since he was a rip, did that make him more guardian angel?

"No, it's all good." I walked back to sit on the edge of the bed, not trusting my knees. Jack was a grown man. Who happened to be dead. I needed to pull it together.

"To have gone for so long without anyone to talk to," Jack said in a voice so sweet it would turn vinegar to sugar, "how lucky am I that my first conversation is with someone like you?"

Not an angel.

I fought the urge to fan myself.

"Um . . . thank you?"

"You're welcome." He fingered the chain on his pocket watch, the upward pull of his suppressed smile barely noticeable.

I couldn't even manage a normal social exchange with a dead guy.

"Em?" Dru knocked on my door.

Feeling like I'd been caught doing something naughty, I jumped up from the bed. "Yes?"

"Who are you talking to?"

"No one, just . . . oomph—" I backed away from Jack and managed to trip over my ottoman in the process. "I was reading out loud."

"Open the door. I want to show you the baby bedding I bought."

"Sure, just a sec." Staring at the doorknob, I realized I hadn't locked it. It didn't really matter if Dru came in or not because she wouldn't be able to see Jack. But the thought of trying to have a conversation with her while he stood next to me . . . no way.

I scrambled to my feet and turned to tell him he needed to disappear.

He was already gone.

In addition to bedding, Dru purchased possibly every article of gender-neutral baby clothing in the entire town of Ivy Springs. She sorted it into groups on the four-poster king-sized bed she shared with my brother, and the cream lace coverlet was completely hidden underneath the piles.

"Emerson, I wanted to apologize," Dru said, folding up a tiny T-shirt imprinted with the words SPIT HAPPENS.

"For what?"

"Running you off when Thomas and I, uh, celebrated our pregnancy news." Her face turned the same tomato red as the bedroom walls. Mine grew hot, and probably the same color as hers. I welcomed the cool breeze flowing through the open window and stirring the pale window sheers. Dru cleared her throat and continued. "We could've been a little more discreet."

"It's okay," I mumbled, ducking my head and kneeling to retrieve a tiny sock that had escaped to the hardwood floor.

"No, it isn't. This is your home, and you should feel comfortable in it."

"I do." I smiled up at her. "You and Thomas are going to be wonderful parents. And I know how long you've . . . wanted a baby."

Dru rubbed her midsection as tears formed in her eyes. I stood and focused intently on finding the mate for the sock in the pile of clothes on the bed. According to Thomas, they'd started talking about babies on their honeymoon. It was never openly discussed, but I knew the past few years had been filled with disappointment.

"You know," she said softly, her voice trembling, "we decided we're going to name the baby after your mom or dad. Clarissa if it's a girl, Sean if it's a boy."

I would not cry. I just wouldn't. "I know they'd love that," I whispered. "I mean, I know they *would've* loved that."

"So, it's okay with you?" Dru asked, removing her hand from her stomach and picking up a chenille blanket.

"Why wouldn't it be?"

Dru fiddled with the blanket's fringe, twisting and untwisting. "You'll have children one day. I didn't know if maybe, you'd want to . . ."

"Me? No way," I said, trying to laugh it off, failing. The only way I'd ever experience children would be vicariously, as the spinster aunt living in a tiny house with thirty cats. And possibly some dead people. The muscles in my face wouldn't cooperate with the smile I tried to force. "I don't think I'll ever get married, much less have children. Whether I want to or not. That's all so . . . normal. I'm not."

She put down the blanket and reached out to take my hand and give it a comforting squeeze. "Thomas told me you're seeing them again."

"Bad news travels fast." My stomach dropped all the way down to my shoes. I pulled my hand away and turned back to the bed to continue sorting through the tiny clothes, searching blindly for the elusive sock with the yellow chick on it.

"Maybe it's not bad news. Maybe it's serendipitous, perfect timing. Thomas really seems to think Michael will be able to help you."

"Or he could end up being as bad as all the rest of them." Or worse. Because from our first conversation I'd hoped for so much more from him, and now I didn't know what to think. "How did you two find him anyway?"

She shrugged and took more clothes out of a paper shopping bag. "You'd have to ask your brother about that. And don't change the subject."

"What subject?"

"The subject of your future. Your happiness." She wadded up the bag, fiercely crunching the brown paper, and threw it to the ground. "You're one of the most compassionate, generous people I've ever met, which means if you want to be, you'll make an excellent mother. You have so much to offer. Don't sell yourself short and hide in a hole instead of living your life!"

I froze, waiting for the flying pigs to descend. Dru *never* yelled.

"I'm sorry." Her hand flew to her mouth. I shouldn't have. I'm sorry."

"Don't be. I—I, just, thank you. For everything." I paused, pressing my lips together, blinking furiously. "That's how I know what a phenomenal mom you're going to be. Because you've been one to me. So thank you."

This time the tears spilled over. I grabbed the SPIT HAPPENS shirt and held it across my chest. "I don't think this will fit. Didn't they have bigger sizes?" I got the laugh I was hoping for and took the opportunity to change the subject. "Looks like the bags are empty. Are all baby items deemed acceptable?"

She nodded, brushing the wetness briskly from her cheeks, getting back to the business at hand. "Will you help me take the tags off everything so I can wash it all?"

"No problem. I had no idea babies needed their own detergent." I handed Dru the pink plastic bottle with the picture of a sleeping infant on it.

"Me neither." She laughed. "We have a lot to learn. Isn't it exciting?"

It was.

When we were finished, a pile of tags and tiny plastic hangers covered the floor, so I stuffed it all into an empty shopping bag and took it down to the Dumpster. Dusting off my hands, I headed up the metal stairs and ran smack into Michael's chest, losing my balance.

He reached out to grab my shoulders, stopping me before I fell. I pulled away quickly. Now wasn't the time to be reminded of our crazy physical connection.

"Hey," he said, his focus shifting from my face to the ground as he hooked his thumbs into the pockets of his jeans.

I crossed my arms and stepped around him to continue up the stairs, irritated that he'd spoiled my good mood.

"Wait, Emerson." I heard his feet hit two steps behind me before I turned and leaned back against the metal railing. We were practically eye to eye.

"What?" I drew it out, trying to sound bored, but my voice trembled at the end of the question.

"About yesterday . . . the Hourglass . . . I wish I could explain."

"Why can't you?"

He scrubbed his hands over his face. "I just can't."

I gave him an irritated growl and turned to continue up the stairs. He grabbed for my hand, but I yanked it away as I spun around. "Why? I 'don't know what I'm dealing with,' so I should just 'mind my own business'—isn't that what you said?" I could feel the sneer curling my upper lip.

"It's more complicated than that."

The desire to kick him in the shins at the answer that was beginning to become his standard was overwhelming. "No."

"What?"

"No." My impulses moved from kicking to punching, spurred on by my own anger and the fact that, before yesterday's incident in my bedroom, I had trusted Michael. "I won't mind my own business. You show up, tell me you *understand* me and that I should trust you. And then you won't tell me the truth."

"Emerson, I'm being as honest with you as I can be, believe me," he said, his palms up.

"Not being completely honest is the same as being a liar."

"I am not a liar," he said. A vein pulsed in his forehead.

"I think you are," I pushed with my words.

"I'm not. What I am is extremely frustrated."

Michael reached out, cupped his hands under my elbows, spun me around, and dropped me to my feet.

"Whose fault is that?" I shouted as he walked up the stairs to the back door, his spine stiff. "Not mine. Maybe you should go ahead and tell me whatever it is you think I can't handle—have you ever thought of that?"

But the door slammed, and I was talking to thin air.

Chapter 12

The next morning I stopped by Murphy's Law for a little liquid energy and a chat with Lily. Lack of sleep was becoming an unfortunate occurrence in my life. I briefly considered ordering chamomile tea. Supposedly, it helped with anxiety, and I had plenty.

Lily stood behind the counter. She saw me coming and called out my usual order. "Double *Cubano* and the biggest empanada we have."

Chamomile?

Right.

When Lily wouldn't let me pay, I shoved my money in the tip jar and walked to the front of the shop to sink into an overstuffed pumpkin-colored chair. Outside, a man wearing khaki pants and a T-shirt bearing the logo of a landscaping service pulled summer annuals from the intermittently spaced planters lining the street.

He replaced them with delicate pansies in dusky crimson and two shades of purple. A Davy Crockett look-alike stood beside him, his calves disappearing into the middle of the planter. Rips and solid objects didn't really mix. I was glad Davy was out of his century and not just fashion challenged.

The coonskin cap really would've been over the top.

As I watched them both I noticed a sign taped up on the outside of the plate-glass window of the coffee shop. The sun shone at the perfect angle to make the thick black words stand out clearly: HELP WANTED. The heavens broke open. I wanted a job so I wouldn't have to ask Thomas for extra spending money, and my favorite coffee shop in the world was hiring. Could I get a job smelling and selling the elixir of life?

Lily brought over a tiny espresso cup and my empanada and then lowered herself gracefully onto the edge of the chair across from me.

"Why didn't you tell me you were hiring?" I asked.

She frowned, and I gestured toward the sign. I watched her read it through the glass, backward letters and all. "I didn't know *Abi* decided to hire anyone. I thought she was going to keep working me to death to save money."

"Your powers of observation astound me. One of your many superpowers." She frowned at me. Needing to be on her good side, I changed the subject. "You think your *abuela* would hire me?"

"I don't know why not. Coffee runs through your veins instead of blood. I think it stunted your growth." I looked for something to throw at her, but the empanada was the only thing I could see, and I wasn't willing to give it up.

"Is she here?" I struggled to get out of the chair. It seemed to have eaten half of my body. "Can I talk to her?"

"She ran over to the bank for some change. And why are you even asking? You know if you want the job, it's yours." Lily twisted her long dark hair up on top of her head, fanning herself with her order pad, looking more like Cleopatra on her barge than a barista at a coffee shop. She carried glamour as casually as some women carry a purse. "You think you can start tomorrow? I need a break."

"Only if you can free me from this beast of a chair," I said, wiggling as I tried to get some leverage. "What do you feed this thing? Customers?"

"Relax." Lily let her hair fall around her shoulders and grinned at me. "I kind of like having a captive audience. How's it going with Thomas and Dru?"

Since I wasn't going anywhere without help, I took a sip of my espresso, sighing with pleasure. Rumor had it Murphy's Law was the best place in the States besides Miami to get a *Cubano*, an espresso shot sweetened with sugar while brewed. "Better than I expected. They're pregnant."

"Pregnant? That's great," she said before tilting her head and narrowing her eyes at me. "Or is it?"

"It is. Dru threatened to put me under house arrest if I tried to move out. She said she knows somebody at the police department who can get her one of those ankle bracelets."

Lily's voice turned wistful as she leaned back in her chair. She'd never get stuck. "Family is important."

The two of us shared the no-parent thing. Her parents were alive, but her father's involvement with the government hadn't allowed him or her mother to escape Cuba with Lily and her grandmother. Except for some extremely distant cousins in South Florida, she had fewer family members than I did.

"Any news from your parents?" I asked.

"No. Not since last Christmas." Her eyes filled with sorrow I recognized. She changed the subject quickly, the way she always did whenever her family came up. "You never gave me details about the restaurant opening. Spill it—any developments on the social front?"

"Nope."

She gave me a look that clearly indicated she didn't believe me. "That was an awfully quick answer."

"When did y'all start selling your own brand?" I hedged, squinting up at the sign announcing the price for freshly roasted coffee beans.

"Last spring. Dish. Now." She perched on the edge of her seat, eager for the details. "You *did* meet someone."

"It's true." Lily knew me too well. She wouldn't stop until she got it out of me. "But there's no point talking about it. He's off-limits."

"Why?" She pulled her head back in dismay. "Don't tell me there's a girlfriend?"

"It's one of Thomas's rules—the guy sort of works for us. Plus he's older than me, but only by a couple of years. Thomas thinks a high school diploma puts the guy in the speed-pass line for the nursing home. The thing is, every time we're together there's all this crazy . . ." Unable to come up with a solid description, I made wordless circles with my hands. I guess I could've told her we almost made the circuits blow at the Phone Company, but figured I should probably keep that to myself. "I feel this . . . pull toward him."

And it scares the bejeezus out of me.

"Em, that's a big deal for you," Lily said softly. She knew how hard it was for me to relate to people sometimes. "If there's really a connection there, don't you think Thomas would understand, make an exception?"

"I don't know if it's mutual. Besides, I think Michael agrees with Thomas. He's the one who told me about the no-mixing-business-with-pleasure rule."

"Michael," Lily said in a sultry voice before she giggled. "Nice name. You could always go all Romeo and Juliet if you had to. Keep your love a secret."

"Yeah, because that worked out so well. There's no love there, Lily." And for me there probably never would be. No matter how much Dru protested, I didn't think I had anything to offer.

"Abi's back. Let's go talk to her. I bet you won't even have to fill out an app."

"I don't see her." I craned my neck to look toward the kitchen door. She walked in two seconds later. I looked back at Lily. "Okay."

She laughed uncomfortably and pushed herself out of her chair, but stopped in her tracks when I called out to her.

"Lily?" She turned back to face me. I gestured to the chair. "Help?"

Chapter 13

*T*homas wanted to watch *The Godfather*. Again. I refused to surrender.

"But *The Philadelphia Story* is my favorite." When he started to protest, I switched tactics. "Your wife is with child; you're supposed to be catering to her every need."

"She's right, Thomas." Dru nodded wisely. "And violence isn't good for the baby."

"The baby hasn't even grown fingernails yet—how is he going to know we're watching a mafia movie?"

"*She* is going to be sensitive just like her mother." Dru looked up at him with wide eyes. "Surely you don't want to take the risk?"

As the music that accompanied the title credits to *The Philadelphia Story* started, the doorbell rang. On my way back from the kitchen, snack bowl in hand, I called, "I've got it," into the living room, and shuffled to answer the front door. Probably the pizza.

I opened the door to Michael, his hands shoved deep into his pockets, a look of misery on his face.

"Hey." I hadn't heard a peep from him in two days, and I felt supremely awkward. I pulled my robe closed over my purple striped sleep pants and tank top, putting the bowl of popcorn between us. "Did you need something?"

He eyed my bunny slippers. "Just you. Can we talk? Please, Emerson?"

"Give me a few minutes," I said, keeping my voice neutral. "I'll meet you downstairs."

The small lobby was deserted except for Michael when I found him there ten minutes later. I'd exchanged my robe for a sweat jacket, brushed my teeth, and at the last second sprayed on some perfume.

I left my bunny slippers on. Just to be cheeky.

I led Michael to the patio on the side of the building. It shared the same street view as the restaurant patio, as well as the same type of wrought-iron fence. Sitting down across from him at a glass-topped table, I waited for him to speak.

"I was wrong."

Not exactly what I expected.

"Noble of you to apologize," I said, inwardly cringing at the sarcasm in my voice, even though in my experience it was always best to run the defensive.

Michael leaned back heavily in the chair. "Listen, if you don't want to work with me, I can try to find someone else to help—"

"No. No, I want you." The words were out before I could stop myself. Michael's smile was so wide, it exposed a dimple in his left cheek that I hadn't noticed before. "To work with me."

"Good. I promise from now on to keep any feelings I might have to myself."

Feelings? What kind of feelings?

"There was another reason I wanted to talk to you." He hesitated, drawing a deep breath. "You said you wanted the truth, and I want to tell you everything I can. Seeing time ripples from the past is only part of your gift."

Gift was a really subjective term.

"There's more?" I asked.

"This is going to sound impossible. Just hang with me. You've seen people from the past. Have you ever seen anyone . . . from the future?"

"I only see people who are dead. Dead people from the past. People from the future aren't dead. How can a rip from the future show up in the present? Which would be their past, I guess."

Wrinkles appeared on Michael's forehead, I assumed from attempting to follow my logic. Understandable. I couldn't follow it either.

"It's not so much past, present, and future." The creases grew deeper as he tried to explain. "It's more fluid than that, almost parallel."

"Then it's inevitable?" I asked, defeated. "I'm going to have to deal with people from the future?"

He nodded. I felt like I'd been slapped across the face.

"Have you seen people from the future?" I asked.

"I started out seeing rips from the future, but now I see them from the past, too."

Great. A whole other group of people to look out for at parties.

"That's the craziest thing I've ever heard," I said, my voice edging closer to hysteria. "How did you know they were from the future? Did they show up in a hovercraft? With a trusty robot sidekick?"

"No." He shook his head. His face grew more worried by the second. "At dinner you asked me about the first time I saw a rip from the past. I told you. But the very first rip I saw was from the future. We'd gone to Turner Field to watch the Braves play the Red Sox in an interleague game. The guy in line in front of me had on a World Series shirt. Something about the year— and the team that won—was off."

Michael had been staring off in the distance as he relayed his experience. Now he focused on me.

"Two thousand four or two thousand seven?" I asked.

"Two thousand four." He grinned. "When I reached up to touch his sleeve, my hand connected with his arm and he dissolved. I freaked, and my mom took me to the hospital. That's how the Hourglass found me. They pay people to research that kind of thing."

"People from the future. How strange. My rips show up in pilgrim bonnets or powdered wigs. But . . . people from the future. How strange," I repeated. "Have you ever seen anyone you know?"

"Not exactly." He looked away. His avoidance put my already overloaded senses on full alert.

"Michael?"

He said nothing but refocused his eyes on mine.

"Michael, who have you seen? Tell me."

"I think this is a mistake," he said, leaning forward to stand up. "Just forget it. You don't really want to know."

"No, I think I do." I reached out to stop him, putting my hand on his shoulder then jerking away when the tremor started traveling up my arm. I repeated the question softly. *"Who did you see from the future?"*

He exhaled and leaned back in his chair before he answered.

"You."

Chapter 14

Staring at Michael, I wondered which one of us was the nut job. I practiced my deep breathing, although I don't actually know how to do deep breathing that is in any way official. But the chances were good I would pass out cold within seconds if I didn't try.

Michael's voice was cautious. "Em, it's okay."

"Don't call me Em." The nickname suggested way too much familiarity, which made sense, considering he knew me before I met him. Placing my forehead on the glass tabletop, I banged it a couple of times, mumbling under my breath.

I convinced myself not to run from the patio screaming, mostly because I would have to come back eventually. I did live upstairs. I was also pretty sure I wouldn't be able to run in my bunny slippers. The fact that he saw the jazz trio at the party gave him some validity. Just a little. But now he was talking about people from the future, specifically me. I raised my head, trying not to whimper.

"I should've broken that more gently," Michael said. "It's just that when you found me you told me to—"

"Stop! Please don't talk about anything I've said to you unless the words have been uttered in the past twenty-four hours. By me." I pointed to myself for emphasis. "This me. *If* this is true"—I emitted a hysterical giggle—"how did you know who I was? Why did you believe me?"

"You were very convincing. You knew things about me, kind of like I know things about you now."

"Like what?" The thought was intriguing enough for me to forget we were talking about the impossible.

"Let's see. You're a baseball junkie, an out-of-place Red Sox fan like me, but you think designated hitters are a joke," he explained, watching my face for my reaction, clearly enjoying the upper hand even in the midst of my breakdown. "You listen to bluegrass when you're alone because you don't want anyone to know you like it. You had a belly ring, but you took it out before you came home and Thomas found out." He grinned and cut his eyes to my middle. I forced myself not to squirm. "And . . ."

He was dead on so far. I wondered why he stopped.

"What?"

"I'm not ready to give up all my secrets. Have I been wrong about anything?"

"No." I sniffed. "Although the designated-hitter opinion is still in development."

"You don't have to think about it anymore. Now you know what you decided."

"Whatever. So, when me from the future found you"—that just sounded insane—"what did I know about you?"

"Why should I tell you?" He was having a little too much fun.

"What if this is the only chance you get?" I pointed out. "What if the information you give me right now, in this conversation, is the only time you ever tell me what it is I eventually tell you to get you to believe me?" I hoped he would answer without making me explain that again because I was having a hard time keeping up with myself.

Michael's grin grew wider, and I had the feeling he was on to me. "You told me that my favorite ice cream is spumoni, that I got stitches when I was seven and my scar is in a really interesting place—you knew where—that I had a teddy bear named Rupert I wouldn't part with when I was little, and that the first time I saw you, now, in the present, you would . . . take my breath away."

"Well." Heat crept up my chest to my face.

He looked up at the night sky, speaking his next words so softly I almost couldn't hear them. "You were right."

Deep, slow breathing, Em. Deep, slow breathing.

"When I found you . . . was I a time ripple?" I asked after a quiet moment.

"That's a little complicated," he said, drumming his fingertips on the glass tabletop again.

"Why is that your favorite answer for everything?"

He didn't respond.

Dealing with my own anxiety, I found I couldn't keep my legs still underneath the table. I wished urgently it wasn't see-through. I took a breath to steady myself, knowing what I was about to ask meant either I was truly crazy or my world was about to be turned upside down.

"You said I came to you from the future. I can only think of one way that could happen if I didn't appear to you as a rip." Another hysterical laugh escaped from my lips, this time for a really good reason. Or a really bad reason. "Christopher Reeve and self-hypnosis? Doctor Who and his phone booth? Hermione and the Time Turner?"

"Doctor Who had a police box." He kept his gaze level. "But I'm glad to hear it's not a foreign concept."

"Holy crap. You really expect me to just *buy* this?" I leaned over to put my head between my knees, shaking so hard my chair rattled. I vaguely wondered if I saved any of my medication or if I'd flushed it all. Michael could put it to good use.

"You asked me the question—"

"I know!" I sat up, closing my eyes. Before I spoke again, I lowered my voice. "Can you do me a favor and lay *all* the information on me *now*? I don't need any bonus material to throw me over the edge later."

Or down a flight of stairs, under a bus, and straight back to the mental ward.

"Okay. I know it sounds impossible—" he began.

My eyes flew open. "Time travel? Yes, it does! How? Why me?"

Michael frowned. "It's kind of . . . genetic."

"Like a *disease*?"

I could tell he didn't like the analogy. "If you want to go the disease route, you could compare it to addiction. Addiction is genetic. What each person is addicted to might be different, kind of like one son is an alcoholic, the next son is a drug addict, the next is addicted to gambling, and so on." He pressed the heels of his hands to his forehead. "None of that sounds good."

"Nope."

"Look at it this way. You have a special ability. Seeing ripples is like a symptom." He growled in frustration. "I mean, an indicator. The fact that you've only seen people from the past so far indicates you're able to travel to the past."

"Mmm-hmm. So if I want to go somewhere in the past, I can? What do I have to do? Close my eyes and picture where I want to go? Click my heels together three times and say, 'Neolithic Age'?"

"It's a little more—"

"If you say 'a little more complicated than that,' I *will* scream. What about you? Can you go to the past?" Was I having this conversation? I pinched my thigh, really hard. I *was* having this conversation. "Or can you go to the future because you can see people from the future?"

"I can go to the future on my own and travel back to the present. You can go to the past on your own and travel back to the present. But if we travel together, we can go anywhere on the timeline. We're sort of . . . two halves of one whole."

"Two halves of one whole?" I blinked slowly, twice, and then leaned in close to examine his face. "Do you do drugs? Pot? Acid? What? I asked my brother if he got you fresh from rehab, but I really didn't think it was a possibility until now."

"I don't do drugs, and you aren't crazy." He leaned toward me now, placing his hands palm down on the table. "Considering all the other things you've experienced, is it really so impossible to believe?"

I stared at his fingers, watching the heat from his hands fog the glass. Was it? Almost four years ago I started seeing people from different time periods who disappeared when I tried to touch them. So, no, time travel wasn't impossible to believe. That didn't mean I *wanted* to believe it.

Except for the connected-to-Michael thing. That part still appealed to me.

"The connection," I said, looking up at him. "Is that why we practically short out when we touch each other?"

"Our abilities complement each other. It can create a deep bond. That's why there's so much . . . chemistry between us." He shifted in his chair, staring at the stained concrete patio floor.

A welcome wave of relief flooded over me. I was grateful I could attach my feelings for him to something, even a scientific connection. Chemistry. I thought about the amount of energy we produced when we accidentally touched and had a brief vision of what it would be like if our lips met. Would the world explode around us?

When he started speaking, I made myself focus on what he was saying, pushing away thoughts of fireworks and detonation.

Michael continued, his embarrassment either overcome or well hidden. "The man I told you about, my mentor from the Hourglass, he and his wife had the same abilities we do, the same connections."

Tucking the word *wife* away to think about later, I asked, "What are the other connections, besides the physical one?"

"Strong emotional ties, a visceral pull toward each other."

I didn't have any trouble believing that. I was more drawn to him every time I saw him. More than I was willing to admit, even to myself. "What does all this have to do with the Hourglass? Why won't you tell me anything about it?"

"I have my reasons," he said. "There are things you can't know yet—"

"You said you'd tell me everything," I accused. "I need to know *everything.*"

"I did tell you everything. About you." He stood abruptly, staring over the edge of the patio down onto the street. "You've seen time-travel movies. Parts of them are true. Events can be manipulated, but usually not without consequences."

Michael turned back and crouched down, balancing on the balls of his feet at my eye level. "I'm not just here to help you understand what you see and why. I'm here to watch out for you and to . . ."

He broke off. I got the feeling he almost revealed something he didn't want to share.

"Don't stop now," I said.

"This is where the visceral thing comes in." He took my hands in his. "Either you trust me or you don't."

I didn't know about trusting him. I did know I didn't want him to stop touching me. I was getting used to the intensity. He leaned closer. I lost myself in the depths of his warm brown eyes, wondering if his lips would be warm, too . . .

Michael slowly inched forward before losing his balance and tipping to one side. He uttered a low curse under his breath and stepped away.

"You . . . You rule breaker!" My mouth dropped open, and I propelled myself up and out of the chair, poking him in the chest. "You almost kissed me!"

Michael backed up into the wrought-iron fence. "No, I didn't."

He didn't mean it. I took a step closer and spoke in a whisper. "Liar."

Running his hand over his face, he groaned in defeat. In one movement he turned so I was the one with my back pressed against the cold metal. The benefit was that my front was pressed against Michael.

He bent down, burying his face in my neck. I reached back to grab onto the iron bars behind me to hold myself up. My jacket slipped off my shoulders. I was pretty sure I was on fire, and at that moment I would have sworn that bursting into flame was a glorious way to go.

I'd never touched alcohol—doesn't mix too well with crazy pills—but I knew at that moment what it must feel like to be drunk. Everything in my world shifted, and I knew I would trade every breath I'd ever taken for more of him. In a heartbeat.

Then, from the corner of my eye, I saw a red blinking light.

Security camera.

Chapter 15

I don't think it will make a difference if you destroy it."

I'd pulled a table umbrella from its stand and was using it, rather ineffectively, to knock the camera off the side of the building.

"Really, I'm sure the footage is stored in a computer somewhere." He had two fingers over his lips, making every effort to hide his burgeoning smile.

Slamming the umbrella to the ground, I fisted my hands on my hips and glared at him.

He let go with a deep belly laugh. It would've been contagious if I weren't so furious. My senses were reeling. I felt *denied*.

"Sweetheart, listen." The term of endearment stopped me cold. Nothing else would have. I could not explain away the affection in his eyes because I felt it, too. "We're in dangerous territory here."

"Right now the only thing that's dangerous is me, especially when I get my hands on Thomas."

"Emerson—"

I tilted my head to one side. "I think you have nickname clearance now."

I tried to appreciate his smile without focusing on his lips.

"Em, it was a good thing you saw that camera when you did." Michael sounded as if he were trying to convince himself. "We could have had a major disaster on our hands."

"Right now the earth could fall off its axis, and I wouldn't give a rat's behind."

Michael's gaze skimmed over my bare shoulders, and he reached out to gently pull my jacket around them. "I've known since before we met how it would be between us. But knowing didn't prepare me for you. I'm sorry."

"I wish I could say *I* was sorry."

"The rules about . . . fraternization . . . are in place for a reason." He gestured to the fence and then closed his eyes. "This can't happen again."

I'd never had a real relationship. Back before my world went pear shaped, I indulged in the occasional fantasy involving a movie star or pop singer like any other normal teenage girl, but the last few years had been spent in an on-again, off-again with Joe Pharmaceutical. I had no idea how normal relationships worked to begin with, and Michael and I were far from normal. Talk about going from zero to sixty in eight seconds or less.

I should contact the *Guinness Book of World Records*, category: "making up for lost time."

Michael ran his hands over his face again. "We don't need to be confused when there's a bigger purpose."

"I'm not confused at all." Just worked up. "And what bigger purpose? It's not like we're saving the world."

He said nothing.

"Michael?"

I considered flipping him over my shoulder again to make myself feel better. I told him as much.

"I think it's time you explain that particular trick."

Michael and I sat on the flat section of roof outside our bedroom windows. We'd reconnected after going back to our respective lofts; it was late after all, and I didn't want my brother to ask any questions. Considering Thomas and his spying habit, I was already going to be in for it due to the evidence captured by the security camera. I hoped he would believe nothing happened.

Not that it did. Of this I was painfully aware.

We kept a safe amount of distance between us. No matter how far away Michael sat, I still felt an insatiable pull toward him. It grew stronger all the time, as if our centers were connected. Made it hard to concentrate.

"How did you become a teenage ninja?" He didn't bother to hide the teasing in his voice.

"I took martial arts as my physical education elective at school. I was the best in the class. Once the semester was over I pursued my black belt at a private studio. I passed the test for brown right before I came home." I sensed his doubtful look rather than seeing it. The streetlights didn't quite shine high enough to light our perch above them, and the moon was a waxing crescent. "I know. It was a shock to me, too, but it was a healthy way to take out my frustrations."

"It's not been very healthy for me," he said, his chuckle quiet in the night air.

"I've gone easy on you. Tell me, will my ass-kicking abilities come in handy when I'm 'saving the world'?"

"It's not the whole world, exactly."

"Just the contingent forty-eight states?"

He sighed. "I'm not talking geography."

"Details, please."

Michael pulled his legs up, resting his forearms on his knees, his long fingers intertwined. "I'm trying to keep you out of trouble, Emerson. And that involves my keeping quiet for now. It's not easy for me, but this is the way it has to be."

"Not easy for you?" I scoffed. "How about you spill the information, and I'll take care of myself?"

He looked up at the sliver of moon hanging in the sky. So did I.

"Michael, you need to understand I've been asking questions for the past four years. In my head, out loud, every way you can think of. And I've never gotten any answers until you came along."

"We can't cover four years in one night." He slid his hand across the roof toward me, palm down.

I slid my hand toward his, palm up, the shingles rough on the back of my hand. Our fingers barely met, yet every inch of my skin responded. The desire to close the distance so more of me could touch more of him was overwhelming. My breath caught in my chest, and I looked at him.

He pulled away without looking back.

I left my hand open to the night sky. "How long before you tell me everything?"

"Not long, I promise. Can you wait?"

"Do I have a choice?"

He didn't answer.

"You have no idea how frustrated I am." About so many things.

"Give me until tomorrow. Tomorrow, I promise. I just want to make sure we do this the right way. Trust me?"

"Yes," I answered, breaking my own rule.

Chapter 16

You want a ride to work?" Thomas asked as I grabbed my backpack. I was wearing my trusty pink rain jacket because it was raining. Again.

"No, it's not that far." My hair was already wet anyway. I'd had some difficulty motivating myself to wake up and shower and hadn't had time to dry it. After I'd climbed in my window last night I could still sense Michael, could almost hear him breathing on the other side of the wall. It took sleep a long time to pull me under, my thoughts racing too fast for my brain to keep up.

As I walked to Murphy's Law, I wondered why I had never seen Michael in a car. How did he get around? Probably he snapped and appeared places at will. Or maybe he time traveled where he wanted to go.

Or maybe he was delusional, and I was one small step away from buying it.

I snorted out loud, not even bothering to be embarrassed as a man in a Confederate soldier uniform looked at me strangely. He probably wasn't really there anyway. I'd have liked to kick him just to see, but I didn't want to take the chance.

Time travel? Saving the world? Had I fallen into a straight-to-DVD release? How could I believe Michael was telling me the truth? It was all so crazy. If I had learned about rips before I experienced one, I wouldn't have believed it. Lots of unbelievable things happened. Every day. Things like gravity.

But time travel? Saving the world? At seventeen?

I pushed open the door to the coffee shop so hard I almost knocked the welcome bell from the doorframe. "Morning," I mumbled to Lily as I walked past her, reaching greedily for the espresso machine.

She leaned over to peer into my eyes before saying with a hint of disgust, "You look like something I'd scrape off the bottom of my shoe."

"Great, thanks. Not all of us can be naturally gorgeous. I bet you can't even tell when you have sleepless nights."

She shoved me out of the way and took over. "Let's keep you away from heavy machinery until you get your groove on. Why no sleep?"

"The list is way too long." And if I gave it to her, she'd call for the men in white coats. "Let's just say I'm facing a challenge."

"Does it have anything to do with Michael?"

I grabbed the cup of espresso she offered and threw it back in one scalding, exhilarating moment. After I could feel my tongue again, I held out my cup for a refill and said, "Sort of."

"Sort of."

"I'm not ready to talk about it."

"Hmph." Lily turned to start another espresso, and as if the day weren't already off to a rip-roaring start, an image began to take shape behind her.

Just beyond the register sat a table full of teenagers in poodle skirts and letter sweaters. I knew they had to be ripples, because Murphy's Law had slick, modern furniture instead of the leather booth with the Formica table where the couples were seated. They joked with a waitress in a pink nylon dress, a gingham-checked apron tied around her waist.

Pretty sure that wasn't the standard uniform.

"Em? Emerson?" Lily snapped to get my attention. "Where did you go?"

"The nineteen fifties, if those shoes are any indication." Saddle oxfords. Really.

"What?"

Crap. I'd said that out loud. "Nothing. Just a movie I watched last night. Thinking about it. Sandy and Danny. Beauty School Drop Out. Greased Lightning."

"Okay." Lily looked at me strangely as I sang "Shama Lama Ding Dong" under my breath. "I'm going to go pull some piecrusts out of the freezer. You'll be all right out here by yourself?"

I was busy staring at a dude with enough grease in his hair to cook a pan of biscuits.

"Em?"

"Yes. Yes. Go ahead." I nodded serenely as she walked into the kitchen.

The second she was gone I scrambled to look under the counter. I had to find something long enough to reach the rips so I could make them disappear. No way could I work a whole shift with the entire cast of *Grease* two feet away from me.

"Jackpot."

I popped up, threw my body across the counter, and proceeded to stick a long-handled rolling pin into all the rips I could reach. It wasn't easy—they started running once Biscuit Boy went down. Busy rip jousting like Don Quixote fencing windmills, I was too distracted to notice Lily backing into the swinging door from the kitchen while balancing a wide metal tray of piecrusts. A millisecond before she turned around I popped the last rip, slid back across the counter, and chucked the rolling pin over my shoulder.

"What was that?" Lily almost dropped the doughy circles as she whipped her head toward the noise.

"Rats. I think you have rats. Really big ones." I held my hands two feet apart as an example and then leaned against the counter, trying to catch my breath. "Huge. You should probably have Abuela check that out."

Lily raised one eyebrow, put the tray down, and wiped her

hands on a dish towel. "You're obviously not okay. Are you going to talk to me or am I going to have to drag it out of you?"

Avoidance. I let out a sigh. "I can't have feelings for him."

"Why?"

So many reasons. "Number one: I'm not the girlfriend/boyfriend type. I'm the crazy girl at the lunch table in the cafeteria type."

"Em, that was a long time ago. That doesn't have anything to do with who you are now."

It had everything to do with who I was now.

"Number two: He might be his own brand of crazy."

"Crazy like he's a serial killer, or crazy like he attends Star Trek conventions in full costume?"

"That's only crazy if you dress like a Klingon," I pointed out.

Lily rolled her eyes.

"Neither one of those." I pushed myself away from the counter, retrieved my espresso cup, and took a slow sip. "Maybe he has a secret, and maybe it's too outrageous to believe. But everyone has secrets, right?"

"Not everyone." Her body tensed, and she twisted the dish towel in her hands. "I don't have any secrets. My life is an open book. Do you have a number three?"

"Um . . . yes." I picked up the sugar dispenser and dumped a couple of tablespoons' worth into my cup, looking at Lily with my peripheral vision. "Number three: Thomas has his 'no fraternization' rule, and Michael seems perfectly willing to enforce it."

She lowered her shoulders and chewed on her bottom lip for a few seconds before responding. "That could be a good thing. It gives you time to get to know him before you decide how you feel."

"I guess."

"Take advantage of it. You don't have to rush things. If he's worth it now, he'll still be worth it in a month. Or you could just take advantage of all that pent-up frustration and roll out those piecrusts for me." Lily walked around the counter and headed for the corner of the café, scooping up the rolling pin from where I'd sent it flying moments before. She rinsed it off in the sink, dried it, and patted it down with flour.

I watched her with my mouth hanging open. "How did you know where that was?"

"What? Um . . . that's where I keep it." A slow flush spread up her neck to her cheeks. "Why do you ask?"

We stared at each other for a seemingly endless moment.

"No reason."

She held out the pin.

I pushed up my sleeves, took it, and started rolling.

When Lily and I walked out together at the end of our shift, the sun was shining through the disappearing gray clouds, reflecting off the puddles gathered on the asphalt. The humidity was stifling, making my hair feel heavy.

I shoved my jacket into my backpack and grabbed a ponytail elastic out of a side pocket. Stopping above the last step to the sidewalk, I held my bag between my knees and the elastic band in my mouth, twisting up my hair with my hands while I tried to keep my balance.

I froze midtwist when I saw Michael across the street. He was leaning back against a sleek black convertible with the top down, two fingers covering his lips to keep from laughing. He did that a lot. I wondered if it was a habit before he met me.

Lily let out a grunt of appreciation. "Mmm. Santa came early, and look at the deliciousness he brought with him." She smoothed down her hair and rooted around in her purse, pulling out a breath mint. "Adios."

"Hold it." I reached out to grab the strap on her bag, pulling her back. "That deliciousness isn't available for sampling."

She turned to face me, eyes wide. "Is *that* the challenge you were talking about?"

"The challenge that's off-limits. And occasionally a pain in the ass." And possibly insane.

"Oh, girl." Lily shook her head, looking back at Michael with obvious admiration. "I am so sorry."

"What are you doing anyway? You never approach guys. I realize he's exceptional, but really?" He might be a pain, but he was *my* pain. Sort of.

Lily looked at me and shrugged. "Exceptional is an under-statement."

"Later," I murmured as I jumped the last step and ran toward him, barely looking as I crossed the street.

"Hey." The breathless thing was happening again, but I didn't care.

"Hey," he replied. I wanted to put my hands on him as a test, to see if the connection existed on a busy street in the middle of the afternoon. I reached a finger out to boldly touch the curve below his smile.

He reached up to grab my arm. "Are you trying to get me fired? Or kill me?"

"You would be of no use to me dead." Although I couldn't breathe when he touched me, so I guess it all depended on who kicked the bucket first. He still held my wrist, and my whole arm was vibrating.

I almost wished he were telling the truth about the whole time-travel thing. He was way too pretty to be delusional.

"Get in." Michael let go of my arm, grabbed my backpack, and opened my car door. I slid into the leather seat. As he shut the door and walked around the car, I looked back toward the front of the coffee shop.

Lily, her mouth hanging open, still stood in the exact same spot.

Chapter 17

"When did curbside service become part of the deal?" The bucket seats in the small foreign car put us precariously close to each other. At least the sky spread out above us gave the illusion of space. He steered away from the town square and turned down the radio.

"I have to go away for a day or two. I thought if we were both buckled in, I could have an actual conversation with you before I left. It's important. So don't touch me." He made a noise that resembled a growl. "I mean, again."

"What are we talking about now?" I was ready to do something. At least we could start my . . . time-travel training. I made a mental note not to say that out loud.

"I've got a couple of things I want you to read." The wind rumpled his hair as he steered with one hand, turning to reach into the tiny backseat with the other. He gave me a hardcover book with the title *Space Time Continuum and Wormhole Theories*, in addition to a thick, worn three-ring binder with tattered and coffee-stained pages inside. "Concentrate on the binder—move to the book if you have time. It's theory, not fact. The facts are in the binder. Don't let it out of your sight."

One wish granted, even if it was just reading material. Maybe the books held some kind of scientific proof that would help me believe him. Like I would understand it if I saw it.

Michael turned down one of my favorite back roads. It ran parallel to a lake. I took my hair down from the ponytail and rested my head back against the seat, looking up at the trees along the shoreline that were tinged with color. Autumn always fascinated me—so much beauty in dying. Leaves holding on until the bitter end, finally going down in a blaze of glory, almost as if they were trying to convince us to keep them alive.

I looked at Michael's profile out of the corner of my eye, attempting objectivity. Crazy connection or not, any girl would be drawn to him, as evidenced by Lily's reaction. Straight nose, strong chin and jaw, and then there was that pesky mouth of his. I closed my eyes, enjoying the warmth of the sun peeking through the trees and the wind in my hair. I recited multiplication tables in my head to keep my thoughts under control and my hands to myself.

I don't know when I fell asleep, just that I awoke when I heard the engine cut off. We were parked on the side street by the lofts.

The sun hung only slightly lower in the sky, so I hadn't been out long. I stretched and opened my eyes to Michael, who appeared to be in pain. His brows pulled together over his dark eyes, and there was a hard set to his mouth.

I froze midstretch. "What's wrong?"

"Nothing," he said, his voice rough.

I didn't think I had crossed any boundaries since I touched him before I got in the car, and none of my roommates at school ever claimed I talked in my sleep.

"I'm sorry about before, on the street—"

He shook his head. "It wasn't that."

"Then what did I do?"

"Besides fall asleep?"

"I'm sorry. It's not the company, but we were up so late, and the sun felt so good." I stopped. Why was I defending myself? Michael wasn't too big on the explanations, so I had no idea why I was trying to clarify anything to him.

He looked away from me to focus on the side of the building. "You seem so vulnerable when you sleep. I don't get that from you a lot."

I shifted uncomfortably in my seat. "I almost cried at dinner the other night. Was that not vulnerable enough for you?"

"There's a difference. At dinner you were sad; today you're . . . soft." His eyes returned to my face. What I saw in them made me catch my breath.

"As long as I didn't drool."

One corner of his mouth twisted into a half smile. "I wish I didn't have to go."

"Don't."

"I have to. It's probably not a bad thing. I don't know how I would handle another incident like the one we had last night on the patio," he said uneasily.

"When will you be back?" I reached down to grab my backpack and the books he gave me. And to hide my flaming face.

"I can't say for sure, but maybe by tomorrow. I hope you're a fast reader."

I opened the car door. I needed to get out, needed to put space between us. "Please. Faster than a speeding bullet. Even with the whole"—I twirled one finger in a circle beside my head, giving him the international sign for crazy—"thing, I was ranked in the top five of my junior class." I shut the car door for emphasis. "Actually, top three."

"Funny, gorgeous, and a genius. What a package." He backed out of the parking space, smiling as he drove away.

I loved that he left crazy off the list.

I loved it even more that he would never think to add it.

Chapter 18

The binder Michael gave me overflowed with detailed information, making me cross-eyed. I gave it all I had for half an hour, decided I needed sugar and caffeine, and went to grind some beans I'd snagged from Murphy's Law for a fresh pot of coffee.

Instead of watching it drip, I did my good deed for the day and cleared the countertops of all the piled-up papers. I pinned tiny white cards with dates and times for obstetrician's appointments scribbled on them to the corkboard on the wall, threw away old newspapers, and saved unopened bills. I'd just finished spraying down the counters when a long beep sounded to tell me my coffee was brewed. I leaned down to put the spray cleaner under the sink and spotted something barely sticking out from underneath the cabinets.

Dru's key ring.

Maybe the excitement of the pregnancy was making Dru forgetful, because it was totally unlike Dru to lose anything. Yet her keys, including the master, lay on the floor right in front of me.

By accident.

Or by fate.

I wanted to know more about Michael. I didn't expect anyone from my family to be home for at least another hour, and since Michael was out of town, what kept me from slipping next door, sliding the key into the lock, and taking a quick look around? Maybe Michael left a candle burning. Maybe he forgot to turn off his iron, or the oven. Maybe he left his dishwasher running and it was flooding the place, or a thirsty plant desperately needed water.

Maybe I was way out of line.

I held the key ring by the master key, swinging it back and forth in front of my eyes. Yes or no, yes or no. I was saved from any further contemplation of breaking and entering when the phone rang. Dru sounded more harried than I'd ever heard her.

"Em, thank goodness you're there. I didn't have Michael's cell, and the guys are coming from the storage place to pick up the master for the building so they can deliver his sofa. But I don't have my keys because I couldn't find them this morning and he's not answering at his loft and I think I left them—"

"Calm down," I said, laughing. "I have your keys."

"Oh, thank goodness." She took a deep breath. Good choice. "Can you let the movers in?"

My smile spread wide enough to rival the Grinch's. "Absolutely."

The delivery guys did their job quickly. To justify the excuse to linger, I set off to look for any plants affected by drought.

Even though he'd lived in it for only a few days, the apartment smelled like Michael. Clean, like laundry fresh from a clothesline with a hint of something else, maybe pheromones. I caught a whiff of his citrusy cologne and almost forgot what I was doing. I gave myself a mental smack.

Focus. Here to spy.

Dru furnished Michael's place with items from her stock storage, and the design was simple. It suited his personality. The only concession was a complicated-looking computer. I bumped the corner of the table it sat on with my hip, jostling the mouse. When the computer blinked to life, the screen showed that it was password protected.

Every loft had built-in bookshelves. Most of Michael's were filled with modern decorative accessories, courtesy of Dru. Two held personal items. On the first was a book of poetry by Byron, along with novels by Kurt Vonnegut, Orson Scott Card, and Jack Kerouac's *On the Road*. I realized I'd never asked him about his major. Probably wasn't time travel. I didn't think our local college was quite that progressive.

The second shelf held photographs. One obviously of his family when he was younger—his dad wasn't in the picture. Another showed an adolescent Michael laughing with an older man at a lake, fishing paraphernalia scattered around. I peered closer. No resemblance.

A stack of photos lay facedown on the shelf. I flipped through them. Graduation shots, a group on a ski trip, someone's eighteenth birthday party, and then, last in the pile, a girl wearing a princess costume with dark auburn hair and a wide smile. At first I thought it was Michael's sister, but something about the girl in the picture was different, maybe the perfect shape of her oval face or her porcelain skin. Jealousy rolled in my stomach. She looked mysterious and exotic and . . . tall.

In the kitchen, I opened a couple of cabinets and the fridge. Nothing much, unless you counted energy drinks and frozen dinners. A box of Fruity Pebbles sat on his counter. Men.

A moment of hesitation stopped me at his bedroom door. People were less likely to be careful with what they left lying around in their bedrooms. I had no idea what I was looking for, but I was afraid of what I would find. I took a deep breath and clasped my hands behind my back.

If the scent of Michael when I opened the front door hadn't already prepared me, when I walked into his bedroom I might have just shoved my face in his pillow and stayed. His bed was made and, as I thought, situated directly on the other side of the wall from mine. No wonder I couldn't sleep.

More books took up space on his bedside table, in addition to a docking station that held his iPod. I leaned over to check out his taste in music and noticed a pad of paper with some scribbling on it.

Bingo.

I eyed it upside down for a second then unclasped my hands to pick up the pad and look at it more closely. When I did, a few business cards fell to the ground. I scooped them up, slightly panicked because I didn't know if they had fallen from between the pages of the notebook or the tabletop. I gave them a quick glance. They all said the same thing:

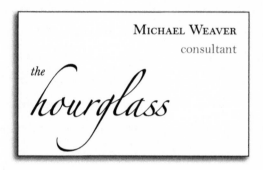

On the back was an address just outside Ivy Springs proper. I shoved one in my pocket, stacking the rest in a neat pile. I tried to decipher the words on the pad, but they were in some kind of shorthand or code. Michael seemed to be a master at hiding things.

"What are you looking for?"

I let out a squeak and jumped, almost dropping the notebook. Jack stood beside me with a half smile on his lips.

"You scared me!" I was embarrassed to be busted, even by Jack, who didn't have anyone to tell. I looked down at my hands and saw my fingers still clutching the notepad. I flung it back on the bedside table, mortified when I had to pick it back up and flip it over so it would look as it did before I touched it. "How did you get in here?"

Jack pursed his lips, hesitating before answering. "I can move between rooms."

I considered what that meant, and my skin became gooseflesh. "Like from my bedroom to my bathroom?"

"No, no," he answered, shaking his head before reassuring me. Still keeping his distance, he took a step closer. "As tempting as it might be, I would never do that. I respect you too much."

I couldn't look away from him. His pupils weren't exactly black, just a shade lighter, and his irises were less blue today and more gray. "So you've been in Michael's room before?"

"I have," he concurred.

Uh-oh.

"Have you ever talked to him?" My forehead broke out in a sweat. Jack might have someone to tell about my snooping. What if he'd appeared to Michael, too?

"No," Jack said, his eyes growing wide. "Only you."

"Good." I hadn't realized rips could pick when to reveal themselves. I'd have to ask Michael about that later. "Seen anything interesting?" I prodded.

"Such as?"

"I don't know," I shrugged it off. "Who he talks to, what he does?"

"He seems to type on that a lot." Jack pointed to the computer with one hand, leaving the other behind his back. He then pointed toward the portable phone on the desk. "And he speaks to someone on that quite frequently."

"Have you heard him say any names?"

"I've heard him mention you a few times." Jack said the words carefully, watching me, as if he was weighing my reaction.

"My name?" I asked. "In what context?"

"Just that you were nice . . . no"—he stopped, considering—"you were coming along nicely . . . and that all was going according to plan."

I turned to stalk blindly out of the bedroom, angry with myself for being hurt by his words.

"Where are you going?" He followed close behind me.

"None of your business." I stopped. I had no reason to be so rude to him. I turned back around to apologize, catching him off guard. He sidestepped to avoid the bedside table.

I froze.

"What's wrong?" Jack asked.

I took a hesitant step toward him. "Why do you avoid solid objects? I've noticed it before, but it didn't sink in."

"I don't avoid anything," he answered, stepping fluidly away from me.

"But you do. Except for the other night, you were sitting on my bed—I felt your weight pushing down my mattress. How did you do that? And why are you always holding your hands together that way, like you're afraid to touch anything?"

"I'm not afraid," he protested, pulling his hands apart quickly, dropping one to his side and tucking the other into his vest. "It's simply a habit."

"I don't think so." I took another step closer, lifting my hand and reaching gingerly toward his chest.

"Stop. Stay where you are," he warned, his voice full of fear.

Squeezing my eyes shut and taking a deep breath, I moved forward to slide my hand through his form.

Chapter 19

I met resistance.

It wasn't solid matter exactly, more like thick mud or wet sand. Jack twisted out of my way at the same time I jerked away from him.

"What the hell?" I looked at the traces of the substance on my hand. Whatever it was, it sort of . . . glowed.

When I looked up, Jack was gone. I got out of Michael's apartment as quickly as possible, not even bothering to lock the door behind me. I had no idea what to do next.

Besides wash my hands.

Even though I was more than freaked out by Jack and his semisolid state, the address for the Hourglass was burning a hole in my pocket. I could be there in less than twenty minutes.

I had to risk it.

After a thorough hand scrub in my bathroom sink, I threw some essentials and dark clothing—in case I needed to blend—into a bag, as well as the binder Michael told me not to let out of my sight. I twisted up my hair to keep it out of my face before stopping in the freshly tidied kitchen to pour my coffee into a travel mug. I wrote a quick note for Thomas and Dru and left the loft with Michael's card in my hand.

Thomas had installed GPS in Dru's SUV for her birthday. All I had to do was enter in the address listed on the business card. I checked the gas gauge, then took a deep breath, putting the vehicle in reverse. I was a decent driver, but I didn't do it very often. Good thing driving a car was like riding a bicycle.

Or whatever.

Jack. If he wasn't a rip, what was he? What if he'd existed for so long that he picked up some matter along the way? If that was the case, why hadn't Scarlett been semisolid, too?

I could ask Michael, but for reasons I didn't exactly understand, I wanted to keep Jack to myself. My face grew hot just thinking about it.

I'd expected the Hourglass to be in some kind of an office building. Instead, the GPS system led me through downtown to rolling green farmland and rural country estates. I lowered my window to let in the breeze, along with the smell of harvested hay and other earthy things. Soon, the GPS indicated I'd reached my destination, and I stopped, noting the property was lined with a stone fence guarded by an iron gate. It stood open.

Tall oaks blocked the view from the main road. A gravel drive curved beneath them, leading to something I couldn't see.

I'd have to take a chance.

One benefit of being a survivor was that there was no fear when it came to taking risks. What could happen? I could go to jail for trespassing. Couldn't be worse than a mental hospital. Whoever lived behind the stone fence could capture me and hold me prisoner while performing experiments on me. Not unlike a mental hospital. I hesitated, my turn signal blinking so brightly it felt like a beacon for the security officers and guard dogs I imagined hiding just beyond the property line.

I *needed* answers.

I needed to know if Michael was telling me the truth—and what he was still hiding.

I took a deep breath and drove through the gate.

Chapter 20

*W*ondering if I had entered the wrong address in the GPS, I looked at the business card again to make sure I was in the right place. A Greek Revival style plantation house spread out in front of me—big, rambling, and red brick, with tall white columns flanking the wide front door. No armed guards, no dogs, nothing like I expected. Part of the driveway extended past the house, creating a small parking area under some trees.

After I pulled in, I decided in my typical fly-by-the-seat-of-my-pants fashion that if anyone asked, I was going to be "lost." I hoped no one would have the opportunity to look in the car. Lost and a fancy GPS system didn't go together. I decided to case the joint—since I was such a superspy and all.

Sliding out of the car into the humidity, I hurried to hide myself behind the trees. The sunset burned orange on the edge of the horizon, all Creamsicle and heat. In the scant amount of daylight left, the outline of a stable as well as some other outbuildings rose against the backdrop of dark forest.

I crept closer.

Perspiration formed at the base of my neck and ran down my back as I slid along the side of the house, ducking at the occasional low window. The effort I expended to stay quiet combined with the heavy air made me glad I'd pulled my hair up. Once I reached the corner of the house, I used the bottom of my shirt to wipe my forehead. The leaves might be changing, but it didn't feel like fall was almost here.

The back of the property reminded me of one of those grandiose 1980s television shows I had seen in reruns. A well-lit lap pool was lined by pencil-thin evergreens in urns. Four columns stood at each corner of the Italian ceramic tile patio. A three-tiered stone terrace extended from the back of the house. Tiny café tables with matching chairs and plush outdoor furniture were scattered about, along with electric torches and more evergreens in urns. It certainly didn't feel like Top Secret Time Travel Headquarters.

I ducked behind a retaining wall when I heard voices. I could barely make out the shape of two people at the other end of the patio. They were leaning over the railing, and their voices carried. Distinctly male.

One stood out.

Michael.

Moving closer, I placed my back against the stone retaining wall and slid down into a sitting position. Might as well get comfortable. As comfortable as I could get against rocks.

"So what's she like?" asked the voice I didn't recognize.

"Frustrating. Unbelievable." Michael sighed. "More than I ever thought possible."

There was a brief silence. "What does she know?"

"Pretty much everything, except why I need her."

"How did she take it?"

"How do you think she took it? How would you?"

I stiffened. I had a feeling I knew who they were talking about.

"You *have* to tell her the rest." The unknown voice carried urgency.

"The timing is wrong, Kaleb. She's starting to trust me."

"You need to fill her in before something happens." Kaleb's voice was rougher, more gravelly than Michael's. I wished I could see Kaleb's face. I wondered if it matched his voice. "She needs to know what's going on. You can't let her go into this blind."

"I'll take care of it." Michael sounded as if he were speaking through gritted teeth.

"Do," Kaleb said. At least he wanted me to be able to protect myself instead of keeping me in the dark. I liked him. Whoever he was. "Remember, we're a team. I'll handle the files; you handle her. A lot is on the line for a lot of people."

"I made a promise, and I'm going to keep it. I'll do whatever it takes to get him back, whatever the sacrifice."

"You think she'll go for it?"

Michael paused before answering. "I can't be sure. But I wouldn't doubt it. She's pretty amazing."

The sound of surprised laughter echoed off the stone wall. "Mike! Are you into her?"

"I can't be. You know the rules."

Kaleb snorted. "That wouldn't stop me."

"I know. Besides, I'm not into her." Michael's voice was firm. Kaleb must have given him a doubtful look, because Michael repeated, "I'm not into her. I have my reasons."

My stomach dropped a little.

"Brother, I can *sense*. I *know*. If this girl is as 'amazing' as you say she is, you're just being stupid. But I keep forgetting, you're all about chivalry and honor," Kaleb said in a singsong voice.

"You should try it sometime," Michael answered quietly.

"Just *please* don't tell me you're holding back because of Ava."

"Kaleb," Michael said, sounding frustrated, "I've already told you how things are with Ava—"

He stopped talking when light flashed on in one of the upstairs windows, throwing a yellow square on the stone terrace floor. "I'd better go back inside," Kaleb said in a rushed voice. "Tell her—don't treat her like a kid."

"Go!" I heard Michael make a hissing sound through his teeth, and then a door closed.

The light in the upstairs window went off.

I sat for a minute, trying to process. I couldn't swear they were discussing me; no one said my name. Call it massive paranoia, which was entirely possible, or incredible intuition—I was pretty sure I was the "she" in the conversation.

But who was the "he"?

Sneaking away from the terrace, I crept back the way I'd come. I didn't hurry, giving Michael time to clear out so I could avoid running into him. As I neared the front of the house I got curious and peeked in one of the low windows.

On one wall hung several photographs. Even though they were lit from above, a strange reflection shone off the faces, making them hard to see. Scanning them one by one, I paused when I reached the last picture in the row. Something about the face seemed familiar. Before I could place it, another light went on inside the house, causing my shadow to stand out in sharp relief on the grass. I flattened myself against the wall until the light went off again, then I took off in the direction of the car, flinging the door open when I reached it.

I let out a scream.

Someone was already sitting there.

Chapter 21

Be quiet," Michael whispered. "Are you trying to wake the dead?"

"What are you doing?" I managed to choke out, clutching my hand to my chest, my heart pounding.

He'd turned off the inside car lights, but I could still see his angry expression in the fading light. "I think the better question is what are *you* doing?"

I briefly considered telling him I was lost and tried to think fast. Nope, nothing. I shook my head, gasping for breath.

"How did you find me?"

"I wasn't looking for you. I was looking for the Hourglass," I said. "I got the address from the business cards on your bedside table." Okay, not helpful. "Dru's keys. Just sort of . . . there on my kitchen floor . . . needed me to let the couch guys into your loft. I'm sorry."

Spies should be able to endure torture and still keep their secrets. I spilled mine out like pennies from a broken piggy bank.

Michael sighed and leaned back on the headrest. "Great. What else did you find?"

"Nothing really."

Except a picture of a gorgeous girl and some notes written in code.

"It's not safe for you to be here," Michael said, reaching up to grip the steering wheel. "We need to get you off the property before anyone sees you."

"You mean someone like Kaleb?"

"Kaleb is the least of your worries right now."

"At least he thinks I should know what's going on," I taunted. "He's never even met me, and he gives me more credit than you do."

Michael shook his head in disgust and motioned to the seat beside him. "Get in." When I didn't move, he reached out with both hands to pull me across his lap, dumping me in the passenger seat. "Did they teach you to eavesdrop at boarding school, too?"

"What makes you think you can manhandle me?" The heat from his touch racing across my skin didn't do a thing to cool me down. He cranked the car. I looked at his face, now fully illuminated from the light of the dash. "And I didn't mean to eavesdrop. I was in the right place—okay," I amended when he raised his eyebrows, "the wrong place at the right time."

More head shaking.

Michael drove slowly down the long driveway, not switching on the headlights until we reached the main road. He turned in the opposite direction of Ivy Springs.

"What about your car?" I asked.

"We'll pick it up on the way back."

"On the way back from where?" Ah, my old friend, anxiety—throwing itself into the blender with sheer terror and embarrassment.

"My place," he said, keeping his eyes on the road.

"Isn't it in the same direction as my place?"

"No," he answered with forced patience. "I meant I'm going back to my place at school. And you're coming with me. There's someone I need you to meet."

"Can't it wait? Who is it? You have a place at school?"

"Would you please stop asking questions for one second? I have to figure out how to handle this." The tiny muscles in his jaw tightened.

I waited exactly one beat. "When you left today, why didn't you tell me where you were going?"

Michael let out a loud groan of frustration. "Didn't I just ask you to stop asking questions?"

"You asked me to stop for one second. You should have been more specific if you wanted longer." Having a big brother taught me quite a bit about arguing with the intent to wear down my opponent. Like a rat terrier with a pork chop. "Why didn't you tell me you were going to the Hourglass?"

"Well, Emerson, I obviously didn't want you to follow me." He turned up the radio in a noticeable ploy to silence me.

"I didn't follow you. Exactly," I argued, turning it back down.

"No, you invaded my privacy and then happened to end up at the one place I wanted you to avoid." He kept his voice controlled, but anger simmered beneath the surface. "You should have stayed away."

I briefly wondered if I should be afraid instead of mad. Michael had basically carjacked me and was driving somewhere unknown, against my will. That equaled kidnapping. I dug deep, searching for any indication I was scared.

Nope. Just pissed.

We turned down a small side street behind campus. The houses I could see were early-twentieth-century bungalow homes, all well appointed. We pulled into the driveway of one of the nicer ones. It boasted a low-pitched gabled roof, black shutters, and a wide front porch.

Michael came around to open my door. I didn't move or speak as he took my bag and started for the house. When he realized I wasn't with him, he turned back to the car, blowing out a gust of air that lifted the hair from his forehead. "Emerson? Don't make me come and get you."

I followed him to the front door.

I tiptoed behind him through a dark entryway into a high-ceilinged room with elaborate moldings and wooden floors. A long mahogany table in the back of the room boasted laptops and multiple mugs of coffee in different stages of use. He placed my bag on a side table and dropped down onto one of the leather couches.

"Am I supposed to sit?" I asked, pointing to the cushion beside him. The leather reminded me of a worn baseball glove. "Or did you prefer I wait on the porch?"

He reached up to grab my sleeve and pulled. I landed a little closer to him than I would've liked at that moment, but I didn't move.

"I guess you're still mad."

Michael tilted his head to look at me, his lips twisted in disapproval.

"This whole thing is so unfair," I protested. "You're keeping secrets. Secrets about *me*. I know it, you know it—why aren't we talking about it?"

"Isn't the information about your ability enough to digest right now?"

"*The info is digested*, Michael. As a matter of fact, it's so digested it's getting ready to come out as a big pile of sh—"

"Don't get snippy with me." His eyes flashed a warning.

"I'm not snippy, *I'm mad*," I returned through gritted teeth. "And your personal health is in danger if you don't fess up about what's going on."

"I *really* underestimated you."

"What's *that* supposed to mean?"

Michael stared at me for a moment. "You're too brave for your own damn good. You have no idea what kind of situation you put yourself in tonight." He stood, pacing back and forth in front of the couch. "Seeing you at that house . . ."

"What are you talking about? Fill in the blanks," I snapped.

His wide shoulders slumped over in defeat. In one second, all the anger disappeared. "If something had happened to you tonight, it would've been my fault. Kaleb warned me not to treat you like a kid. I did it anyway, and I'm sorry."

I struggled for words, but none came.

"I can't take another step without involving you." He clasped his hands behind his head, closing his eyes. "Tonight, when you overheard Kaleb and me, we were talking about—"

"Michael?" A soft voice called from the entryway.

He dropped his hands and his eyes flew open. "Dr. Rooks?"

A woman stepped into the room. A drop-stinking-dead gorgeous woman. Her bronze skin was flawless, her dark hair cropped close to her head. Probably she didn't bother with her hair because nothing could compete with her face. I knew I was staring, and I hoped my mouth wasn't hanging open.

"Emerson, this is Dr. Rooks, the person I wanted you to meet. She's a theoretical physicist, and she teaches at the college. She's also kind of like a housemother."

I doubted seriously there'd ever been a theoretical physicist and housemother in the history of the world who looked like this one. She appeared to be in her late twenties, tall, with delicate features and wide eyes. When she turned her head to smile at me, her tiny nose ring caught the light, taking me by surprise.

"Lovely to meet you, Emerson." Something about the lilt of her voice made me think of warm rays of sunshine and tropical breezes. "Are you visiting?" she asked, puzzled.

I didn't know how to answer, so I looked at Michael. He checked the grandfather clock in the corner.

"It's almost midnight," he said to me. "You should probably call Thomas."

I didn't move.

"Please? I don't want either one of us in trouble."

"I'll call, but we're not finished here. I'm going to tell him not to expect me until tomorrow morning." I stood to retrieve my cell phone from my bag, silently daring him to contradict me, at the same time shocked by my own defiance. "Is that a problem?"

"It's your life."

Dr. Rooks smiled as I excused myself.

Michael didn't.

I stepped into the hallway to make the call, my hands shaking as I dialed. Thomas didn't answer. Relieved, I left him a quick voice mail. Better to beg for forgiveness than to ask for permission and all that. Dr. Rooks and Michael were whispering furiously when I reentered the room.

"Um, we were just discussing where you could sleep," Michael explained as they stepped apart, but the flush creeping up his neck told a different story. "Dr. Rooks is going to set up an air mattress in her room."

"Upstairs." She gestured to my bag. "Are you ready now?"

I looked at Michael. I didn't want to pitch a fit, but I wasn't above it.

"Go on," he told her. "I'll bring her up in a while. We have some things to discuss."

Chapter 22

*H*ere." Michael handed me a tall glass of ice water he'd gotten from the kitchen, then sat down on the couch beside me. "Are you sure you don't want anything to eat?"

"Stop procrastinating. All I want are answers." I rested the bottom of the glass on my thigh, watching the condensation drip down the sides to form a cold, wet ring on my jeans. "You were getting ready to tell me something about Kaleb."

"Yes, Kaleb." He blew out a deep breath. "His last name is Ballard. He's Liam Ballard's son."

It took me a second to connect the dots. When I did, my jaw dropped. "The same Liam Ballard who founded the Hourglass?"

"The same. Liam Ballard was my mentor. He's the one who died six months ago."

"Michael," I breathed out. I didn't tell him I was sorry. It never helped when people apologized for something they had no control over.

His eyes tightened, and the same mix of sadness and anger I'd seen on his face when he'd first told me about losing Liam reappeared.

Dropping his head back to stare at the ceiling, he fed me facts instead of feelings. "Years before Bennett shut down their parapsychology department, an offshoot formed."

"I read about the Bennett lab closing down." I ran the tip of my middle finger around the rim of my glass. "Not enough funding or respect."

"Liam opened the Hourglass to serve the private sector. For a moral purpose." He raised his head but didn't meet my eyes. "It had one until he died. You know what it's like to have an ability with no idea what it is or how to use it. Liam wanted a safe place for people like us to get help. A place where we could figure out a way to make a difference in the world instead of doing damage to it."

"You left. You aren't part of the Hourglass anymore," I realized.

"When Liam died, Jonathan Landers took over." Even Michael's profile displayed anger. "As much as I want to be loyal to the Hourglass and Liam's memory, I refuse to be part of it with Landers in charge."

"Why?"

"For starters, he's obsessed with getting to Liam's research. Kaleb's been keeping it under lock and key, trying to smuggle it out of the house when he can, but Landers or his minions are always in the way. There's something specific he wants. He has an agenda. I can *feel* it."

"Why didn't you stay at the Hourglass house to keep an eye on him?"

"I had other things on my plate." He looked at me, and I felt remarkably like a hamburger with a side of fries. "Besides, Kaleb has a better reason to be in the house than I do. It's his."

"If the two of you are friends, why were you so worried about being seen there tonight?"

"Because Landers doesn't know where I am or what I'm doing, and I don't want him to know. I've been trying to keep you off his radar." He raised his fingertips to his temples, rubbing them as if he had a headache. "And you practically walked up to his front door and knocked."

I didn't mention how close I'd come to doing just that.

Michael leaned his head from side to side, stretching his neck. I wondered if his muscles were as tight as mine, and what he would do if I reached out to massage his tension away. Instead of touching him, I bit the bullet and apologized.

"I'm sorry. For going to the Hourglass, and for not trusting you, and spying on you." I held my hands up in a gesture of surrender. "All of it."

"I'm sorry for acting like some kind of overprotective freak without giving you a reason. But we're invaluable to someone like Landers. If he could, he'd use me to travel to the future to manipulate the present—find cures for diseases, the economy, the energy crisis."

"Is that why you were worried about his finding me? Did you think he'd send me back in time to . . . buy Google stock or something?" Surely that wasn't what caused Michael to be so secretive. Or so angsty. "Did you think I'd go along with it?"

"No, it's nothing like that at all." Shifting on the couch, he leaned his body toward mine. Close enough to make my heart skip a beat. "It's a sense I have. The guy's obsessed with the past, and I was afraid he'd persuade you into seeing things his way. I hoped that wouldn't be the case, but I couldn't be sure until I'd met you, spent time with you."

I looked into his eyes, wondering what he saw when he looked back at me. Turning my head away, I worried my bottom lip between my teeth before asking my next question. "And what's the verdict?"

"I trust you," he said. "Enough to ask you for help."

"How can I possibly help you?"

"I need you to stop Jonathan Landers."

"Stop him from what?"

"From murdering Liam."

Chapter 23

"You need me to do what?"

"I need you and your ability to travel to the past so I can keep Jonathan Landers from killing Liam. I can't do it without you."

I sat back, taking a pillow from the couch and holding it over my chest like a shield. Tremors started in my legs, working their way up my body, through my stomach, out to my arms, and to the tips of my fingers. "I don't understand."

"If we can keep Liam from dying, Landers can't take his place as the head of the Hourglass."

"How? It's already happened. If we tried to change it— wouldn't that create like a . . . a paradox or something?" I knew nothing about time travel except what I gleaned from *Back to the Future* marathons on cable and *Lost* reruns, but paradoxes seemed basic. And, up until now, fictional. I clutched the pillow more tightly. "How can you stop someone from dying—especially if he's already dead?"

My chest ached at the possibility.

"There's a theory, called the Novikov Principle. It's a scientific loophole that would allow us to save Liam without altering time. No paradoxes. Liam was killed when there was a fire in his lab. It burned everything in the place beyond recognition."

"When you found the search pulled up on my computer . . ." I stopped. I never would've found the facts I needed in a news article. "I'd just finished reading about it."

"Did you read how thoroughly the building was burned? No identifiable body parts were found." The tendons in his knuckles protruded against the thin skin of his fingers. "Just a few charred bones."

I felt sick to my stomach. How terrible, to die that way. "I didn't get that far."

"The Novikov Principle wouldn't allow us to change the past, just affect it without producing any inconsistencies."

"I'm not following. What kind of inconsistencies?"

"Everyone believes that Liam's dead. To keep him from dying, we go back in time. Before anything happens to him we get him out of the lab." His hands relaxed as he explained. "To keep up the appearance that he's dead, we replace him with someone else. Then he goes into hiding and stays out of sight."

I swallowed furiously but nausea won out, rising in my throat.

I couldn't have heard him correctly. "Are you suggesting we let *someone else die* in his place?"

"No!" He faced me. "Since Dr. Rooks is a theoretical physics professor, and she's part of the science department at the college, she has keys, which gives me access to cadavers—"

"Stop." I took a moment to breathe. When I was sure I wasn't going to lose the contents of my stomach, I motioned for him to continue. "Why do we have to keep up the appearance that he's dead?"

"So that nothing changes. There will still be bones for evidence. And as long as Liam stays completely hidden for six months, until the exact moment in time that we go back to save him, the fact that he's actually alive won't affect the timeline. Probably." I caught a faint glimmer of hope in his voice.

"So if there were ever an event that could be altered without some sort of cosmic world-changing side effect, this is it?" I asked, trying not to think about the cadaver part.

"This is it. Especially since no one was ever able to prove conclusively that the few bones found in the lab were his."

Reaching out for my glass, I took a slow sip of water, thinking. "Saving Liam isn't just about stopping Landers. Is it?"

"Liam was like a father to me. The only father I've ever really had."

"I can see why you'd want him alive." Michael's real father abandoned him, and then his surrogate father had been murdered. I'd want justice, too.

"I don't want to do it just for me. It's for his wife, his son, all the people at the Hourglass he's helped, all the people who he had the potential to help. I never knew until I met him how much good one person could do."

"I understand."

He tilted his head and looked at me through his dark lashes. "I know. The future you understood, too. Who do you think told me about the Novikov Principle?"

Even though I did understand—probably better than most people—why he wanted to save the life of someone he loved, I couldn't make my brain process his words. I exhaled, the tremors running through my system causing my breath to come out shaky.

"You wanted answers. You just got them," he said with concern, leaning closer, not helping my breathing at all. "Are you sorry you asked?"

"You're talking about bringing someone back from the dead," I said softly.

"I know it's unbelievable." Michael took my hands in his. "But it's true."

"And I thought the concept of time travel was strange."

I tried to think clearly but found it impossible with his hands on me. Encircled in an electrical current, I looked up at him, and a thousand unspoken words passed between us. The longer he held my hands, the more intense the connection.

"I need to think about this." I pulled away and scooted to the far side of the couch, exhaling deeply and closing my eyes. My brain had stretched so far in the past couple of days I didn't see how it could hold anything else.

The possibility of altering time kept circling my thoughts. Bringing back someone you loved from the dead. Wondering if even the idea flew in the face of the universe and tempted it to a crueler fate than ever.

Exhausted and overwhelmed, I fell asleep.

Chapter 24

The glass revolving door spins, faster and faster, bringing with it arctic air and the smell of pine. I watch as it detaches from the building, still spinning, transforming into a snow-covered sled drawn by horses as black as death. As quickly as it appears, it pitches over the side of the mountain, leaving nothing but the sounds of screams hanging in the air and the mustard-yellow smell of sulfur. Beside me stands a figure, a body with no face, only holes where eyes are supposed to be, replaced with burning coals.

"No! No!" I jerked upright, and the sweat gathered at the base of my spine went cold. Michael still sat beside me. I crawled into his lap, shaking furiously, too scared to be embarrassed. The electrical current returned. This time it was comforting instead of unsettling. Concentrating on breathing instead of gulping for air,

I forced my gasping to subside to something manageable enough to allow me to form words.

"I'm sorry," I managed to choke out. "I'm okay."

"Liar." Michael rocked me back and forth, consoling me. For once he didn't seem to care how close we were. I knew I didn't.

I rested my forehead on his shoulder. He rubbed my back in small circles as I concentrated on regulating my breathing. The grandfather clock in the corner sounded twice, echoing into the room.

In the silence that followed embarrassment replaced the fear.

"Don't."

"What?" I pressed my face into his chest, hiding.

"I can tell you're self-conscious, and I don't want you to be." He lifted my chin. "I'm pretty sure you've had that dream before. What was it about?"

"It's not that I don't want to tell you, I just . . . I can't."

"Em?" My hair had come out of the elastic. He brushed it over my shoulder before resting his fingers on the back of my neck. "If you need to talk, I'm here to listen."

My pain reflected back to me from the depths of his eyes. The emotional part of our connection grabbed me by the throat. I had the feeling he already knew what I was going to say.

"My parents. The day they died."

He tucked me securely into the curve of his arm, and the electricity between us calmed to a subtle hum.

I took a deep breath, shuddering as I released it. "We were

on vacation, a ski resort. I'd started seeing the rips a couple of months before we went—my parents didn't know what to do. I think they wanted to get me out of town to see if things would stop."

He was listening, watching me carefully, maybe wondering if I was going to break.

I wondered the same thing.

"We were hurrying to catch the shuttle bus to the expert run. I couldn't find one of my ski poles. I told my mom to go on with my dad, that I was old enough to ride a shuttle by myself." I winced as I remembered the tone of voice I'd used. "She'd been in overprotective mode ever since her only daughter started showing signs of losing her mind."

"You don't seem like the kind of girl who'd go for overprotective." He took my hand in his.

"I hated it. But she wouldn't leave without me. We were still arguing when we walked through the lobby. I wasn't paying attention, and someone slammed into me. I dropped my backpack. Stuff went everywhere. My mom was frustrated, and I told her to go ahead. She did."

Almost as if it was yesterday, I could feel the cold wind as the revolving door spun. I could see my mom stepping into it, her blonde hair blowing around her face, her expression somewhere between pity and disappointment.

"Best the authorities could figure was that they either hit a patch of ice or someone ran them off the road. The shuttle bus went over the side the mountain into a half-frozen lake." My lips started to tremble. "Crashed through the ice. Took three days to recover all the bodies."

Michael said nothing, just held my hand more tightly. I rested my cheek on his shoulder. But I didn't stop talking.

"The last thing I said . . . The last thing I said to my mother . . . was that I didn't need her. I told her I didn't need her to hover, that I could take care of myself. I said I didn't need her. I've never told anyone that. Not even Thomas."

It had been too horrible to say out loud. Sharing it meant reliving it.

"But you loved them," he said. "And they loved you."

"I know."

We sat, motionless—the only sound in the room our breathing and the ticking of the clock. I could feel his chest rising and falling.

"Oh no, Emerson." Michael sat up straight. His skin went pale underneath his olive coloring. "I'm such an idiot . . . Liam . . . if anyone ever had the right to change something in the past, it's you."

"Stop." I shook my head.

"We could try to find a way . . ."

"Is there?" My voice broke. "Is there a way?"

"I don't . . . I don't know." I could tell by his eyes that he did know. He knew it was impossible.

I swallowed hard, biting the inside of my cheek, willing the tears not to fall. "If you changed that path it would change others, too. Paradoxes can't happen, right? Besides, there were funerals."

Bodies.

I tried to make my tone light and failed miserably. "Unless there's some other theory up your sleeve?"

"No." His thumb brushed a lone tear from my cheek. The care behind the gesture almost did me in. "I wish it could be different. I wish I could change things."

"I told you because I wanted to, not because I want you to help me change anything." I gave him a small smile. "Besides, I can take care of myself. Been doing it for years."

"Emerson, you just shared your deepest secret with me. I value that. Don't make light of it."

If he wasn't already holding my heart in the palm of his hand, I would have taken it out and given it to him right then.

I closed my eyes, took a deep breath.

I wished things could be different, too.

Chapter 25

I awoke to the sun fighting its way through the slats of the hor-
izontal wooden blinds covering the windows, close to claiming
victory. The room held enough light to tell me we missed our
early start back to Ivy Springs.

Too bad.

I'd spent the night in Michael's bed. I wiggled my toes, grateful he'd at least removed my shoes before tucking me in—still
fully clothed—before he returned downstairs to sleep on the
couch. The boy had propriety on lock. I inhaled deeply, noting his
pillow smelled as good as he did. I resisted the urge to bury my
face in it.

As my eyes adjusted I took in my surroundings. Definitely
not as posh as the loft, more college boy, but neat-and-tidy college
boy. A blue-and-green watchman-plaid comforter coordinated

with navy walls. His desk held a silver gooseneck lamp in addition to a sleek laptop like the one in his loft. An acoustic guitar displayed on a stand in the corner sat beside a well-stocked bookshelf. The whole combination felt very . . . Michael.

I gave in to my urges, turning my face to the side and deeply inhaling the scent of his pillow. A soft knock sounded on the door. Growing warm with embarrassment, I fanned myself for a second before I called out, "Come in."

Michael cracked opened the door, grinning. "Hey."

Waking up to his face felt extremely personal. Maybe it was because last night I opened up to someone besides a family member for the first time in four years. Or maybe it was just because it was him.

Or it could be the pillow thing.

"Shower's through that door. Towels are under the sink. I'm going to check out the breakfast situation." He dropped my bag inside the door and left before I could say anything.

I showered and dressed quickly, glad I always carried a travel toothbrush and makeup essentials in my purse. I returned to his room to find Michael sitting on the bed, holding two mugs of coffee. He scanned my all-black ensemble.

"Did you go emo and I missed it?" he asked, grin still in place.

I smoothed my hand over my shirt and said primly, "I didn't know what the Hourglass was going to be like. I brought these clothes in case I needed to blend in with the dark."

"You look like a miniature burglar."

"Don't forget I can kick your ass."

"Sorry." He wasn't, really.

"I feel bad about running you out of your own bathroom," I apologized as I took the empty chair by his desk.

"No problem. Plenty of extra showers around here." I noticed his hair was damp as he held out one of the mugs. "Sorry, it isn't a *Cubano.*"

"No problem. Caffeine is caffeine," I said, taking it, pleased he remembered my preference in morning beverages, struck by morning-after awkwardness. I didn't know what to say next.

He interrupted the silence. "There's food in the kitchen whenever you're ready to go down."

"Sounds good. I should probably call Murphy's Law, too. I can't believe I've already missed work, and it's only my first week on the job." Lily was probably crazy with worry. Or convinced Michael had kidnapped me to force me to be his love slave. If only the answer was that simple.

"I already called. Told them we got stuck here. They gave you the day off, but that could have something to do with a girl yelling in the background that she would take your shift if you were still with 'Delicious'?"

"Thanks." I took a huge gulp of coffee and swallowed, even though it was scorching hot, focusing on the carpet.

"Are you ready to get back?" he asked. I didn't raise my eyes, but I could hear the amusement in his voice. "Or do you have some time today?"

"I'm all yours." It slipped out before I could stop it. "Er . . . I mean, I think I'm going to be in trouble either way, since I spent the night with you . . . here, I mean, spent the night here." I stopped talking and sighed deeply. "I have time."

Kill me now.

"Good." Michael stood, his smile wide enough to split his face in half. "Because we need to fill Dr. Rooks in on who you really are."

Chapter 26

A back staircase led into a sunny kitchen with oak floors and lemon-yellow walls. Michael joined two guys at a table, but I stopped when I saw Dr. Rooks standing at a kitchen island with a ceramic tile top, slicing fruit. I'd never seen anyone cut through the tough brown skin of a pineapple so expertly. Thick pieces piled up, making the kitchen smell like an oceanside bar, causing my mouth to water.

"Good morning."

"To you as well," she said in her melodic voice, taking a fat orange from a bowl beside her. "Michael said you and he had a late night talking."

"Um . . . I'm sorry you got the bed ready for me and I didn't come up."

She put the knife down on the tile and peered at me from

under her ridiculously long lashes. "I didn't even take it out of the box."

My mouth fell open, and she laughed.

"It's not like him, and I must say I was rather surprised, considering. But think nothing of it." I wondered what she meant by "considering." She grinned and handed me a piece of fruit. "He's a special young man."

Heat crept across my cheekbones. I leaned forward to keep from dripping the sweet pineapple on my shirt, holding my hand underneath it. It tasted even better than it smelled. I chewed while I struggled with what to say next. "That's not . . . I mean, we didn't . . . It's not like . . . *that* . . . between us."

"I'm sorry. I shouldn't have assumed." She pierced the thin skin of the orange with the knife. "I thought what I sensed between you was rather strong. Perhaps I was mistaken."

A paper-towel holder shaped like a bunny stood on the counter, ears sticking up from the cardboard tube, oversize feet keeping the roll in place. I ripped one off to wipe the juice from my hands. "I just wanted to apologize for any trouble, Dr. Rooks."

"Cat." Smiling, she went back to slicing the orange. "No trouble at all."

She was so cool I almost considered becoming a physicist. Almost.

An argument erupted at the table.

"Batman wins. No supernatural powers—just straight will— the desire to right wrongs." A guy with dreadlocks and soulful eyes speared a silver-dollar pancake. He had on a Hawaiian-print shirt. "All he needed was determination."

"That's such a lame argument, Dune. Superman, hands down. He's *Superman*. Who's better than Superman?" A boy with spiky black hair shot with neon green streaks shoveled in a forkful of the biggest plate of scrambled eggs I'd ever seen. He pushed his thick-framed black glasses up. "Unless we count the X-Men as one person instead of a team—"

"Hey, guys," Michael interrupted when he saw me watching, "I hate to stop this scintillating breakfast discussion, but I want to introduce you two to Emerson. Meet Nate Lee and Dune Ta'ala."

"Hi." Good thing my cheeks were still red from my conversation with Cat. I felt like a beauty contestant, on display and awaiting judgment.

Nate's mouth dropped open to give me a tantalizing view of half-chewed egg. Dune's expression mimicked Nate's—with the exclusion of the food. They weren't looking at me, but just past me.

What was with these two?

I got my answer when I heard a female voice behind me. "Well, well. So very nice to meet you."

I turned to see who could dish out such excessive sarcasm so early in the morning.

The girl from the picture.

I had a dilemma. I could find absolutely no good reason to slap the girl standing in the kitchen doorway.

And I really wanted one.

Her legs were ten miles long. Thin, but with curves. Lots of curves. Her face was plastic-surgery perfect, but I had a horrible feeling most of it was natural.

Or all of it.

She wore impossibly high heels and an impossibly short skirt, and her dark auburn hair was pushed back by a pair of designer sunglasses perched on top of her head.

Michael stood, stepping between us. "Emerson," he said, his voice guarded, "this is Ava."

I smiled, but I was pretty sure I just looked like I was baring my teeth. "So very nice to meet you, too."

As we stared each other down, I realized I was being petty, immature, and unreasonably jealous, but any girl who has ever faced competition over a guy knows what it looks like when she meets it head-on.

I had a horrible feeling I was going down.

Twisting around to the kitchen island to take a section of orange gave me a moment to compose myself. When I turned back, Ava and Michael sat together at the table, her hand on his knee. I turned back around.

I'd squeezed my orange into juice.

Taking another paper towel from the bunny holder, I used it to wipe away the stickiness dripping through my fingers. Dune broke the silence with his deep voice. "So, Emerson's moving into the Renegade House?"

"Just a day trip," Michael answered. "Nate, close your mouth."

"I thought you guys got here last night? I heard voices late," Nate said after swallowing loudly.

I turned around in time to see Michael move Ava's hand back to her own lap. She poked out her bottom lip, and I wondered what I was missing.

"Cat, there's something I need to talk to you about," he said. "Alone. Do you have any time today?"

"I do." Cat's forehead creased slightly as she looked from Michael to me, then back at Ava. "Let me take care of some things upstairs and I'll be right down."

Dune stood and pushed his chair back. It screeched on the hardwood floor, the sound putting me on edge. *More* on edge.

"I should go get our gear together. Water's waiting." He disappeared for a second before popping his head back into the room. "Nice to meet you, Emerson." He looked at Ava and was gone again.

"Water?" I asked. "What does he mean by that?"

"Oh, just that Dune's got some skills when it comes to aquatics," Nate answered. "Legendary skills."

"He's got some legendary skills of his own." Michael pointed at Nate. "Not only is Nate a mass consumer of protein, he's—"

"Ah, let's save the details for another time. As for the protein, I'm trying to build bulk. It's not going very well." Nate pointed to his bony chest and grinned. He unfolded himself from his chair, all skinny arms and knobby knees, and followed Dune. Leaving me alone with Michael and Ava.

She stared at me coldly before sweeping her hair over her shoulder and returning her attention to Michael. There was nothing cold about the way she was looking at him. "I need to see you. In my room."

She *lived* here?

My stomach dropped. Now I understood Cat's comment. She was surprised Michael had brought me here, considering Ava lived in the house. Last night I'd curled up on his lap and poured my soul out to him.

I'd been emotionally naked with him on the couch while Ava had been asleep upstairs.

And from the way she was looking at him, they were way more than friends.

Chapter 27

Michael's gaze moved from Ava to me, lingering on my face, probably assessing the damage. "Let me get Em . . . erson taken care of. I'll be up in a sec."

Take care of me? Is that what he'd tried to do last night?

He was still staring at me when Ava stood up.

"Don't be long." She walked past me without a glance.

I thought of her picture on the bookshelf in Michael's loft and kind of wished I'd swiped it.

Because I really wanted to throw darts at it.

I dropped into a vacant chair, crossed my arms and my legs, and waited for Michael to say something.

"Um . . . I guess I should explain."

"Explain what?" A definite undercurrent of something unpleasant in my voice betrayed my light tone.

"Who all these people are. I told you the Hourglass did consult jobs and mentoring." He pulled out the chair beside mine and started to sit down. I gave him the evil eye, and he put his foot on the seat instead, resting one forearm on his leg as he explained. "You saw last night how big the house and grounds are."

"I did."

"Dune's from Samoa, Nate is from New York, and Ava's from California. They're boarders who came here to go to the school Liam set up." He kept his eyes on mine. "Other kids go there, too, but most of them moved here with their families."

"There's a school attached to the Hourglass?" I asked, liking the idea but not happy about the timing of the discovery.

"Liam staffed it. Being educated by teachers who understood us was the only way a lot of us are able to get a decent education. Nate and Dune were asked to leave school after Landers figured out they weren't going to go along with the way he ran things. That's when they moved in here."

I couldn't fathom it. Never having to explain anything because everyone around possessed qualities as strange as yours. Not needing to make excuses to leave a classroom because a flapper girl from the 1920s chose to perform the Charleston beside your teacher while he lectured on the reproductive qualities of frogs.

"The place must be amazing."

"Most of the time. That many varied abilities in the same square footage . . ." Michael grinned. "I'll tell you some stories sometime."

After meeting Ava, I didn't foresee a lot of time with Michael in my future. Of course, he knew way more about the future than I did, not that he was sharing the information. "Nate called this the Renegade House. Why?"

"It's his name for those of us who were booted out by Landers. Since we're working against him, we're renegades."

"But Ava didn't get the boot? And did the two of you hook up before or after you started living together?"

"Whoa." Michael pulled his head back in surprise. "It's not like that. I only asked her to move in a couple of weeks ago."

"Oh." I chewed on the inside of my cheek, concentrating on keeping my face expressionless. "Well, then."

"I mean," he backpedaled, "she was still at the Hourglass trying to help Kaleb, but I didn't want Landers to have access to her anymore. I needed to keep her away from him."

"Aren't you just a knight in shining armor?" My voice dripped syrupy sweetness, and any warm, fuzzy feelings left over from last night completely disappeared into a vacuum. "Wherever do you keep your horse? And who scoops up the crap it leaves behind?"

He hurried to explain. "No, no, no, it's not the same thing as us—"

"Stop." There was no us. "You don't owe me the particulars, Michael. You really don't."

"But Em—"

"Don't. Really." I tried to rein in my emotions. I had no reason to be so pissy. If anyone had a right to be mad, it was

Ava. Apparently, I was now the other woman—poaching in her territory.

Cat stuck her head around the corner, effectively putting an end to the conversation. "Are you ready to talk now, Michael?"

"He's ready. I'll go outside." I stood and walked toward the back door.

"Wait," Michael said urgently.

I stopped but didn't look back. "What?"

"The thing I gave you yesterday . . . did you bring it with you?" he asked.

"You told me not to let it out of my sight." I glanced at him over my shoulder. "It's in my bag."

"Would you get it and bring it down? And"—he paused, looking at Cat from the corner of his eye—"take your time."

"Sure."

I hurried up to Michael's room but descended the stairs quietly with the binder, coming to a standstill just outside the kitchen door.

"Did you find her?"

"It's more like she found me," Michael said softly. I pressed myself against the wall outside the kitchen.

"How did she take it?" Anxiety laced her voice.

"She just found out a couple of days ago."

"Is it like it was for Liam and Grace? The chemistry between the two of you?"

He didn't speak.

"I knew it. I could feel it. Michael—"

"I never understood before, but now that I've met her . . ."

"Does she know?"

Again, Michael was silent.

I realized I was holding my breath. Did I know what?

"What's taking her so long?" Cat asked. A scraping sound accosted my eardrums. I jumped and clutched the notebook more tightly to my chest.

I made coming-down-the-stairs noises and entered the kitchen, as breathless as if I'd been running. Cat stood by the table, and she practically snatched the binder from my hands, cradling it to her chest as if it were inlaid with precious jewels. The way she held it made me wonder why Michael had trusted me with it. Now I wished I'd understood more of what I'd read. I turned to leave.

"Em, wait. Sit down?" Michael gestured to the empty seat beside him. I stared at him for a moment. He pulled the chair out. "Please?"

I took the seat he offered, clasped my hands together, and put them on the table. Cat said, "Michael just told me what you can do."

Her words sounded accusatory, and after the way she'd grabbed the binder, I couldn't help going on the defensive. "I'd apologize, but I'm not happy about it either."

"No." She reached out to touch my hand, her eyes wide, full of amazement. "Forgive me. I'm . . . overwhelmed. This changes so many things. Opens up so many avenues—I can barely believe it."

Too frustrated to listen to her talk in circles, I asked, "What kind of avenues, specifically?"

"You're half of a unique pair. I've never met anyone besides Liam and his wife who can do what you and Michael can. That changes things for me, for my gift." She removed her hand from mine and placed it on top of the notebook. I caught a glimpse of sadness in her eyes as she sat down. "Did you have a chance to read the information explaining how it is that you and Michael travel?"

"I tried, but I didn't understand most of it."

"I'll try to make it simpler for you. One of the many theories about time travel is the wormhole theory. Wormholes connect two points in space, like a bridge." Cat opened the notebook reverently and flipped to a diagram that might as well have been written in invisible ink. She traced her finger across a line of equations. I wondered if I should be taking notes. "See?"

I felt my eyes grow as big as saucers, and she stopped, closing the binder. "Sorry, I didn't mean to get too technical. Here are the basics. The bridges can connect you to a different time, but they must be made stable and held open for travel to happen. This is accomplished by using negative matter, also known as exotic matter. Simple enough?"

Sure.

"What does all of this have to do with your ability?" I asked.

Cat was silent for a moment. "I create exotic matter."

"Like in a lab or something?"

"Like this." She closed her eyes, and then cupped her hands as if holding a handful of water. An inch above her palms, a swirling purple sphere appeared. It wasn't solid, more like a gas, pulsing and spinning, giving off a slight mist. Everything else in the room went dark. I could focus only on the energy in Cat's hands. I leaned forward, closer and closer, drawn to it in a way I couldn't explain.

I kind of put a damper on the display when I leaned so far forward that I fell off my chair.

Cat gasped and put her hands together. The spinning ball disappeared, and the room was full of light again.

Michael leaned over to help me up. I was too shocked to be embarrassed or to respond to his touch. "Em kind of needs a warning before you spring things like that on her."

Now I understood the superhero discussion at breakfast. The inhabitants of the house were discussing their fictional peers.

No problem.

"How"—I paused for a second—"did you do that?"

"Body chemistry?" Cat acted like it was no big deal. "It's hard to explain. Science has always intrigued me, especially the study of negative and positive matter, wormholes, black holes . . ."

She'd just produced matter. *Matter*. With her *hand*. I could barely believe it, but I didn't see any way the spinning purple sphere could have been a trick.

"Creating true exotic—or negative—matter is generally considered impossible. It's a very volatile substance." Cat sounded as if she were repeating a lecture she'd given hundreds of times. "Liam taught me what we could do by combining our unique talents. In the simplest terms, I opened bridges, and he traveled through them."

"I believe you, about all the science stuff." I waved the thought away with my hand. While I was interested to learn how she and Liam Ballard put all the pieces together, right now I was more intrigued by her personal journey. "How did you figure out you could do it—create matter?"

"I grew up on an island. As a child, I used to sneak out of my bed at night to lie in a hammock that hung between two palm trees on our property." Cat's dark eyes took on a dreamy quality, and I was there with her, hearing the surf rolling in and out, feeling the warm breezes soothe me as I rocked. "I would stare at the stars above me and wonder what it would be like to float among them.

"One night I dreamed I could hold a galaxy in my hand. I watched it form, felt it orbit, as if I created it myself. Breathed life into it. When I woke up, what you just saw was spinning in my hand as if it was meant to be there."

"How old were you?" I asked.

"Eleven. I knew what I could do was special and needed to be tested. I learned as much as I could in high school, graduated at sixteen, and went straight to college on scholarship as a physics major. I volunteered to be a teaching assistant so I would have access to a lab." She paused, her lips parted in a slight smile. "That's where I first met Liam."

"How did he know what the two of you could do together? The time-travel thing?"

"He had some . . . outside resources." The slight smile disappeared, and her voice turned businesslike. "You and Michael haven't talked about the logistics of traveling at all?"

"No." Because up until the purple ball formed in Cat's hand, I'd half hoped he'd made the whole thing up, so I hadn't asked. Now I hoped he was telling the truth, because if he wasn't, my hallucinations had taken a whole new turn. For the worse.

"Give her the ring," Cat said, inclining her head toward Michael's hand.

He removed the ring from his thumb and passed it over to me. I held it up to the light, and for the first time I noticed a continuous series of tiny number eights inscribed in the band.

"What does the number eight carved into a silver ring have to do with time travel?"

Michael took the ring back, careful not to touch my skin as he did. "It's an infinity symbol, not an eight, and the ring isn't silver. It's duronium—a metal that hasn't been identified on any periodic table."

I thought for a moment. "So, if I'm understanding this correctly . . . our genes plus the duronium ring plus Cat's exotic matter equals time travel?"

He nodded.

"Piece of cake. Not woo-woo freaky at all." I stared at the ring on his hand for a long moment. "And how am I supposed to come up with one of those puppies? I'm guessing I can't shop for it online?"

"We'll take care of it," Michael said.

"You do that." I turned my attention to Cat. "Michael told me there were others out there who have special abilities. What kinds?"

"All kinds." She tilted her head toward Michael as she asked, "Do you want to explain this one?"

Her tone indicated that it wasn't a matter of who wanted to field the question, but more if it should be answered at all. More secrets.

"Yeah," he said as he drummed his fingers on the table. "There are other places like the Hourglass. Not many, but others," he said. "Some of them have certain . . . areas of expertise. They might attract those who have spirit-hunting skills or transformation abilities . . ."

I drew in a sharp breath. He trailed off, turning to look at me. As he shifted in his chair, the full length of his leg pressed against mine underneath the table. The fact that I wasn't hyperventilating from such close contact was a testament to how overwhelmed I felt by what I'd just heard.

"I'm sorry," I said weakly, shaking my head in case my ears needed clearing, "but did you just say . . . spirit-hunting skills and *transformation abilities?*"

"Bad examples. I shouldn't have gone there," Michael said hastily, standing. I wondered if the accidental touch made him get up or if the topic of conversation did. He moved away from the table to pace, twisting his thumb ring as he walked. "It's not my goal to freak you out."

"Too bad," I answered. "Because that one was so solid it didn't even touch the net."

Swish.

"Emerson, none of what we do is easy or clear-cut." Cat's voice carried a hint of exasperation, making me feel slightly stupid. "Just listen to what we have to say, and at least try to understand. It can't be that hard to wrap your brain around."

Michael snapped his head toward Cat. Her spine straightened, and her irritated look disappeared. "I'm sorry. I've lived in this world for so long I forget how foreign it can look from the outside."

Michael continued to stare at Cat, his expression so intense it made me nervous. She broke the gaze, and he turned to me. "The Hourglass has a specialty, too. Everyone there possesses an ability that involves the manipulation of time."

I was still trying to interpret the look he'd directed at Cat, so it took a second for Michael's words to break through. "I thought you said we were the only ones who can travel?"

"We are." He sat down beside me again but moved his chair a little farther away. "But time as a concept is fluid. It can be slowed down, sped up, stopped."

I thought of the most impossible, movielike scenario I could. "So if someone were shooting at me and I had the ability to stop time, I could pluck the bullet out of the air before it hit me?" I asked, laughing.

He didn't crack a smile. "Does the fact that such a thing is possible upset you?"

"No more than any of the rest of it," I mumbled, the laughter dying in my throat. I dropped my head into my hands. "Why is it I suddenly feel I'm on the more normal end of the freak spectrum?"

"I keep trying to tell you normal is relative," he said. "Do you need a second?"

I needed a millennium. "Can I . . . Can I do those other things? Stop a bullet?"

"All indications are that your ability is traveling to the past."

"That's enough," I said, feeling a little better. Although stopping a bullet would be a handy skill for a girl to have. "So what about everyone else?"

"Nate is kind of like Oliver Twist mixed with David Blaine." Michael wiggled his fingers as if coaxing a rabbit out of a top hat. "Thievery skills with illusionist abilities. He can slow things down, speed things up, including himself—all depending on his needs."

"How did he end up here?" I asked, frowning. "That doesn't seem like the kind of ability Liam would've encouraged."

"He didn't encourage it. Not for financial gain anyway. But there are other reasons to need stealth."

"What about everyone else?"

"Dune can influence water. It's handier than it sounds. Ava . . . well. She's still trying to figure some things out." Michael gave me an apologetic smile that faded as he glanced toward the back stairs. "Speaking of Ava, I have to talk to her. Then we can head back to Ivy Springs."

"I'll be right here."

Seething with envy.

He disappeared through the doorway leading to the stairs. It sounded as if he took them two at a time. I focused my attention on Cat. "What are Nate and Dune doing today?"

"A consult job I set up. Dune can control things like the tide and the direction a river flows. It's helpful when we're looking for certain things, but it's not something he can use very often. He's also a research genius, which comes in handy . . ."

She continued, and I tried to pay attention, but my mind strayed to Michael in Ava's room. What were they doing up there? She said she needed to talk to him. I really hoped they were talking. I really wished she weren't so gorgeous. I really wanted to go upstairs and listen outside her door. I hadn't told Michael when he questioned me the day before, but I *had* learned how to eavesdrop at boarding school. From the other students. Not the teachers.

I realized Cat was silent and waiting for a response to something she'd said.

"What? Oh my word, I'm so sorry." I sat up, horrified, my hands flying to my mouth.

"It's fine—I promise. I know your mind is elsewhere."

"That obvious?" I covered my face to hide the blush I felt coming on.

"I understand the way it is between the two of you," she said in her lilting voice. "It was the same way with Liam and his wife."

"What do you mean? How was it?"

"Cataclysmic." Cat let out a chuckle at my facial expression and gave me a gentle pat on the shoulder.

I heard heavy footsteps coming down the stairs, slower than they had been going up. Michael entered the room alone, his face drawn. "If we don't leave soon, your brother's going to send out a search party."

"Considering I haven't talked to him since yesterday, it might include torches and pitchforks."

"You ready?" He looked toward the back door. "I want to get out of here."

"Let's go."

It seemed as if there was trouble in paradise.

I could only hope.

Chapter 28

I dropped Michael off at his car, and we planned to meet at Murphy's Law once we got back to Ivy Springs. I owed Lily an explanation. Before going into the coffee shop I checked my voice mail. Seven messages from Thomas.

My ass was grass, and big brother was the lawn mower.

I parked and crossed the town square, trying to figure out what in the world I was going to say to Lily. I paused outside Murphy's Law to try to come up with a good story. Or at least a decent lie.

Through the plate-glass window I could see her leaning against the counter, staring off into space. Her fingers held a pencil that moved at a furious pace across a pad of paper. I opened the front door and the jangling bell caught her attention. She shoved the pencil and drawing into her apron pocket and put her hands on her hips.

"Girl."

The emphasis she placed on the word asked a hundred questions at once.

"It's not what you think," I said defensively.

"Then I'm very disappointed for you."

That made two of us. "I haven't been with him since he picked me up here! Last night, I had to go out for . . . something, and I ran into Michael and it got late and we lost track of time and—"

"You don't have to explain anything to me." She took the dishrag from her shoulder and began polishing the counter needlessly. "Your secrets are yours to keep."

"Lily, please." I reached out and pulled the cloth from her hand. "I'm not trying to keep anything from you. This . . . thing . . . with Michael is more than complicated. Please believe me."

"It's okay. I understand. But you have to throw me a bone and tell me if the personality is as hot as the package."

I gave her a slow grin before faking a heart attack, clutching my chest, and backing up a few steps. Falling against the counter, I slid to the floor, twitched a couple of times for effect, and then burst into giggles.

"You are not right," Lily said, but she laughed as she pulled me to my feet. I handed her the dishrag and reached behind her for a to-go coffee cup. I was starting to drag after the long night. Being around Michael kept my energy up, and now that he wasn't close to me it felt like I was coming down from an adrenaline high.

"Can I talk to you seriously for a sec?" I pulled the lever on the coffee machine that dispensed the bold blend, inhaling deeply when the liquid began to fill my cup.

"What's up?"

"Do you ever wonder what your life would be like now, if your parents were here instead of in Cuba?"

"Yes." She pulled up the bar stools she kept behind the counter in case things were slow and she had a moment to sit. "All the time. Are you wondering what it would be like if yours were still alive?"

"I am." I clambered onto my stool. Lily and her long legs made everything look so effortless. I practically needed a stepladder. "I wonder about the whole depression thing, too. If the accident never happened, if my parents had been there for me to lean on—would I have been able to handle everything better than I did?"

"You'll never know. And you can't go back in time. No one can."

I didn't see any point in correcting her.

"The thing is, Em, you don't know if you struggled with the depression because of your circumstances or if it's a chemical thing. You might have to deal with it again. So you do everything you can to keep yourself well, whether that means meds or counseling or . . . whatever." She threw up her hands. "Vigorous exercise . . . I don't know."

We both laughed. Lily knew I didn't like to talk about my depression, but whenever we did, she always made a tremendous effort to affirm me, and my choices. Another reason to love her.

"What do you think about the supernatural?"

She frowned. "You mean like werewolves or ghosts?"

"Maybe, but more like superhero stuff—special abilities like mind reading or precognition."

Or manipulating time.

Raising one eyebrow skeptically, she asked, "Did you walk away from your drink last night? Did somebody slip you something?"

"Lily, I'm serious."

She chewed the nail of her pinky finger, silent for a moment, frowning. "I don't have an opinion."

"You have to have an opinion," I argued. "Are you really going to tell me you haven't ever thought about it?"

"No, I haven't. And I really don't want to think about it now," she said firmly.

"Hey, it's cool." I'd never seen Lily react that way to a simple question. "I just wondered."

"When do you see Delicious again?" Lily shifted on her stool, folding the cloth in her hands in half.

"He's going to meet me here so we can go talk to Thomas. He wasn't very happy his little sis spent the night out."

"Does your brother have a gun? If so, get Delicious a bullet-proof vest. That boy is way too pretty to have a big hole in him."

"No," I said, laughing at the thought of my straightlaced brother with a firearm. "Thomas doesn't have a gun. I'm sure everything will be fine once we explain."

At least I hoped it would.

"Explain about how you just lost track of time," Lily said. "Right?"

"Um . . . right."

I had been keeping my own counsel for years. I didn't know what it was like to truly confide everything in a friend, and here I was, wishing I could tell Lily all of it. There were too many secrets in my life.

The bell jangled again as someone entered the coffee shop. I knew it was Michael when my energy level jumped ten notches. He walked up to the counter, smiling at Lily.

"Michael," I said, "this is Lilliana Garcia."

Lily, usually articulate and poised—the perfect example of grace—just sat on her stool and giggled.

"Nice to meet you, Lilliana."

"Call me Lily." Her voice did the Marilyn Monroe thing, and I wondered if Michael had that effect on every girl he met.

"Nice to meet you, Lily." He flashed another smile, and I heard her whimper under her breath. When he looked at me, his expression softened. "Em, you ready to face the music?"

"Ready as I'll ever be." Lily stared at Michael as if she would scale Mount Everest and swim the English Channel if he asked. I snapped to get her attention. "Lily? *Lily?*"

"Yes?" She dragged her eyes away from him and cleared her throat before she spoke. The husky voice was wasted on me anyway. "Yes?"

"Unless Thomas locks me in my room, I'll see you tomorrow."

"Good luck." Her fingers fluttered in a feminine wave. "Bye, Michael."

We turned to leave, and I noticed Lily making wild gestures to get my attention behind Michael's back. When I looked over my shoulder, I was treated to a mimed performance of a full-blown body slam. And maybe some French kissing, but I closed my eyes before I could be sure.

I dragged him from the shop into the afternoon heat before Lily embarrassed herself, or me. We walked through the middle of the town square, passing a bubbling fountain and several wrought-iron benches on our way to Dru's car. I'd miraculously parallel parked it in a spot without a coin meter. Michael's convertible sat right behind it.

"You think you can work some of your magic on my brother?" I asked as we waited for a rusty pickup truck to pass before we crossed the street. The exhaust from its tailpipe lingered in the air, and I wrinkled my nose as we passed through it.

"What are you talking about?"

I pressed the remote for the keyless entry, and the car chirped. "Don't even try to tell me you didn't notice Lily's reaction to you. She *never* acts like that around guys."

He rolled his eyes and reached out to open my car door for me.

"I'm serious about working the magic," I said as I climbed into the SUV, the heat from the leather warming the backs of my legs.

"I think you're a little optimistic about my skills. I can't imagine your brother is going to be too thrilled about your spending the night with me, even if I can morph into Houdini."

"I didn't spend the night with you. I mean not, *spend the night*, spend the night." Now my face felt as warm as my legs. I stayed quiet for a moment, staring at the steering wheel and waiting for my embarrassment to subside. "Anyway . . . about going back to help Liam. It isn't safe, is it?"

"There's definitely a huge amount of risk involved," he answered, leaning over to rest his hand on the frame of the open car door, his wide shoulders blocking the light of the sun.

I leaned back, glad I didn't have to squint up at him anymore. I preferred an eyes-wide-open view. "People at the Hourglass know what you can do. What if word gets out that you found a partner, someone who can help you change things?"

"Remember, Kaleb's still on the inside, and he hasn't heard anything," Michael said, rapping his knuckles against the driver's window. "Jonathan's probably too busy covering his tracks right now to listen to any rumors."

"So he's busy," I said, feeling tiny beads of perspiration form on my forehead and upper lip. "That doesn't mean he doesn't know about me."

"We've taken precautions," he assured me. "There's no way anyone at the Hourglass could know anything, except for Kaleb, and he won't say a word."

Getting hotter by the second, I cranked the SUV, turning on the air and adjusting the vents. "What about Liam's wife?"

"When you have a bond like theirs . . . that close . . . After he died, she got really sick." Michael looked across the street toward the fountain.

"Is she all right? Did she die?" I couldn't imagine coming out of hiding and finding out the person I loved was no longer in the world.

He looked back at me. "Not sick like that."

"Oh." My kind of sick.

"If we can bring him back, she'll be okay," Michael insisted. A breeze blew through the open door, erasing the remnants of the truck exhaust, bringing the scent of mums. "Everything will be. I have to believe that."

I hoped he was right. "Do you really think Jonathan Landers will stop if we save Liam?"

"No. He's had a taste of power. I think what drives him so hard is his desire to be like us, even though he knows he can't. If he finds out you were involved, I can't promise he won't come after you." His expression grew fierce. "But I can promise I'll do everything possible to keep him from getting to you."

The way he said the words caused a shiver to run over my skin. I focused on the windshield, tapping my fingers on the steering wheel.

Weighing options.

If everything Michael and Cat had told me was true, my ability would allow me to save a man, a man with a wife and a son. A man whose whole life had been about helping others. Not only had he started a school for people like me, he had also provided employment. A future.

Then there was Jonathan Landers. If Michael was to be believed, Landers exploited those with abilities, used them. I guessed he had no problem feeding on insecurity and fear to convince people to do what he wanted. Before I met Michael, I would've been a perfect target.

It was a clear-cut choice.

I looked into Michael's eyes, touching his arm to make sure I had his full attention. "I'm in."

Michael jumped, either from the shock of my fingers on his skin or my words. "Are you sure?"

"How can I say no to saving someone's life?" I pulled my hand away, tucking it under my leg. "And if I help . . . well, it's a good reason to be a freak."

"Em, you aren't a—"

"Michael. I am a freak. So are you, so is Cat, so are Dune and Nate, and so is . . . whoever else the Hourglass has helped." I didn't want to make Ava part of this conversation. "But for the first time in my life, it's actually okay. Now I'm a freak with a purpose."

"Tell me why. Why do you want to help?" I felt the weight he gave to the "why." It was almost as if the reason for helping was more important than the act itself.

"Not because you pressured me, or because of anything you said. Maybe it's just the thought of what Liam's life meant when he was alive. He was exactly like me, and he made a difference."

That seemed to be the answer he was looking for. His eyes searched my face. "Promise me that you're sure."

"I said I'm in, and I'm in. One hundred percent. Don't ask me again. Okay?"

"Yes, ma'am." Michael gave me a mock salute, but I sensed admiration beneath the teasing. "If you're in, we need to tell your brother. Everything."

I tapped my fingers on my leg. "Do I have to?"

"Thomas trusts me. I have lots of reasons not to betray that trust." Michael reached out and laid his hand on mine, stopping me from tapping. Heat shot up my arm. "What do you think he'll say?"

"He'll probably get over the fact that I spent the night out pretty quick. I mean, comparatively speaking, there's no competition." I grinned. "But seriously, Thomas won't get in the way of any choices I make."

"Even dangerous ones?"

"We'll find out, I guess."

He squeezed my hand. "Okay then. Are you ready?"

"Nope." I squeezed back. "Let's go."

Chapter 29

I had to hand it to my brother. Maybe he believed I'd experienced some sort of relapse and had somehow used my feminine wiles to rope Michael into my delusions. Maybe he was faking the calmness to keep me from going even further off the deep end. Or maybe he'd been all ramped up to take me down for spending the night with Michael, and my news threw him for a loop. Whatever it was, he seemed to be taking the whole "apparently I can time travel and by the way I'm off my meds" thing in stride.

Dru was a little bit harder to sell.

"You're saying," she said, looking from me to Michael, her cool blue eyes intense, "that together you can break the boundaries of time?" She kept her voice composed, but it sounded forced, the way a parent might speak to an unruly toddler in public.

I nodded. Dru knew I could see random dead-ish people since the first time it happened, but while Thomas believed me immediately, it took her a while to come around.

She was quiet for a moment as a waiter cleared the table beside us. When he blew out the candle in the centerpiece and left, walking through the jazz trio on his way to the kitchen, she continued. "So you're trying to tell me that the things you saw weren't ghosts, but people from the past?"

"Sort of."

"*Sort of?*" Her voice hit a higher pitch than usual as more of her composure slipped. She held up her hand. "I need a minute."

Michael had chosen the restaurant as the place to spill the beans. He'd hoped being in view of the public would help curb the intensity of any strong reactions. Didn't look like it was working for Dru.

Smoke from the extinguished candle drifted over to our table, briefly covering the smell of tomato sauce and baking bread coming from the kitchen. My stomach growled, and I thought about asking for a basket when it came out of the oven.

Instead, I stuck to the business at hand. Hoping I'd given Dru enough time, I tried to explain more clearly, realizing again how unbelievable it all sounded. "The fact that I can see time ripples is a symptom that I'm a time traveler. I mean an indicator."

Her gaze jumped from me to Michael. "And you can time travel, too?"

"Yes."

"Uh-huh." She slumped back in her chair, checking out of the conversation.

"Could Dru or I see rips?" Thomas asked.

I looked over at the jazz trio and answered for Michael. "No."

"So when you met Emerson the first time, when she came to you from the future, how did you know she was a time traveler instead of a time ripple?" Thomas asked, leaning closer to us over the table, keeping his voice low. At least he seemed to be following.

"Rips disappear if someone touches them. Time travelers know exactly what and where they are. And they're solid."

I sat up straighter in my chair. "How solid?"

"The same as we are now."

An uneasy thought crowded my mind. If rips were vapor and time travelers were solid . . .

What was Jack?

The thought disappeared when Thomas asked Michael his next question. "What would happen if someone who wasn't born with the ability to travel attempted it? Assuming they could come up with exotic matter and something made of duronium. Could Dru or I do it?"

"Only people born with the innate genetic ability can travel without serious consequences."

"What kind of consequences?" Thomas asked.

Michael's face was grim. "Death by disintegration."

"Ouch," Thomas said, sitting back and loosening his tie.

"What have you seen? When you've traveled to the future?" Dru interrupted. She'd been so quiet I'd almost forgotten she was at the table. "What kind of world do we live in?"

I knew she was thinking of the baby.

"I can't say. I have to keep what I've seen a secret. But babies were still being born, every day"—Michael gave her a comforting smile—"and then going on to lead spectacular lives."

"What's the next step for you two?" Thomas asked, but not before reaching out to wrap his hand around Dru's. "Do you have a plan?"

"I've got to fill Dr. Rooks in on what I want to do," Michael said, turning serious eyes to my brother. "If she agrees and Emerson has your permission, we're going to try to save Liam Ballard."

Thomas looked at me with concern. "Are you on board with this?"

I nodded.

"If—really, really big if—all this is . . . true," Dru said, worry clouding her expression, "I hope you're completely aware of what you'd be risking."

"I am fully aware." I searched my gut once more to make sure the words I spoke were true. The answer came back the same. "I know I'm doing the right thing."

Thomas reached over to touch me lightly on the arm. "Do you think you and I could talk for a second? By ourselves?"

"Dru," Michael said, standing and stepping around my chair, steadying himself by placing his fingertips on the table. "I wanted to ask you about one of the art photos in my loft. I wondered if you had contact information on the photographer. Can we go look at it?"

"No problem. But if it's a photograph, I can guess who took it. Have you met Em's friend Lily?" Dru asked as they left the table together. She cast a worried look over her shoulder as they walked to the door, her dark hair hiding half of her face but none of her concern. The phantom musicians seamlessly transitioned from a Cole Porter classic to a Billie Holiday standard.

Once the heavy wooden door closed behind Michael and Dru, Thomas looked at me intently. "Truth time."

"I've been telling the truth since we sat down, Thomas. You think I could make all that up?"

"Not that." He pulled a green packet of sugar substitute from a ceramic holder on the table. "You know I believe you, at least I hope you do. What I'm talking about is the way you sounded when you two were explaining everything."

I crossed my arms over my chest and waited.

"Even though I've been your legal guardian for the past four years, you've pretty much made your own decisions about how you run your life. The only exception was when you were . . ." He paused, his face cautious as he tried to figure out how to put it delicately.

"Committed." I said it for him. "It's okay. It's not a dirty word."

Thomas acknowledged the word but didn't expand on the subject, just continued folding and refolding the tiny green packet in his hands. "You're almost an adult. I can't really tell you what to do anymore."

"I'm not following."

"You and Michael." He ripped the packet open and poured the contents on the table in a grainy pile. "Listening to the two of you, watching you together, I'm guessing your connection goes further than sharing a supernatural ability."

"We haven't crossed any professional lines." Looking away from him, I felt the blush start beneath my skin. "It's not like that."

"It's not like that *yet*, you mean. What about last night?"

I'd hoped I'd gotten away with last night.

"Thomas. Please." I wanted to crawl under the table and hide. Anything not to participate in this conversation. "Nothing is going on."

"Hey, you're the one who tried to knock a security camera off the side of a building. That's a lot of pent-up frustration."

I'd wondered when he was going to bring that up. "You have nothing to worry about. No rules have been broken."

Thomas traced a circle in the white granules on the table before looking up at me. "But you have feelings for him?"

"There are a lot of complications."

Rules. Trust. Ava.

"I thought something like this might happen. That's why I made sure Michael would adhere to the rules, both the Hour-glass's and mine." Thomas sat back in his chair, assessing me the same way he'd evaluate a foundation before buying a building. "I don't want you to get hurt."

"I won't," I said. "My relationship with Michael is professional. We've never even come close—"

I stopped when Thomas pursed his lips.

"Well, except for that one time on the patio, we've never even come close to doing anything inappropriate." I looked down at the sugar substitute, then absently brushed it to the floor, immediately feeling guilty for making a mess. "Even though he's amazing, and thoughtful . . ."

My brother's lips pursed so tightly they almost disappeared.

"Anyway, nothing is going on." I dusted my hands and placed them on the table, staring Thomas dead in the eye. "So it doesn't matter."

"But see," Thomas said, reaching out to take my hands in his, "I think it could matter. Be honest, Emerson. Does the way you feel about him have anything to do with why you're helping him?"

"No. It doesn't," I protested when he gave me a knowing, superior, older-brother look. I tightened my hands around his for emphasis. "Liam Ballard has a family, a wife and a son. I could save him. After everything, you have to understand . . ."

"I know why it appeals to you. I worry about you, not physically, although that's part of it." His face contorted in pain, reflecting mine. "How can you go back and save the life of someone else's parent without thinking about going back to save the lives of your own?"

"Michael and I already had that conversation." I focused on the chandelier centered in the ceiling, not wanting him to see the hopelessness I felt. And to keep the tears from falling. "There's no way. This is some crazy once-in-a-lifetime opportunity. I know it's impossible to change the past. Except for this time."

We sat quietly for a moment, both deep in our own thoughts, remembering our loss. Thomas cleared his throat. "You know what Dad always used to say whenever we faced a big decision."

I resisted an eye roll as we said the words together. "Do the next right thing."

"Exactly. Whatever the next right thing is for you, Em, I'm behind you."

"The right thing is helping Michael. After that"—if there is an after that—"we'll just have to see."

Thomas let go of my hands and looked in the direction of the front door. "Wonder what's keeping them?"

"I'll go check," I said, grateful for the opportunity to exit the conversation before I said something I shouldn't. I nodded my head toward the kitchen. "Why don't you make yourself useful and score me some of that bread and marinara? Don't you own the place or something?"

As I crossed the town square, I replayed everything Michael had said to my brother and Dru in my head, my mind sticking on one particular subject.

Travelers were solid, and rips were vapor.

Jack. Not solid, not vapor, but somewhere in between.

Michael, Dru, and Thomas would have to wait. I needed to take care of some business. Now.

Chapter 30

*C*ome out, come out, wherever you are!" I called softly as I opened the door to my room. "Jack? Don't tell me you're getting all shy on me now."

Silence.

I opened my closet door, my bathroom door, looked under my bed.

Nothing.

I sat down in my armchair to think. Unlike the leather in Dru's SUV earlier, it felt cool against my legs.

What if, when I touched Jack, I'd scared him away for good? I twirled a strand of hair around my finger, wondering. If I had, it would solve a big problem, because I still hadn't decided if I should tell Michael about him.

Besides, what was I going to say? By the by, there's this

partially solid glow-in-the-dark guy who likes to hang out in my room? Was I going to admit why I'd never mentioned him to Michael? The attention and interest Jack gave me felt good. Now that I thought about it, maybe good enough to offset the fact that Michael had the lovely Ava as an alternative, when I had no one.

Except whatever Jack was.

How could I explain that without looking like a complete jerk?

If Jack disappeared, it wouldn't be an issue, and I could go back to worrying about other things, like the possibility of dying while attempting to time travel so I could stop a murder.

Stuff like that.

So much had happened since I returned to Ivy Springs. I leaned back and closed my eyes. My whole world felt upside down. A month ago, I didn't know what rips were. I didn't know what my ability meant. I didn't know Michael existed. Things were a lot simpler.

And a lot less interesting.

I waited a few more minutes. Figuring Jack for a no-show, I knocked on the door to Michael's loft. No answer. I returned to the restaurant to find Thomas and Dru at the table. Alone.

"Where's Michael?" I asked, looking up at the clock hanging above the bar. I'd been gone for only fifteen minutes. Surely the man possessed more patience than that.

"He left." Dru's eyes darted to meet Thomas's before she looked back at me. "This, um, woman, came up to his loft to find him. She said there was an emergency."

"Woman?" Please mean Cat. "Tall and gorgeous? Supershort hair?"

"No," Dru said apologetically. "Tall and gorgeous, but long auburn hair."

Ava. "What kind of emergency? Did she say?"

Dru nodded. "She mentioned a name before I left them alone . . . Kaleb."

"Michael insisted you stay here." Thomas cleared his throat and took my cell phone from the table where I'd left it when I went to the loft. He dropped it into his shirt pocket. "That you not try to contact him and that you keep a low profile. He was adamant it was for your own safety and told us that if you tried to follow him, we should stop you."

"Of course he did," I muttered. I dropped into my chair, overcome with jealousy. And worry. Whatever happened must have been big for Ava to come to Ivy Springs to get Michael.

I folded my arms on the table and laid my head down on top of them, fighting tears and exhaustion. I'd just made a huge decision, agreeing to help Michael save Liam, and I itched to act on it. I'd felt so connected to him when we sat down to talk to Thomas and Dru. Now he was back to keeping things from me.

I sensed Dru gesturing furiously to Thomas. When I looked up, she and I sat at the table alone. "Michael said he'd call you as soon as the problem was resolved. I'm sure things will be fine."

I nodded.

"If it makes you feel better, he didn't seem happy to see her."

It didn't.

I felt hurt that he left without saying good-bye, and angry that my brother and Dru seemed to be so accepting of Michael's "orders" for me. I also felt too defeated to argue. For now.

Dru sighed and reached out to pat my hand. "When was the last time you ate anything?"

The pineapple at the Renegade House. "Breakfast."

"Let me take care of you, okay?" Dru asked in a gentle voice. "I know you hate it, but I need to practice for when the little one gets here."

"Not fair." Mentioning the baby was the worst kind of blackmail.

I let Dru take me home, feed me the marinara sauce and bread I'd smelled coming from the restaurant kitchen, and even make a bed for me on the couch, knowing she did it only to keep an eye on me.

Even though my body had reached the point of exhaustion, my brain wouldn't shut down. So many thoughts kept my mind whirling: Jack, and who, not to mention *what*, he really was. Lily, and the secrets between us. Michael, and where he was. What he was doing. And with whom.

Circling around and around, never finding any answers, I fought sleep, holding out hope the phone would ring.

Talk about pissed.

I woke up confused. I'd slept in three different beds in the past few days. I preferred Michael's to all of them. Probably because of the pillow.

He never called. Or he did and Dru or Thomas answered because I was asleep. Maybe one of them turned off the ringer. I reached out for the portable phone on the coffee table, fumbling to see the caller ID.

Nothing.

I might not know where Michael was, but I had a pretty good idea how to find him. I threw the covers back and made a beeline for my room, taking the phone with me, just in case.

"Hold it." Thomas stepped out of the kitchen with a box of Fruity Pebbles in his hand, blocking my way. "Where are you going?"

"To take a shower."

He angled his body to keep me from stepping around him. "What about after that?"

"Why does it matter?"

"You're not going to look for Michael, are you?" Thomas asked the question as if he already knew the answer.

"I guess it all depends," I said, fisting my phone-free hand on my hip. "How long are you supposed to keep me away from him?"

"Did he call?"

I shook my head.

"Em, he was serious. I don't know if he knew what kind of

situation he was walking into when he left, but he didn't want you to be involved."

"I need to go to the coffeehouse to check my schedule," I said in a monotone, not meeting his eyes. "Am I allowed?"

"Don't be this way," he pleaded. I knew he hated lording any kind of authority over me. But he still did it.

"I'm your sister. You're taking Michael's side over mine. How could you?" I figured it wouldn't hurt to layer on some guilt now to pave the way for forgiveness later.

"I am on your side. So is Michael," he said self-righteously. "His intention is to keep you safe."

I still held the cordless phone in my hand. I really wanted to throw it at my brother's head. Growling in frustration, I pushed past him, slammed the door to my room, and locked it behind me.

I showered quickly and chose not to argue with my hair, leaving it loose and wavy. I didn't want to think about why, but I took special care with my makeup and clothing, wearing tighter jeans than usual and a close-fitting green T-shirt with a scoop neckline. As accessory challenged as I am, I even threw on a matching pair of earrings. Dru's shimmery powder still sat on my dresser, and I used a little to highlight my . . . collarbone. Trying not to feel like a hooker, I grabbed a pair of strappy-heeled sandals and pulled them on as I half ran, half hopped to the front door.

I didn't see Thomas, but as I turned the knob to leave I heard Dru clear her throat from behind me.

"What?" I spun around to face her, leaning back against the front door hard enough to make it creak. "I'm going to Murphy's Law. I already cleared it with the prison matron, even though her panties were in a wad about it."

"Work? I know what I would do in your situation." She scanned my outfit, then handed me my cell phone and her keys. "Don't make me regret this. And stop insulting my husband."

I took the keys and gave her a quick hug. "You're going to be such an excellent mother."

"If you were my child, I would staple you to your bedroom wall."

I blew her a kiss and shut the door softly behind me.

Chapter 31

I couldn't get in touch with Michael—his cell phone kept bouncing straight to voice mail. I drove like a maniac to Murphy's Law, parking illegally at the curb. The pickup line for orders snaked almost to the front door. Lily threw me an apron as I walked behind the counter and then did a double take.

"Wow," she said, giving me the once-over. "Okay. Wow. What are you going for with this look? Are you headed for a Playboy Bunny convention? Because whatever you're doing, I can guess it's not making coffee."

"I'm throwing my hat in the ring, staking a claim, making my intentions known. It's kind of like . . . a dog peeing on a fire hydrant."

"I could've done without that visual." She assessed my outfit as I tied on the apron. "Why do you feel the need to put all your goodies on the front line for a man?"

"It's more for the competition," I answered, twisting my hair up and sticking a pencil in it to keep it out of my way.

Lily shook her head and added a shot of espresso to a latte.

I threw up my hands. "What? Do I look that bad?"

"No, you look that good," she said, spooning foam into a mug. "I just want your self-respect to be intact when all this is over. I assume Michael is your fire hydrant?"

"Yes." I picked up the order pad to see what was next and then poured milk into a metal cup before attaching it to a steamer. "I'm sorry for bailing on you yesterday," I said over the hissing noise. "You've been here two mornings in a row, haven't you?"

"No worries. Vanilla latte?" she called out to the crowd before turning back to start the next drink. "Just help me get through these orders, and I'll forgive you."

We worked in silence for a few minutes until the crowd dissipated. Lily picked up a glass of ice water and downed half of it before asking, "Where are you headed?"

"I don't know exactly. There are a couple of places I think he might be. Or he could be someplace else altogether. That's why I came to talk to you." I was done with secrets. My best friend needed to come clean. Even if it meant I had to do the same. "I wanted to ask you to help me."

"Help you?" she asked, crunching down on a piece of ice and narrowing her eyes.

"Help me . . . find him." I wouldn't chicken out. I wanted everything out in the open. "The *way you find* things."

Lily choked on her ice before seizing my arm and dragging me toward the back office. She yanked me into the room and slammed the door behind us.

"What the hell, Lily?" I rubbed my arm where she'd grabbed it.

"How do you know?" Lily's breath came out unevenly.

"I don't know anything specific," I confessed. "I just had an idea."

"I've tried so hard to keep it a secret." She stared at me with wide eyes. "When you asked me my opinion about the supernatural the other day, I got the feeling you were on to me."

"Actually, I asked you the question about the supernatural stuff because of *me*." I opened the door, sticking my head out to check the shop for customers. Only a couple of people sat in the orange chairs by the front window. I pulled my head back in and shut the door.

Lily sat down on the edge of the desk. "Please don't tell me you're a vampire. Vampires are so overdone."

"I swear on every coffee bean in the universe that I'm not a vampire," I promised her, laughing. "But . . . I can . . . sort of . . . see people from the past. Talk to them."

"Is that what you saw that day in the cafeteria? A ghost?"

"Yes, but it's a little more complicated than that." I smacked my forehead with my hand when I realized I'd just given her Michael's standard answer to me. "It would take a while to explain, and I'm kind of in a hurry. But am I right? About you?"

"Em, there's so much tied up in what I can do—what I promised my *abuela* I would *never* do. It's not dowsing. It's not like I use a divining rod, or even a pendulum, even though I wear this one." She fingered the tiger's eye pendant that always hung from a silver chain around her neck. I thought she wore it because it matched her eyes. "The short answer is, yes, I can find things."

"Why is it such a secret?"

"I don't know all the reasons." Lily's mouth turned down at the corners. "But Abuela has very strict rules about what I can actively look for. Inconsequential things, like my keys or a recipe she's misplaced, occassionally. But a living, breathing human? Never."

"But the other day—you knew she was back from the bank before you saw her."

"I knew the bank bag was back. And I knew Abi had the bank bag. I've developed loopholes over the years."

"Have you ever talked to anyone about it?" I thought of the Hourglass. "Like a professional?"

"A professional *what*? Abi would kill me if she knew I told you." She inclined her head toward the front door. "I'm sorry I can't help you find Michael. I know you're in a hurry. Go."

"I'm not if you want to talk—"

She shook her head. "Let me think about everything. Figure out what's okay to share and what isn't. Figure out what I want to ask you."

"I'm glad you told me. After everything I've been through, everything you've seen . . . you're still here. I'm here for you, too."

Lily reached out to grab my arm and pulled me into a hug. "I should've told you earlier. You might not have felt so alone."

"No. I understand why you couldn't." I hugged her back. "Thanks for trusting me. I won't tell anyone your secret."

"Ditto."

We broke the embrace and looked at each other for a long time before I turned to leave.

"Em? Wait."

"What?"

She held out her hand, her signature moxie back. "The apron doesn't go with the outfit."

Chapter 32

I figured I'd start at the Renegade House. It was almost too easy. His car sat out front. He'd had access to a phone yet failed to call me.

Payback time.

Taking a quick glance in the rearview mirror, I yanked the pencil out of my hair and shook it out. I got out of the car and marched toward the porch. Before my heel hit the top step the door flew open.

"Why is it *impossible* for you to do what anyone asks you to do?" Michael wore the same clothes he'd had on the last time I saw him. They were wrinkled, as if he slept in them—except he didn't look like he'd done any sleeping. His eyes were bloodshot, his chin stubbly. I wondered briefly how it would feel against my face if he kissed me.

Then I remembered I was mad.

"Why is it impossible for *you* to call someone when you're supposed to?" I reached up with both hands and gave him a good shove to the chest, feeling a jolt of electricity that ran all the way to my toes. "My brother practically handcuffed me to the furniture. I spent all night worried, wondering what was going on."

"Easy. I need you to stop yelling." He rubbed his eyes with his fists. "It's been a long night. I apologize for not calling, but it took us forever to find Kaleb."

"Us?" I asked, my voice thick with jealousy.

"Us. Me, Dune, Ava, and Nate." He leaned back, propping one foot against the side of the house. "We had to split up and take it place by place. He went barhopping in downtown Nashville. Luckily, he didn't drive."

"Is he even old enough to get into a bar?"

"He's almost eighteen, but not quite. Fake ID. He uses it to do lots of things he shouldn't. It's easy to tell when Kaleb is hellbent on destruction. A friend called here, and Ava answered. She couldn't get me on my cell, so she had to come to the loft."

Had to, my rear end.

"Come inside." Michael pushed himself away from the wall and gestured to the screen door before pulling it open. "But I'm warning you ahead of time: it's not very pretty. Kaleb is my best friend. I hope you don't judge him on what you're about to see."

He held the door for me, and I followed him into the living area. The smell hit me first. Part brewery, part gas-station bathroom.

"Whoa."

Even though the room was dim, from the doorway I could see one foot hanging over the arm of the couch. A big foot, the ankle attached encircled by a tattoo resembling barbed wire. I walked quietly around it to take in a sprawled-out, snoring figure.

One huge bicep featured a tattoo of a dragon's head; the other bicep, a forked tail. Taller and broader than Michael, Kaleb had the most defined abs I'd ever seen. The flannel blanket wrapped around his waist would've been a perfect size for me; on him it looked like a hand towel.

"Why isn't he wearing clothes?" I whispered the words to Michael.

He grimaced and whispered back. "You don't want to know."

I wrinkled my nose and started breathing through my mouth. Taking a step closer, I noticed Kaleb's face, probably beautiful when he wasn't hung over. His black hair was cut short, and he had a small hoop earring in each ear, kind of . . . sexy pirate. I jumped back when he groaned and opened one violet-blue eye.

Kaleb struggled to focus. The circles underneath his eyes were deep, or it could've been the shadow of his black eyelashes. "Am I dead? Are you an angel? Damn. You're smokin' hot for an angel. Come 'ere," he slurred.

Not hungover.

Still drunk.

I hurried to stand behind Michael when Kaleb reached out for me. More like swiped at me with a hand the size of a frying pan. He was scary big, mostly naked, and reminiscent of an escaped convict.

"Hey, Mike. I did it again." Kaleb grinned, and his face lit up. I could see how, clothed and sober, he could possibly be endearing. Right now . . . not really.

"Yes, Kaleb, you did it again," Michael said, sounding very much like a tolerant but exasperated kindergarten teacher.

"Who came to get me? I know she wasn't there." He pointed to me and smiled wider. "I would have remembered her."

"I did," Michael said. "So did Nate and Ava."

Kaleb put his hands behind his head and closed his eyes. I tried not to stare at his chest. "Ava? Why did you have to bring the Shining?"

"The Shining?" I asked.

"Stephen King reference," Michael said to me. To Kaleb, he said, "Because Ava's the one who answered the phone. She came to get me."

"Came to get you?" Kaleb frowned and opened his eyes to squint at us. "Where were you?"

Michael pulled me forward to stand beside him. "With the angel. This is Emerson."

Kaleb sat up quickly, turning three shades of green before grasping the blanket tightly around his waist, leaping up from the couch, and making a run for the door.

I looked up at Michael. "Okay."

We walked up the stairs as I tried to ignore the sound of retching coming from the downstairs bathroom, glad I'd skipped breakfast. "Great first impression."

"He's really not that bad." Michael's blinds were open and sunshine filled his room. "That's not true. He's worse than this sometimes."

"I meant me, not him. You told him my name, and he ran to the bathroom to throw up. You don't have to explain his behavior. Who am I to judge?"

"In the past six months I've watched him go from nice guy to hard-ass." Michael sat down in his desk chair and put his head in his hands. "It was bad enough when Liam died, but then his mom . . ."

"Got sick," I supplied.

"It was more than that." He hesitated before raising his head. "After Liam died, she . . . tried to kill herself."

I swallowed. Really hard. "Wow."

"Luckily, she didn't succeed. Grace has been in a coma ever since. For a while she had private nurses around the clock. Landers allowed her to stay at the Hourglass house."

"That's why Kaleb stayed," I said, finally understanding why he would remain in the same house with the man he suspected of killing his father. "To watch out for his mom."

"Right." Michael's face was troubled. "But her doctor suggested a long-term care facility. She's being moved today."

"That sucks." I knew way too much about long-term care facilities. I wondered if Kaleb did. If he knew what he'd have to deal with when he visited.

"That sucks," he agreed. "Kaleb used to be so different, so focused. He was a champion swimmer. The pool you saw at the Hourglass was put in for him."

That explained the swimmer's body, especially the shoulders. And the six-pack.

Eight-pack.

My edit button worked for once, and I kept my mouth shut. I pulled myself up to sit on the desk, the square edge scraping against my jeans. "You never told me what his ability is. Can you?"

"I might as well," he said, settling back in his chair. "He won't. Do you know what an empath is?"

"I know what empathy is."

Michael picked up a pencil and tapped the eraser end rhythmically on his desk. "There's a difference. An empath is supernaturally in tune with other people, sometimes whether he wants to be or not. Empaths aren't held by time or space, so they can feel the emotions of anyone, anywhere, in any time. But Kaleb mostly feels the emotions of people he would otherwise connect with in some way. He can read me because he's like my brother."

"Why did he call Ava 'the Shining'?"

"Have you read the book?"

"No, but I've read about it, and the movie." I avoided horror, especially horror that involved ghosts and psychopaths. I was exceedingly grateful for the Internet, the easily accessible plot synopsis, and the fact that it allowed me to consume popular culture in an informed but distanced way. "Ava doesn't keep an ax in her room or write on doors with lipstick, does she?"

He gave me a look. "Kaleb has a thing about nicknames. He claims Ava's mind is just as fractured as the dad in the book, and that she's just as resentful of authority. She tends to do whatever she wants to do whenever she wants to do it."

"Are all Kaleb's nicknames that involved?"

"No. He just really has a problem with Ava. Maybe because of the way she is around me."

"Um . . . Kaleb's going to stop blowing groceries anytime now, so maybe we should talk about him while he's not in the room?" I suggested. I didn't want to discuss the competition.

"True." He dropped the pencil on top of his desk. "I think the reason he's so tough on the outside is because he's so open on the inside. Everything about him—the way he looks, the way he dresses—is intentional. He tries to keep his distance from people because if he can he doesn't have to feel what they feel. What happened to his dad was bad enough. Dealing with his mom's breakdown almost killed him."

"Is he able to feel her emotions now?"

"No." He shook his head. "Not since the suicide attempt. He blames himself, says he never saw it coming."

My heart broke for Kaleb. His father might be dead, but his mother was alive, and he couldn't reach her. At least he didn't have to be inside his mom's crazy. Seeing it from the outside had to be hard enough.

"Part of his problem is that he can't always identify why people feel the way they do. He can misread emotions—think they're directed at him and then find out they were toward someone else," Michael said, rolling the pencil between his palm and the desk. "He told me once the reason he loves to swim is because emotions don't pass through water. It's one place he can escape."

I'd want a pool in my backyard, too. "Why did he freak out when you introduced us? I thought he knew about me."

"He did. The fact that you're here with me confirms you're on board to save Liam."

Footsteps sounded on the stairs, and Michael held a finger up to his lips. Kaleb walked through the open doorway, shielding his eyes from the sun coming in the window.

"You look better," Michael said, standing to close the blinds.

A lot better. He'd showered and put on clean clothes. The improvement in smell alone was stellar. He looked back and forth between the two of us, his gaze lingering on me.

It made me feel warm.

"Sorry about downstairs. I'm not exactly in my right mind. Which I don't understand," he said, looking back at Michael, "because I swear I only drank two beers."

Michael raised his eyebrows, saying nothing, and sat down on the edge of his bed.

"Swear," Kaleb insisted in his deep, rough voice. "Do you remember . . . um, who I was with when you found me?"

"Tall girl, dark hair, crazy eyes. She didn't seem to want to let you leave."

"Amy. No, Ainsley."

"New girlfriend?" Michael asked.

"No." Kaleb's gaze slid over to me.

"Random hookup?"

"Mike. A lady is present."

"She might as well get to know the real you." Michael shrugged.

"I don't appreciate what that implies," Kaleb said through gritted teeth.

"You'll get over it." Michael reached out to grab me by my sleeve and pulled me over to the bed to sit beside him. He pointed to the empty desk chair, then back to Kaleb. "Sit."

Kaleb sat.

But he wasn't happy about it.

I watched as his face transformed from the wide smile into something fierce and closed off. His eyes were even more beautiful up close, lending some delicacy to his face, but he still wasn't a guy I'd want to meet in a dark alley. Michael said Kaleb was a hard-ass, but I didn't think that began to cover it.

He was just plain scary.

"Nothing to worry about, Mike." Kaleb tried to play the disagreement off, but his voice remained tight. "No harm, no foul. No strings."

"I know." Michael stood, his tone challenging. I wanted to cover his mouth with my hands. Something told me I didn't want to be within a ten-mile radius if they started fighting. "It's like all your relationships. Hit-and-run."

"Watch it." Kaleb's gaze darted in my direction again as he stood and took a step toward Michael. "I don't need a big brother or a babysitter."

"You did last night."

Jumping between them was as smart as jumping into the middle of a cage match, but I did it anyway, putting a hand on each of their chests. Even in the heat of the moment I had to appreciate the muscle tone of both.

"Stop!" My voice broke, so I tried again. *"Stop!* I know you don't really want to do this, either one of you. Quit acting like babies."

It had been my experience that accusing a boy of being a baby was as effective as throwing a bucket of water on the Wicked Witch of the West. Just as she did after the Scarecrow took aim, the tension melted. Michael sat back down, and Kaleb dropped into the desk chair. Placing one arm on the seat back, Kaleb eyed me. "Hey, bro, do you think you can put Shorty back on her chain?"

I stepped forward with my hands on my hips, only slightly intimidated to find Kaleb almost eye level with me when he was seated and I was standing.

"First of all, no one is the boss of me but me. Secondly, if you ever reference my 'chain' again, I will kick your ass." I jabbed him hard in the chest with my finger. Possibly breaking it. "And thirdly, don't call me Shorty."

Kaleb sat silently for a second, his eyes wide as he looked at Michael. "Where did you find her? Can you get me one?"

I blew out a loud, frustrated sigh and dropped down beside Michael, who didn't even try to hide his smile. "You should probably apologize to Emerson."

"I am sorry." Kaleb grinned at me. "Sorry I didn't meet you first."

Chapter 33

I don't *want* anything!"

The three of us had relocated to the kitchen. Michael peered into the fridge, trying to find something Kaleb would eat. Kaleb responded by putting his face down on the table and covering his head with his arms, only peeking out occasionally to look at me and smile. He definitely had charm.

In spades.

"I'm sure Nate wouldn't mind sharing a half dozen or so of his eggs. Oh yum, you know what would settle your stomach? Baaaacon." Michael drew the word out as he opened the package and waved it in our direction, smiling widely.

Kaleb let out a groan as the scent wafted over to the table. Michael winked at me as if I were his coconspirator. I envied the level of comfort between the two of them, especially after a fight that almost came to blows.

I realized that I was comfortable here, too. I looked at Michael, still digging around in the fridge, and at Kaleb beside me. It felt right. They felt right. I hadn't come here expecting to find a place to belong.

Team Freak. Wonder if we could get jerseys.

The warm feeling of camaraderie faded a little bit when I reflected on the truth. Michael didn't know everything, not really. If he discovered what my life was like four years ago . . . it hadn't been a life. It had barely been an existence.

Footsteps sounded on the stairs, and Ava swung around the corner into the kitchen, her stilettos hitting the hardwood like tiny hammers tapping the floor. She made brief eye contact with me, offering a tight smile before she turned her attention elsewhere.

"Michael?" Ava asked impatiently.

He jumped before pulling his head out of the refrigerator. "Ava. How are you this morning?"

"We need to firm up our Thanksgiving plans." She'd yet to acknowledge Kaleb. "I want to book our flight to L.A. Assuming you're going to accept my invitation?"

Michael looked as nervous as a deer caught in the headlights of a semitruck hauling hazardous waste. "We already talked about that."

"No, we didn't." She frowned, looking genuinely confused.

"It was a couple of days ago. I told you I don't—"

"Just come upstairs, and we'll look at flight schedules. If you're done with"—she waved her hand in the general direction of the table—"that."

Kaleb smirked. "Oh, if you need him, Ava, I'm sure he's 'all done' with me. Michael, make sure you wash your hands before you spread any of my cooties to the Sh— Ava."

Ava cut her eyes around to Kaleb, tilting her head in a challenge. "Drunk," she said.

"Shrew," he replied.

"Kids!" Michael held up his hands in a T shape. "Time out."

Ava shot Kaleb a dirty look and left the kitchen. Michael followed.

He didn't look back.

"Why don't you tell her how you really feel?" I asked Kaleb when they were gone.

"I have from the beginning." Kaleb put his arms on the table and propped his chin on his fist, gazing at me. "Kind of like I'm about to tell you that I might be in love with you."

"Really?" I laughed. "Because of all of our deep conversations and the quality time we've spent together? Or was it just love at first sight?"

"Something like that," he said, teasing.

I thought.

I lost myself in his eyes for a second. When I realized he was waiting for me to say something, I cleared my throat. "So do you have nicknames for everyone? Shorty, Mike . . . the Shining?"

"I guess Mike told you the backstory on that one?"

I nodded, and his grin spread across his face slowly, like honey dripping from a comb. I bet he was used to girls staring. I wonder if he always enjoyed it as much as he appeared to be right now.

"I have nicknames for the people I love and the ones I love to hate."

I wondered if there was some deep, hidden significance to "Shorty." "And Ava's on the hate list."

"We've never gotten along." Kaleb's smile disappeared. He slid his arms across the table and leaned his head toward mine. "Maybe because something inside her seems off, and I can't get past it. She doesn't even know how she feels half the time."

"You'd know, right?" I returned. "I hope you don't mind. Michael told me. About your ability."

"I don't mind. I know all about you. It's only fair you should know about me, I guess." He sat up, the moment of intimacy broken. "No big."

"You don't know everything about me."

"I'd love to hear it all," he said, playing our conversation off as casual, flirty. I didn't bite.

"I don't know about that. The road to where I am now was . . . rough. But I'll give you the details. If you're interested."

Uncertainty clouded Kaleb's eyes as the mood shifted. Staring out the window over the kitchen sink, he said, "I'm listening."

"My parents died in an accident right after I started seeing rips. I was committed to an institution because I let it slip to a grief counselor that I thought I was seeing dead people. Oh, and also because I lost it so completely in the school cafeteria that my best friend had to carry me to the nurse." I gauged his reaction, wondering how much I could tell him. "No one knew what to do with me, so they drugged me into oblivion."

"How did you . . . get better?" He stared at me intently, searching for an answer I couldn't give him, no matter how much I wished I could.

"All those drugs in my system stopped me from seeing the rips. Eventually, the doctors lightened my dosage, and I learned to keep my mouth shut about what I saw. I stopped taking my meds last Christmas. Meeting Michael . . . has made it all easier."

"Did he tell you how my parents met?"

"No," I said. "But Cat told me a little bit about their relationship."

Kaleb leaned back in his chair, propping the sole of one sneaker against the edge of the table. "My dad is . . . was such a typical scientist. Crazy hair, clothes that never matched. My mom always had it together. She used to be an actress. They met when he was a technical adviser on a sci-fi movie she was in."

"What's your mom's name?"

"Grace. Her stage name was Grace—"

"Walker." I interrupted as the resemblance struck me. "You look exactly like her."

"Lucky for me." He grinned. "They married six weeks after they met."

"That's amazing."

"Their connection was unreal, deep. My dad saw rips his whole life, but it didn't start for my mom until they met."

"Did it terrify her?"

"She had my dad."

I wondered if it had really been that simple for her. "How did the empathy thing happen for you?"

"As far as we know, I was born with it. I cried a lot as a baby, but not because of colic. Once my parents figured it out, my mom quit taking acting jobs so she could be home with me all the time, act as a buffer. My mom made my life bearable." He paused, staring down at the floor. I thought I caught a glimpse of moisture on his dark lashes. "I miss her. I miss them both."

"Kaleb, you don't have to—"

"No, it's fine." He looked up at me, his eyes clear. Maybe I'd been wrong. "Anyway, as I got older, I discovered other things that helped, like how quiet it got for me, mentally, when I was underwater. That I could close out a lot if I put up enough walls."

I felt the need to lighten the moment. "Is that why you act like such a jerk?"

Kaleb granted me a grin. "Good call."

"I blocked a lot out, too, after the accident, even after the hospital," I confessed. "Kept my head down. I learned things— self-defense, sarcasm—all designed to keep people out, keep them away."

"Did it work?"

"For a while." I smiled. "It's getting easier to let people in. You should try it."

"I'll let you know how that works out," he said, laughing. Then his face turned serious again. "No one knows this except for Michael, but my dad found a way to isolate the properties of certain drugs to help me filter the feelings, keep me from absorbing everything from everybody. He manufactured a supply for me right before he died."

He took a flat silver coin out of his pocket and began flipping it over and under his knuckles, concentrating on the movement for a moment before fisting it in his hand. "I know what you've agreed to do for my dad."

Directly meeting the blue eyes that matched those of his famous mother, I said, "For your dad. And for you and your mom. No one should have to go through the things we have. If I can change the outcome, make life better, it's like making it right for the whole world."

"My dad gave me this when I turned sixteen. I'd finally accepted who I was. Decided to learn how to use it instead of running from it." Kaleb held the coin out between two fingers so I could see it. It wasn't a coin at all, but a silver circle with a word engraved on it. I leaned closer to read it.

"Hope."

He put the circle back in his pocket and reached out to take my hand. I gave it to him. His was strong, a little rough, and warm. I didn't feel the electricity I felt when I touched Michael, but something else.

Comfort.

"Thank you," he said.

I nodded.

Michael walked into the kitchen alone. I took my hand from Kaleb, but not before Michael saw it. I watched it register.

He didn't like it.

"Did you get your ticket booked?" Kaleb asked with saccharine sweetness, all the cockiness back full force. "Are you traveling first class?"

I spoke up before he and Kaleb could start fighting again.

"Speaking of travel, when are *we* going to travel?" I asked. Meeting Kaleb had only made me more certain I was doing the right thing. There was a face attached to the problem now, making it more real somehow.

"Soon, I hope," Michael answered. "We'll have to fill Cat in, of course, and make sure she's on board."

"What are we waiting for?" I stood up. "Let's go."

"Hold it. Isn't it a little soon?" Kaleb asked. "You just learned about your ability. Are you sure you're ready for this?"

I looked at him. "The sooner we travel, the sooner you can get your dad back."

Kaleb stared back at me. I knew he was trying to read me, probably looking for fear.

He wasn't going to find any.

Chapter 34

I followed Michael and Kaleb in Dru's car as we drove through the college campus and parked in front of the science department. Thomas had studied the classical architecture of the well-preserved stone and brick buildings when he'd decided which direction to take the downtown area of Ivy Springs. Like downtown, the buildings felt stoic, solid, comfortable. And old.

Old and I never meshed well.

A wide staircase led us up to the second floor. The smell of book bindings and chalk permeated the hallways. A deep monotone voice carried from a classroom into the hallway, lecturing about the properties of metals. Papers fluttered as we blew past bulletin boards advertising who knows what. I kept my eyes trained on Kaleb's broad back.

Cat's exclamation of surprise at our appearance broke my concentration. We'd entered some sort of laboratory with tubes and beakers and burners and a whiteboard full of equations. She ushered us in and shut the door.

"Kaleb, after last night I'm shocked to see you among the living. I was quite sure you'd be under the weather until tomorrow at least." Her eyes held a mixture of worry and relief behind a pair of rhinestone reading glasses. I wondered if they were hers, or if she borrowed them from a much older professor, one with blue hair and wrinkles to rival a shar-pei.

"Yeah, sorry about that." Kaleb rubbed the back of his neck as two bright spots of color appeared on his cheeks. "I'm not sure what happened."

She gave him a tight smile that promised more discussion later and turned her attention to Michael and me. "What brings you to the hallowed halls of academia? Did you have some more questions, Emerson?"

"She didn't." Michael stepped in to rescue me. "I have something I need to confess. It couldn't wait."

Cat slid the reading glasses from her nose and leaned back against the lab table. "Confess?"

My heart sped up in anticipation. So much hinged on Cat's acceptance of Michael's plan. He began to explain and I mentally crossed my fingers.

"A couple of months ago, I received a voice mail from someone I didn't recognize requesting a meeting at Riverbend Park." He shot me a sidelong glance. "Just off the main path, in a grove of trees. It was Em. Well, the Em from ten years from now. She told me how and when to contact Thomas to offer my services, as well as what I'd need to know to convince her I was legit. She also told me to research the Novikov Principle."

"What?" Cat breathed the word out, lifting her hands to brace herself against the table behind her. I studied Michael's face, intrigued by his revelation.

"No travel rules were broken," he explained hurriedly to Cat, avoiding my eyes. He said the next words deliberately. "She told me the two of us were a pair. She could help me do *what no one else could.*"

Cat pushed away from the table, causing it to shake violently. Glass rattled and liquid splashed, hissing as it ran into the flame of the burner. "You want to save Liam."

Michael nodded, but didn't speak. The seconds ticked past, and Cat's breathing grew more labored.

"No. You know there's no possibility. You can't interfere with time properties that way. They'll never let . . ." She stopped, shaking her head before continuing. "Slowing down and speeding up for our purposes causes enough trouble, but going back, resurrecting the dead? No."

"You're not thinking about the possibilities," Michael persuaded, taking a hesitant step closer to her. "Have you even considered the Novikov Principle?"

"I won't consider any principle, Michael. It's a no." She slid her body across the edge of the table, taking a quick step back to put the bulk of it between them. "A solid, irreversible no."

Kaleb, standing beside me and listening to the conversation, had remained silent up until this point. I felt his words more than I heard them, the sound of his barely contained rage pushing against my eardrums. "Why? Why the hell won't you help save my dad?"

I put my hand on his arm, even though it was foolish to think I had any hope of holding him back if he decided to go after Cat. His bicep tensed under my fingers, and I expected him to shake me off. He didn't.

Cat looked around the room as if she was seeking the closest exit. "It's not about saving your father. It's about the rules, the things we can and can't do."

Kaleb's long stride devoured the floor space between him and Cat. When he reached her, he pounded his fist against the stainless-steel tabletop, emphasizing each of his words. "Screw the rules."

"Kaleb, please," Michael said, his voice strained. Kaleb didn't move.

The only sound in the room was the hiss of the Bunsen burners and liquid bubbling in a suspended tube. After what seemed like a lifetime, Cat spoke.

"Emerson's never traveled before," she said, looking from Kaleb to Michael. "Are you telling me that you're willing to risk her safety, her life, to have her go back and save someone she's never even met?"

Michael tried to defend himself. "It's not danger—"

"Yes, it is," Cat cut him off. "Michael, you know how Liam died. The timing of what you're proposing would have to be precise— down to the millisecond—to have any chance of being successful."

"We could do it," he argued. "It would take some research—"

"Research? Think about what you're proposing. One false move, and you and Emerson could both be killed, burned to an unidentifiable pile of bones just like Liam. Is that what you want?"

Kaleb hissed through his teeth, stepping back to put himself between Cat and me.

Her words hit me like a physical blow. I wrapped my arms around my waist, my stomach aching with the need to be far away from the building and the conversation. I turned and left without out looking back, weaving my way through the banter of chattering students now flooding the hallway. Dodging backpacks and people, I shot out the double doors and down the steps to ground level. Once I reached the sidewalk, I looked over my shoulder to make sure no one had followed me.

Mistake.

In front of the building, a group of young men roughhoused, passing an old-fashioned pigskin football back and forth. It wasn't old-fashioned to them.

They wore short pants with striped socks and cleats, and I placed their uniforms in the early 1940s. I was already pushing the crazy envelope for the day, and now a whole ghostly football team stood in front of me, lining up to pose for a picture on the wide waterfall of steps leading to the second story.

In lieu of trying to stick my hand into a team of more than a dozen bulky boys, I chose to search for somewhere less populated. To my right, tucked behind the administration building, I found my sanctuary. The Whitewood Memorial Prayer Garden. Two mossy benches flanked an ancient-looking bronze sundial. Flowing willow tree branches created a lush green wall, muffling the sounds of campus life and hiding a small pond. Sinking onto one of the benches, I leaned my head back and closed my eyes, grateful for the warmth of the late afternoon sun on my face.

But as hard as I tried, I couldn't make Cat's words go away.

After I lost my parents, I replayed my version of the shuttle crash in my mind endlessly, imagining what it must have been like to slide down the mountainside into that crystal-clear, freezing-cold lake. I liked to think the end had been peaceful for them.

I knew the end hadn't been peaceful for Liam Ballard.

Heavy footsteps sounded behind me and I turned, expecting to see Michael. I let out a small gasp of surprise when I looked up into Kaleb's blue eyes.

"Michael's chewing Cat a new one for scaring you. I thought you could use these." He sat down, handing me a bottle of water and placing a wet paper towel on the back of my neck. It was so saturated that rivulets of water ran down the back of my shirt. "Are you okay?"

"Me? What about you? Are *you* okay? Cat compared your father to . . ." I trailed off, not wanting to finish the sentence. I took the dripping towel from my neck. Crumpling it into a small ball in my fist, I watched as the water squeezed out through my fingers and ran down the inside of my wrist. The sensation made me shiver.

Kaleb noticed. Placing his elbows on the back of the bench, he lowered the arm closest to me, resting it lightly on my shoulders. I resisted the urge to relax into the curve of his body.

The sun, low in the sky, filtered everything around us through a soft yellow lens. The garden looked like it belonged in a story-book, not like the kind of place in which to have a conversation about death. Pain.

"Kaleb, how could she say something like that in front of you?"

"She didn't mean it," he answered, his expression carefully blank. "Her intention was to make a point, and I'm guessing by your reaction she did."

"I reacted because of you. I'm guessing the two of you are close. I caught the look she gave you after she asked you about last night."

He turned his head away, his gaze skimming over lily pads and cattails to the far edge of the pond. A fish jumped, and tiny waves did a dance with the shoreline. "My relationship with Cat is unusual. Always has been. She's my legal guardian."

"But you don't live with her."

"I'll have to, now that my mom's not at the house anymore. I'm moving some of my stuff in tonight."

"Oh." I inwardly flinched at the pain I saw on his face. "Are you okay with that?"

"I don't know. I mean, I love Cat, but she doesn't know how to deal with me these days. I sure as hell don't make it easy for her. And when I try to read her—her emotions are all over the place." His voice sounded vulnerable, completely wrong for someone with an exterior as tough as Kaleb's. "Fear, guilt, anger, regret. I guess over my dad, or over the fact that she's not even thirty and now she has a ward who's almost an adult."

"I'm sure she doesn't think of you as a ward," I said reassuringly, rolling up the damp paper towel to give my hands something to do. "I think she's genuinely worried about you. How long have you known her?"

"It feels like I've always known her. She's always been there. She's like a sister to me. But she shouldn't have to act as my guardian. Things shouldn't have to be this way."

"She cares about you. A lot of people do."

"What about you, Shorty?" He smiled down at me. "Do you think you could?"

He wasn't talking about friendship. The water from the paper towel practically turned into steam that rose from my skin. "Kaleb, I—things are—I mean, this isn't the right time for—"

I heard the sound of a throat clearing, and I whipped my head around. Michael stood behind us. I wondered how much he'd heard. I realized how we looked from his viewpoint, Kaleb's arm around my shoulders, me looking up at him. I stood so quickly I almost fell over my own feet. Shoving the paper towel into my jeans pocket, I faced Michael.

"Hey!" I said, my voice too loud and too bright for the situation. "What happened with Cat?"

"She wants to think about it." He seemed uncomfortable, looking back and forth between Kaleb and me. "We're all supposed to meet up at the house tomorrow afternoon so she can give us her answer. And so she can apologize."

"She agreed she'd said the wrong thing to Emerson?" Kaleb asked. He stood, too, moving to stand behind me. Close behind me.

"She agreed she said the wrong thing, period," Michael answered, his voice tight. "To all of us."

A cell phone started ringing, and Kaleb jostled to pull his out of his pocket. A picture of a girl with her glossy lips puckered in a seductive kiss popped up on the screen. He held up the phone and gestured awkwardly. "I probably need to take this."

He turned his back to us and answered in a low voice, "Hey, baby."

I wanted to know more about what Michael and Cat discussed, but suddenly all I could think about was escape.

"Okay." I pulled out my keys and began anxiously spinning the ring around my finger. "I'm . . . uh . . . going to head out. Michael, I'll touch base with you later about tomorrow."

I gave half a finger wave to Kaleb's back. Then I turned tail and ran like a coward.

At least as fast as I could run in my heels.

Michael called out, "Em, wait up."

I kept going, still spinning my keys. I didn't look at him when he fell into step beside me. Once again, foiled by my short legs. "What?"

"I wanted to talk to you about—"

"You don't need to ask me if I still want to save Liam. I do. Nothing Cat said changed that. And I don't need you doubting me," I said, unreasonably irritated with him. We reached the car and I turned around to lean against the driver's-side door, bracing myself for an argument. "I can make my own decisions, you know."

"I'm sure you can." He tapped his fist on the roof of the SUV. "But that's not why I followed you. I wanted to ask you . . . how . . . um, experienced are you with guys?"

I froze, my spinning keys slowing to a stop and landing with a smacking thud against my hand. Tilting my head to the side, I stared at him. *"What?"*

Looking at the ground, he used his hands to gesture as he fumbled for words. "I . . . er . . . don't mean it that way, not like the physical . . ."

There was no way I was about to tell him the closest I'd ever come to a make-out session was my adventure with him against the wrought-iron fence. Nor did I think he'd be interested in my middle-school Spin the Bottle disasters. How was my romantic life any of his business? Realizing I still had my hand up in the air, I lowered it, willing myself not to use my key ring like a set of brass knuckles. "Are we really having this conversation?"

"All I wanted to say . . . I know Kaleb can be very . . . appealing." Michael said the word like it was a bad taste in his mouth. "Even though we argue, he's my best friend, but . . ."

"But?" I prodded.

"He's very . . . When it comes to girls . . . he's made some bad . . ." He stepped away from me, shoving his hands into his pockets. "Forget it. I don't have any right to tell you who you should or shouldn't see. I'm sorry."

"I'm not *seeing* anyone. I don't know what you thought *you saw* back there, but it was *just* a conversation." I was torn between being pleased he cared and pissed he thought it was any of his business. "Kaleb and I have a lot in common. We were talking. That's all."

"I get that." His frown lines grew deeper. "But . . . Kaleb doesn't always use his brain when it comes to girls."

"What teenage guy does?" I'd always been told they used quite a different part of the male anatomy. I wondered how this day had spiraled so completely out of control. From my fight with my brother to meeting a drunken Kaleb to revealing our time travel plans to Cat to . . . a discussion of my nonexistent sex life?

Damn, I was tired.

Michael was staring at me. "All I'm saying is that he can be . . . indiscriminate when it comes to hooking up. I wouldn't want you to be hurt."

My sudden headache was fierce, threatening to split my skull wide open and spill my brains out onto the pavement. "Well," I said, "if Kaleb and I hook up, I'll be sure to remember that."

"Oh, no, wait . . . you took that wrong. Emerson, wait!"

Without another word I got in the car and slammed the door behind me, clicking the locks and revving the engine. The last thing I saw as I peeled out of the parking lot was the horrified look on his face.

Chapter 35

The pain in my head caused my stomach to churn in protest. I wanted my bed. And complete darkness.

And chocolate.

I dragged myself up the stairs, opening the door to find my loft empty. Thank heaven. Grabbing a bottle of water, some pain relievers, and a candy bar from Dru's emergency stash, I noticed it was barely eight o'clock. Not too early for nighty-night.

If you were seven.

I didn't care. I was too busy being grateful I wouldn't have to add a confrontation with my brother to the list of the day's defeats. I left Dru's keys on the counter along with a note that I was exhausted and going straight to bed. Seeking comfort, I took a long shower before pulling on underwear and one of Thomas's old soft-as-silk undershirts.

Making sure my windows were locked, I fell into bed. I didn't want to take the chance that Michael would come back to his loft and try to force a face-to-face conversation. I turned out the light and scooted down so that the covers were over my head, closing my eyes and hoping sleep would come with the sheer force of my will.

Growling in frustration, I flipped over onto my stomach, burying my face in my pillow. Maybe taking my thoughts apart one by one would be as effective as counting sheep. I could try to make them jump over a fence and out of my mind.

Was Kaleb really as indiscriminate when it came to girls as Michael wanted me to think? He'd seemed so sincere when we talked. I couldn't imagine that he'd share the things with a random stranger that he'd shared with me, especially the things about his parents. He might be flirty, but I thought he was genuine. Until the phone call from the kissy-faced girl. The way he'd answered practically stamped his forehead with the word *player*.

Add that to the conversation with Michael . . .

I pulled my pillow over my head and screamed.

"Emerson!"

The word was loud, coming from right beside my ear. I choked off my yell and sat up, clutching my pillow to my chest, whipping my head in the direction of the voice. It took me a second to make out the shape standing beside my bed against the light coming in my window from outside, but once I did, I wanted to scream again.

Jack.

"Not now," I moaned in frustration, squinching my eyes shut. I opened them again slowly, hoping he'd disappeared.

No such luck.

"Are you all right?"

I sighed.

"Did you find your young man? Get the answers you were looking for?"

"My young man? Oh, I found him," I grumbled. "And if one stupid boy wasn't enough trouble, I also found his best friend."

"Let me guess," he said, a sympathetic smile on his face. "They're fighting over you?"

"Yes. No! I don't know." I slammed my face into the pillow before answering him in a muffled voice. "It's some kind of . . . competition, and it's totally unnecessary. I just want to trap them in the same room and . . . and . . ."

"What?"

"Slam their heads together until they're unconscious."

He laughed his rich, buttery laugh. "Come now. You must be used to boys fighting over you."

"That would be a big no," I said, but I tucked his words away like a piece of candy into my pocket, to take out later and savor. "Where did you come from? I thought you were gone."

Jack's laughter stopped, and the room grew almost unbearably quiet.

"I looked for you yesterday. Where were you? Scratch that."

Scooping my hair out of my face, I sat up. His eyes were still the same strange blue, if slightly lighter, and they were staring right through me. His hair seemed lighter, too. I held the pillow clutched to me, very aware of how little I was wearing. "What *are* you?"

"That's an odd question."

"Not really." I readjusted, pulling my covers up higher. "Every time I've ever touched rips, they've disappeared. You didn't."

"What's a rip?" he asked, studying me with an expression of amusement.

"What you are. What I *think* you are." I shook my head in irritation. He still wore the same black suit with the vest. Nothing really gave away what time period he belonged in, not even his haircut. His fingers were absent of rings. No visible clues to lock him into any era, except for the silver pocket watch that hinted of a gentler time. "You're from the past. Right?"

He nodded.

"I don't know why you're here, Jack." I leaned forward slightly, wondering what would happen if I tried to touch him. He had to know what I was thinking, yet he stayed still. "Why do you keep showing up?"

"For you."

"What?" I shivered as the air conditioner cut on, the ceiling vent blowing cold air down over my bare arms.

"I feel . . . connected with you. I know all the mysterious turns life can take. I wish I could protect you from them."

"That's impossible." I rubbed my hands over my arms briskly, trying to warm up, wondering how much of the chill had to do with Jack rather than the Freon-cooled air.

"You'd think so, wouldn't you? You are so unique. So innocent." The way he was looking at me didn't make me feel innocent at all. It made me wish Thomas and Dru were home. "Life is . . . ripe with choices. Some less clear-cut than others."

I centered the pillow more directly over my chest. "You're not making sense. What you're saying doesn't—"

"One day it all will." His eyes grew darker for a split second. "And on that day, you'll know that I've done all of this . . . to protect you. All for you."

I heard the front door of the loft open, but I didn't look away from Jack.

He smiled a sad smile and took a step back.

Gone.

I wondered this time if it was for good.

Chapter 36

I don't know what Dru said to Thomas to keep me out of trouble for going to find Michael. I only know that I was grateful. Thomas didn't make a sound the next morning when I asked to borrow Dru's car again, and she handed the keys over willingly.

I got while the getting was good, driving toward campus with the windows down. The air already dripped with humidity, and I was glad I'd put on shorts and a tank instead of jeans and a T-shirt. Blasting the radio, I let the music numb my mind. I didn't want to think about how to handle the Michael/Kaleb situation. By the time I reached the Renegade House I had to give myself a pep talk even to get out of the car.

I walked in without knocking. The screen door banged to a close behind me, announcing my presence. I followed my nose to the kitchen and found Kaleb standing by the stove. He stirred something that smelled absolutely delicious, a wooden spoon in one hand and a huge chef's knife in the other.

"Are you sober?" I asked from the doorway.

He turned and leveled a smile that made me a little wobbly. "I am."

"Good. Because if not, I was going to take the deadly kitchen utensil away from you." I crossed the room and pulled myself up to sit on the counter beside the stove. A cutting board full of green peppers and two uncut stalks of celery waited for attention from the knife. Melted butter and diced onions bubbled in a sauté pan on the stove. "You cook?"

Kaleb was so pretty I was jealous. Pretty, with ripped muscles and a tattoo of a red dragon covering most of his upper body. "Yes," he said. "I cook."

"Do you usually wear a wifebeater and"—I pushed him back a little by his shoulder—"an apron that says 'Kiss the Cook' while you're doing it?"

He leaned so close to me my heart skipped a couple of beats. "I'll wear it all the time if you'll consider it."

"Ha-ha. So," I said, hastily changing the subject and pointing to the cutting board, "what are you chopping up?"

"The trinity: onions, green peppers, and celery. Étouffée's going in the pot. Dune and Nate are on the way back from their consult, and they're bringing crawfish. So," he said, scraping stray bits of cut vegetables from his knife onto the side of the stainless-steel pan, "final judgment's on the way."

My stomach twisted at the thought, knowing all of Michael's plans depended on Cat's answer. We couldn't go without her. "Any idea what she's decided?"

"No clue," he said, raising his eyebrows. "You sure you still want to go?"

"I'm sure."

"I don't believe you." Kaleb put the knife on the cutting board and leaned on the counter beside me. "You were fine yesterday. Today you're nervous. What changed?"

"Are you reading my emotions? We just met yesterday. How?"

He lifted one shoulder and smiled.

"It's really annoying when you do it without permission."

"I can't help it." He picked up the sauté pan and tossed the vegetables a couple of times. I'd never be able to do that without dropping everything all over the kitchen floor or burning myself. "Are you nervous because of something Michael said when he followed you to your car yesterday?"

"Not really." I guessed Michael hadn't shared his hook-up opinions with Kaleb.

"You know, I bet I could take your mind off your worries."

"Oh, yeah?" I asked, teasing.

He put the pan back on the stove and placed his hands on either side of me on the counter, his fingertips touching my outer thighs. "Yep."

"Oh." Shazam. I bit down on my bottom lip.

He reached up to gather my hair in a loose ponytail at the

base of my neck, his forearms resting on my bare shoulders. "I've been thinking about how much I'd like to distract you. Thinking about it a lot."

"Really?" I sounded a little too breathless. My mind scurried to come up with the right words to stop him, but I couldn't seem to find any words at all.

"Really." Kaleb's hands slid down my arms, his thumbs tracing lines from my inner elbows to my wrists. Chill bumps formed on my skin and anticipation ripped through my system. I leaned back, bumping my head on the cabinet behind me.

Smooth.

He laughed, but it made me feel warm instead of embarrassed.

I got only warmer as he moved his hands to my face to hold my head still. I was kind of glad. I didn't want to bump it on the cabinet again.

"You distracted yet?" Kaleb asked.

I was at a complete loss for words. I didn't protest when he leaned forward at a snail's pace, a breath away from touching his lips to mine. In that second I closed my eyes.

And saw Michael's face.

I didn't have to push Kaleb away. He stopped. We opened our eyes at the same time.

"I was afraid of that."

"What?" I asked as I exhaled.

"Michael. And you."

"How did you know? I mean, what are you talking about?"

He frowned, focusing on my face and slowly tracing his thumb along my jawline. "Listen. If this were purely physical, I'd be carrying you upstairs to look for an empty room. With your consent, of course."

I think I squeaked. While Kaleb was ridiculously sexy, he was equally as terrifying. At least to me.

He laughed. "But it's not just physical, which is confusing enough. There's something between you and Mike, even if he won't admit it."

"No, there isn't. There isn't," I protested when he narrowed his eyes.

"Do you feel something for him?"

"Maybe." This time I banged my head against the cabinet on purpose. "I have no idea *what*. I'm sorry."

"Don't apologize. Just let me know when you figure it out." His hands still cupped my face. He leaned over, placing a gentle kiss on one corner of my mouth, keeping his eyes focused on mine. Then he whispered, with his lips still on my skin, "For a chance with you, I can wait."

Michael picked that exact moment to walk into the kitchen.

Kaleb pulled away from me quickly, going back to the sauté pan as if nothing happened. Michael's face was completely unreadable. I wondered for a second if he saw anything. Or cared if he had.

"Emerson?" His voice was empty of emotion. Too empty.

"Yes," I answered, sliding down from the counter. I almost fell when my feet hit the ground, and would have if Kaleb hadn't caught me by the arm.

"Sorry," he muttered under his breath.

"Weak in the knees?" Michael asked.

He'd definitely seen it.

I smoothed down my hair and adjusted my tank top. "I'm fine. It's fine."

"Cat's not here. I went to see her at the lab, and we need to reschedule for tomorrow morning. I wanted to talk to you about our . . . discussion yesterday, but it looks like you've found other ways to amuse yourself."

Then he turned on his heel and walked out of the kitchen.

"Something's up." Kaleb's eyebrows were drawn together in concentration. "His emotions are all over—I think I should go talk to him—"

"No, let me." I put my hand on Kaleb's arm. "You guys have been fighting enough as it is. And I need to settle this."

Chapter 37

Michael."

He was walking out the front door when I caught up to him. I followed him outside. "Where are you going? I thought you wanted to talk."

"Didn't know how long you'd be." He stalked across the wide planked porch, the boards hollow sounding under his weight. "Thought I'd let you finish up."

"Wait!" I reached out, catching the edge of his sleeve. He flinched as I accidentally brushed his skin with my fingers. "We were done. I was done. We weren't doing—"

He jerked his arm free and started down the steps. "What the hell were you thinking, kissing Kaleb?"

"I wasn't kissing Kaleb!"

"I just saw you in the kitchen with him," he said, spinning around after two steps. "And you were *kissing*."

I tried to explain. "It wasn't like that—"

"It never is." He crossed his arms and managed to look superior. "Isn't that the excuse everyone gives when they get caught?"

"Get caught? You say that like I was doing something wrong." I threw the next words out defensively, wanting to wipe away his smirk. "Why do you even care?"

"I only want you to . . . forget it," he said, turning away.

I put both hands on his left shoulder, yanking him around so I could yell in his face. "No, you don't, Michael Weaver. You don't get to unload on me and then reel it all back in without telling me why."

"You can do whatever you want," he said, his voice cold and distant, shutting me down. Shutting me out. "I don't have a right to an opinion."

I still wanted him to have one. And vocalize it. Fighting the urge to push him, I attempted to push his buttons instead. "Kaleb did try to kiss me," I said, sounding like a taunting bully on a playground.

Michael flinched as if my hand had actually connected with his cheek. "Looked like he succeeded to me."

Bingo.

"He stopped." I stood as close to him as I dared. "You want to know why?"

Michael covered his face with his long fingers, his silver thumb ring glinting in the sunlight. "I don't know, Emerson. Do I?"

I said the next words distinctly, hoping for maximum impact. "Kaleb stopped because of you."

"What?" He lowered his hands, his voice soft, incredulous.

"Your best friend is an *empath.* And he didn't kiss me *because of you.*" It was out before I could stop myself. Why couldn't I keep my mouth shut? I growled in frustration and dropped down to sit on the top porch step.

"Um . . . I thought maybe . . . But then Kaleb . . ." He trailed off awkwardly. "I didn't know if you were confusing the way we make each other feel . . . physically . . . with actual feelings."

"Maybe I am."

"Nothing can happen between us, Em." At least he sounded sad about it.

"I know that." I stared down at the white paint flaking up from the porch steps. I leaned over, scratching at it. "I should go find Kaleb and take him up on his offer to distract me."

"Don't."

"Why? 'Nonfraternization' rule or not, I've practically thrown myself at you. One second I think you want me back, then the next I don't know. I barely recognize myself when I look in the mirror because I don't *ever* act like this, and then I meet Ava and—"

The screen door opened behind me, the hinges in desperate need of oil. Grateful for the interruption and an excuse to end my humiliation, I pushed up forcefully from my seat on the stairs, cracking my head on something hard before feeling the sensation of cold slime sliding down my back.

I twisted around to see Dune holding a cooler half full of mud and crawfish heads.

The other half was all over me.

Chapter 38

For a horrible second, no one moved. Everything around me stood out with startling clarity. The dismay on Michael's face, the sludgy water dripping from my tank top, the crawfish heads in my hair.

Michael jumped into action. "Dune, go inside and grab some paper towels. Have Kaleb bring us some ice. She hit her head pretty hard."

"Emerson, I'm so sorry." Dune dropped the cooler onto the porch and reached out to me. Michael waved him away and he took off in the direction of the kitchen.

"Are you all right?" Michael asked, peering into my eyes as he rested his hands gingerly on my shoulders. I couldn't tell if he was trying to avoid the slime or my skin. "Your pupils look dilated. Does your head hurt? Tell me your name."

"Of course my head hurts," I snapped. "Ask me my name again, and I'll turn you into a soprano."

His eyes filled with relief as he let go of my shoulders and stepped away. "At least you're okay."

I was so far from okay.

Pulling a mud-caked strand of hair in front of my face, I crossed my eyes as I looked at it. "Do you have a garden hose somewhere? I can't drive home like this."

"I'm not going to let you wash off with a garden hose," he said, shaking his head. "You can go up and take a shower. I'll wash your stuff."

"So I'm just going to sit somewhere naked while I wait?" I asked. Then I blushed.

Thankfully, at that moment Dune appeared with a whole roll of paper towels. He started ripping them off and dabbing at my hair and my shirt, all the while mumbling under his breath about how sorry he was.

"Dune," I said, grabbing his wrist when his dabbing got a little too personal, "it's fine. I know you didn't do it on purpose. Accidents happen."

His serious sea-colored eyes were full of apology. "I really am sorry."

"How hard did she hit? Do I need to call 911?" Kaleb asked as he burst through the screen door, ice in hand. When he saw me he froze for a few seconds before exploding into laughter.

"Knock it off," Michael said, scolding. "She could've been hurt."

"Are you all right?" Kaleb asked, with tears in his eyes.

I pursed my lips and crossed my arms, surprised to feel a giggle bubbling up in my chest. "Peachy."

He started laughing again. I wondered if I really had hurt myself when I hit my head, because I joined him.

"This really isn't . . . funny." I sat down to try and catch my breath, landed on a particularly slimy pile of crawfish heads, and slid to the bottom of the steps, hiccuping on impact.

Dune gave in, the concern in his eyes dissolving into humor as he doubled over in a deep belly laugh, sinking to the ground beside Kaleb. Michael still stood in the exact same spot, watching the three of us with something that looked like longing in his eyes.

I wiped away the leftover tears of laughter and threw my sopping hair over my shoulder, accidentally dislodging several shells that took flight and landed next to Kaleb.

He and Dune started giggling again, sounding like oversize preschoolers who'd eaten too much cotton candy. I covered my mouth so I wouldn't join them and looked at Michael.

"What?" I asked through my fingers.

"Nothing," he said, shaking his head. "Nothing at all."

Freshly showered, I sat on Michael's bed, waiting for someone to bring me my dry clothes. I'd insisted on keeping my underthings and washed them in the sink, drying them with a hair dryer.

I'd been alone with my thoughts for too long. I kept picturing

Michael's expression before he'd left Dune, Kaleb, and me outside. Almost like he was giving something up.

A knock sounded at the door, and I jumped up to answer, barely cracking it and sticking my head out. "Ava."

She was dressed in a tiny pair of sleep shorts and a white spaghetti-strap tank top. Opening the door wider, I stepped out from behind it, wearing one of Michael's Red Sox T-shirts.

Her eyes took in my damp hair, his T-shirt, and my legs, bare from just above my knees down to my pink painted toenails. I couldn't help wondering how often she made evening visits to Michael's room wearing skimpy pajamas.

"Where's Michael?"

"He's downstairs," I answered, not revealing the specifics of why I was in his room. He could tell her. They could laugh about it together.

"What are you doing in here?"

I had no idea how to explain the crawfish debacle. "Um—"

"Never mind." She shook her head and waved her hand, dismissing both her question and my answer, before leaning down and saying conspiratorially, "Can I give you a little friendly advice?"

"Sure."

"Michael and I have been close for a really long time. I wouldn't want you to do anything that would cause you . . . embarrassment, if you understand what I'm saying." She gave me a pointed look, and her eyes strayed to the hem of Michael's T-shirt.

I desperately wished I wasn't having this conversation in my panties.

"I'm not doing anything . . . This is just . . . I'm only here to help."

"Help who?" she asked. Her eyes stayed on my face, but I could feel her giving me the once-over in her mind. "Exactly?"

"Help . . . to help . . ." The truth hit me like a sledgehammer, and I physically took a step back. She didn't know about the plans to save Liam. I scrambled to come up with an explanation instead of standing there catching flies. "I'm here to help Cat with some things. That's all."

"Oh." Her mouth softened into a suggestive smile. "Well, maybe you should be in her room instead of Michael's. He might . . . need it for something. Later."

A vision of me with my hands around her neck flashed through my mind, taking the green-eyed monster theory to a new level. It hit me suddenly that I had some serious aggression issues.

"Okay, well." I forced a smile. "Good luck with that."

I slammed the door before I did something stupid, leaning against it and attempting to calm my breathing.

I needed to look into anger-management classes.

I needed to get out of this house.

And I really needed to find my pants.

Chapter 39

I kept my fingertips on the hem of Michael's T-shirt, pulling it down as far as I could. Glad I was familiar with the house, I tiptoed down the stairs, stopping short just outside the common area.

Ava and Michael were talking, her voice loud, his soft. I moved back to press myself against the wall beside the wide doorway, swallowing a scream when I felt a solid barrier of flesh behind me instead of the plaster I was expecting.

Kaleb. In the dim light I watched as his gaze traveled up my body, taking in my bare feet, the too-big T-shirt, finally returning to my legs. He let out a low, appreciative whistle.

"Two things. One, you have some *fine* legs. Two, if you were upstairs in my room, looking like that? I sure as hell wouldn't be downstairs with *her*."

Motioning for him to be quiet, I put my shoulder against the wall and leaned my head toward the conversation. Kaleb tucked himself in behind me, so close I could feel his breath on my hair.

"She was in your room." Ava's innate poise saturated her voice. I bet she'd never end up on the receiving end of a bucket of fish heads. "And she didn't have on *pants*."

I could feel Kaleb's gaze move back to my legs. I elbowed him.

"Dune spilled a cooler of crawfish heads and mud all over her." I could barely hear him over the sound of a baseball game on the television. "What was she supposed to do?"

"Go home?"

"She used my bathroom to take a shower. She was waiting for her clothes to dry."

The poise slipped a little. "Were you going to *tell me* she was in your room—half-naked?"

I went ahead and elbowed Kaleb again for good measure.

"Ava." Michael's voice was sad. "You're here because I'm trying to protect you."

Ava sounded confused. "From what?"

"From who. Landers—"

"You're going to bring this up again?" she said, on edge now. "I know what kind of man he is. I've known for a long time."

"If that's true, then you should know why I didn't want you in that house. You kept having blackouts—"

"The blackouts? Is that really the only reason you asked me to move in here?" Michael didn't respond. The sports announcers on the television discussed the first baseman's batting average in depth before Ava spoke again. "Those aren't happening anymore."

"I'm not so sure about that, Ava."

"I don't want to talk about this."

"And I don't want to fight with you."

"You know what? Go ahead and let the little groupie in your bedroom lavish you with 'attention.'" I could hear the air quotes. "Who am I to stop her from feeding your hero complex? Should be easy to get started considering she's naked from the waist down."

I did not like what she was implying about me. At all.

And I totally had on my unders.

I got up quickly, clipping Kaleb in the chin with my head. I started for the common room, but he grabbed me around the waist, lifting me off the ground. If he hadn't, I would have smacked directly into Ava as she rushed out of the room and stomped up the stairs. As soon as I heard her door slam, I started kicking, forcing Kaleb to put me down. I got the feeling he enjoyed my squirming a little too much.

"Where do you think you're going?" Kaleb whispered furiously.

"In there," I mouthed, pointing to the common room.

"You don't want to do that." I raised my eyebrows, and he continued in a low voice. "Come on, Em. He's not your only option."

I took a step back. "That's not what this is about."

He gave me a half smile and shook his head. "Just remember what I said." Then he turned and followed Ava up the stairs.

I didn't know when I'd become the top prize in the pissing contest between Michael and Kaleb, but I didn't want to watch the race. I just wanted my pants.

I stepped into the room. "Hey."

Michael faced me, making every effort not to look below my neck. "I'm sure your clothes are almost dry. I'll bring them up when they're done."

I exhaled. "Can I have them now?"

"You in a hurry?" His stare almost burned a hole through me.

"I've been gone a lot lately. I don't want to worry Dru and Thomas." I fiddled with the hem of the T-shirt and wondered if he knew I was lying.

"Let me guess. You overheard my conversation with Ava."

"Maybe." I looked up at him. "Yes."

"That's too bad." He rubbed his hands over his face, as if he was wiping away the memory of the argument.

"Is it true? Do you have a hero complex?" I stepped toward him involuntarily.

"How's that edit button of yours?" I had the good sense to blush while Michael picked up the remote from a side table and cut off the television in the middle of a double play. The room went dim, the only other light coming from two small lamps on a buffet table. "Ava has a tendency to trust the wrong people. Landers had her snowed."

"Kind of like you had me snowed?" I tried to be angry, but I didn't sound convincing. I was too preoccupied by the way his face looked in the half-light, thrown into shadows. Mysterious. Dangerous. Tempting.

"What are you talking about?"

I imitated him. "'No, Emerson, kissing you would be a big mistake.' Why, Michael? Because you didn't want me to be confused about my reasons for helping you save Liam, or because you didn't want to have to make a choice between me and Ava?"

He moved swiftly. Cupping my face in his hands, he bent forward until he was a second away from touching his lips to mine. My blood rushed through my veins, every inch of my skin shivering and boiling at the same time. I half expected fire to shoot out of the electrical sockets. The lightbulb blew in one of the lamps on the buffet table, sounding a quiet ping into the dark.

I closed my eyes, ready to surrender to the kiss.

Just as quickly as he'd grabbed me, he let me go.

"That . . . wasn't . . . fair." I opened my eyes, swaying where I stood.

"No," he answered. "It wasn't. But now you know. If I wanted to play games with your emotions to get you to side with me, it wouldn't be a hard sell. What I want doesn't have a place in this. Emotions don't have a place in this. They can't."

All the heat I'd felt disappeared, and my mouth dropped open. "I can't believe you did that. You're such a jerk."

"Maybe so. But I don't want you to do anything to please me

or because of any feelings you think you have. I don't want you to do it for the wrong reasons."

"Are there any wrong reasons to save someone's life?"

"No, but there could be regrets."

"My only regret is that I ever thought there could be something between us. Point me in the direction of my clothes. I'll find them myself."

Michael jerked a thumb toward the kitchen.

"I'll be here after lunch tomorrow to hear Cat's verdict. If she says we can go back, I'll still help you rescue Liam. But then you never have to see me again. And I never have to see you."

I thought I caught a hint of regret in his eyes as I left the room.

It had to be a trick of the light.

I slept late. Dru checked on me before she left for work, but the sun shone down from the middle of the sky before I finally got out of bed. I felt like I'd run a marathon or been hit by a truck. It was a familiar—and terrifying—feeling.

What had I done?

I stumbled into the bathroom, turning on the shower to let it heat up while I undressed. Four years of shutting people out, keeping my own counsel, and in less than twenty-four hours Thomas, Dru, and Lily knew all my dirty secrets.

And Michael knew way more than I wanted him to know. So did Kaleb.

I stood under the spray without moving, trying to absorb all the damage I'd done to my life.

Where had my head been? How could someone like me ever trust another person with the complete truth? Way more was "out there" about me than I ever intended to share. At least Dru and Thomas were family. They'd stand by me no matter what. They already had.

Lily had stuck with me for years. Everyone else had cut me off.

I dressed, wishing I could turn off my mind, stop thinking about my circumstances. Relationships were such a risk. At boarding school I'd kept everything light, easy. Always the funny one, but when it came down to building deep relationships, an introvert. The reason I understood Kaleb's protective wall was because I had built a pretty sturdy one of my own over the past few years.

Until Michael came along and blew it to kingdom come.

I took a long look at myself in the mirror. The truth was written all over my face.

I had fallen for him, hard, and I didn't even know until it was already over.

I picked Dru's keys up from my dresser and slipped on my sneakers. I could stop this. It wasn't too late. The protective wall could be rebuilt, brick by brick. Loving Michael wasn't a possibility.

Even if I was already halfway there, I could still make a U-turn.

Even if I thought it might kill me.

Chapter 40

"Where's Kaleb? I thought he'd want to be part of this conversation, too." Cat's face registered surprise.

"He went to get the rest of his stuff from the Hourglass." Michael opened the front door when I knocked without a word. I'd followed him into the kitchen in silence, my heart breaking a little more with every step. "He said to start without him."

We all sat down around the kitchen table. An empty seat occupied the space between Michael and me.

The little-old-lady glasses Cat had been wearing at the college balanced on the tip of her nose. She pulled out a tiny spiral notebook and opened it flat in front of her. "I did some research, looking at every angle of the Novikov Principle. I have to say, Michael, you really did your homework. I think it's a possibility."

Victory.

"Don't get too excited yet," she warned, shaking her head and tapping the notebook. The pages were scribbled with numbers and formulas. "There's more work to be done. We've got to get every element down perfectly, so many—"

We all jumped when the back door slammed open, ricocheting against the wall. Kaleb burst into the room. "Cat, Michael, you'll never . . . the house . . . Landers . . ." He bent over at the waist, hands on his knees, shoulders heaving.

"Did you run the whole way here?" Cat rushed to the fridge to get Kaleb a cold bottle of water, opening it as she handed it to him. He took several long pulls before wiping his mouth with the back of his hand.

"No. Ran out of gas. Couple blocks over. Couldn't stop," he gasped, shaking his head. "It's Landers. He's gone."

Michael sat up straighter in his chair. "Where?"

"What?" Cat asked at the same time.

"No one knows. Overheard a few people talking." Kaleb drained the rest of the water and capped the empty bottle. "Arguing about how no one's been paid in over a month."

"How is that possible?" Michael asked. "Since Liam died, Landers has taken on more work than the Hourglass can handle."

"It was so odd." Kaleb twisted the cap on the water bottle open and closed, over and over, staring down at his tennis shoes. "Like they all realized at the same time that he was gone."

Michael said, "They shouldn't have helped him in the first place."

"You're missing the point." Kaleb's voice grew urgent. *"When he ran, he took the files."*

The tension in the room intensified, pulled tight like a thread.

"But you got them." Michael's tone was as fierce as it had been the day he told me to mind my own business when it came to the Hourglass. "Kaleb, you said you'd get them."

"I planned to. They were in the safe yesterday, when I opened it to get the papers the hospital needed for Mom's admission." Kaleb paused and pain flashed across his features for a brief second. "Landers's guards were in the office, so I had to leave them. Then this morning, the safe was drilled through. Jewelry, stock certificates, still there. Only the cash and the files were taken."

The thread unraveled, and the room went dead silent. Fear wrapped itself around my heart in tiny tendrils. I closed my eyes, knowing when I opened them that everyone would be looking at me.

I was right. "What's going on?"

"My dad kept records," Kaleb answered. I didn't like the sound of his voice. "He'd save things on computer disks sometimes, but these files . . . they were hard copy only. He stored them in the family safe. That's how private he kept them."

I focused on Kaleb. "What do the files have to do with me?"

"If Dad received information about anyone with any type of an ability, even a hint of one, he documented it. Every incident. Every detail." Kaleb's fist crushed the plastic bottle, barely covering my gasp. "Every person."

"Liam documented me." I turned to Michael. "He documented me, and you know because you looked."

"After I met you, that first time. I needed to prove to myself that you were real. I asked Kaleb to open the safe for me. I should've taken your file that day," Michael said.

"It's not just Emerson's file. Think about all the people he has access to now," Cat said. "We have to find him."

"If the Hourglass can't, what makes you think we can?" Kaleb argued.

"We have to. Because we all know exactly who he's going to target first." Michael's face was a controlled mask. "Travelers who can go to the past are rare. Really rare. Some physicists believe they'll eventually be able to travel to the future on their own, gene or no gene. But not to the past."

"That's the very thing that makes people like you and Grace so special. And now that Grace isn't an option," Cat said, "it only makes sense that Landers would look for someone else with the same ability."

"If he didn't know about you before, he will soon. He'll know you're in town, close by. You aren't safe anymore. Not if he has the files," Michael said deliberately. "He has access to every-thing: your records, personal information. Your family's address. My guess is it's only a matter of time before he comes for you."

I fought nausea as terror washed over me. "Oh, no, Michael. Thomas and Dru . . . the baby."

My eyes landed on the phone hanging on the wall, and I

almost knocked my chair over in my haste to get to it, grabbing it off the hook in a panic. It was the old-fashioned rotary type, the receiver attached by a long spiral cord twisted up in knots.

"You have access to more technology than NASA, and this is your phone?" I asked Michael, shaking the receiver at him. Cat and Kaleb disappeared from the kitchen, the door swinging shut behind them.

"It's a secure line, so it . . ." He'd started to answer, but the expression on my face stopped him. I forced myself to concentrate and managed to put the right finger in the right holes as I dialed the number.

One thought pounded against the sides of my brain. If Landers killed Liam to take over the Hourglass, who would he be willing to hurt to get to me and my ability to travel to the past?

I called Thomas on his cell. The clanking sound of machinery muffled his voice. "Em, hold on and let me go somewhere quiet."

I willed him to hurry and tried to figure out how to tell him that a lunatic was on the loose, and thanks to my freaky ability my whole family had big targets painted on their backs. And wombs. Womb.

"What's up?"

"Do you trust me?"

He answered cautiously. "In what capacity?"

I twisted the phone cord in my fingers. "The other day at the restaurant, you said I was almost an adult and you couldn't really tell me what to do anymore."

"I don't like where this is going."

"For reasons I don't have time to explain, you and Dru need to go somewhere safe. A place where no one can find you. Just for a couple of days, until you hear from me or Michael." Silence on his end of the phone line. "Thomas?"

"I'm absorbing."

"We don't have time—"

"You may not," he said, sounding exactly like our father would have, "but I'm not making one move until you give me an explanation."

"The man believed to have killed Liam . . . Michael thinks he could have a 'special interest' in someone with my ability. And now he knows about me. What I can do. *Where I live.*"

"Go home. I'll meet you there. We'll all go somewhere safe together."

"If I go home, I can't save Liam. Michael believes that's the only way we can stop this guy."

"Understand this," Thomas said, exchanging his parental tone for a panicked one. "You are just as precious to me as Dru and our baby. I get your motivation, but—"

"Thomas," I cut him off, and considered asking Michael to leave the room so I could be completely honest with my brother. Instead I turned away and lowered my voice. "My motivation isn't simply about saving a life or a family. The thing is . . . I belong here. I've found my place in the world. If I walk away now, it will be for good, and I can't do that."

"Is Michael with you?" Thomas asked. "Are you somewhere safe?"

"Yes." As safe as I could be. "He's right here."

"Put him on."

He listened to my brother with intense concentration, reaching out to take my hand halfway through the lecture. I was glad the phone wasn't attached to a power source.

"Yes, sir. Whatever it takes. To save time, if you and Dru head for the airport we'll make the arrangements," Michael said. "A guy named Dune will give you a call." He listened for another minute. "You got it. Here she is."

"Everything in me screams that I shouldn't let you do this," he said.

"Everything in me screams that you should."

"I know." A mix of anxiety and reservation strained his voice. "I love you. Be safe."

"I love you back, and I will."

I handed Michael the phone, and he placed it on the receiver.

"You know what we have to do," I said. Nothing like a sociopath on your tail to throw things into a clear perspective. "We have to go get Liam. Now."

"You're not ready. We can't risk—"

"*We can't risk* Landers finding me before we go back to save Liam. *We can't risk* Dru and Thomas and their baby." I wrapped my arms around myself for comfort. "We can't risk lots of things."

Michael pushed the heels of his hands against his forehead. "It was so stupid to leave information about you where Landers could find it."

"There's nothing we can do about it now."

"If we're successful in saving Liam, he can make it all right again." He lowered his arms. "We just have to protect everyone in the meantime."

"What about Lily?" I asked. "Would he target her?"

"He could target anyone to get to you. Do you want her to come here?"

I did, but I didn't think she'd go for it. "No. I'll call her."

"I'll go find Dune. Get him started on the travel arrangements for Thomas and Dru."

I dialed Lily's number.

"Lily, it's me. Something has happened, and I need you to do a couple of things."

"Tell me what you need, sugar." Leave it to Lily to stay cool and not ask questions. She was my best friend for a reason.

"The biggest thing is that you look out for yourself. This would be a good time to keep the baseball bat that lives by the back door pretty close to wherever you are."

She let go with a string of curse words.

"And if anyone asks, you don't know where Michael and I are."

There was a moment of silence on the other end. "I *don't* know where you are."

"It needs to stay that way. No matter what happens." I was terrified of what might be in the files, not just about me, but about my best friend. "Do you understand me?"

She was silent for a beat. "I understand."

I didn't let the tears fall until I'd hung up the phone.

Chapter 41

Michael sat at the kitchen table, laptop open, poring over newspaper articles and college records from six months ago. He had set up a timetable and was trying to find any holes. Dune held another laptop on his knees and searched traffic and accident reports to make sure we'd have clear roadways. Nate leaned against the kitchen counter, holding up a map of Ivy Springs for Dune.

I held an extra copy of the timetable, and tried to hold down the vomit.

Cat was as nervous as a mom sending her baby off to kindergarten. Possibly more, which was appropriate, considering what we were doing was way more dangerous.

"Okay, Michael, you have keys to the car, yes?" He held them up and then returned them to the table beside his computer, and

Cat made a tick mark on the paper in her hand. "I have the keys to the science department."

"You need the identification number for the cadaver you need to steal," Dune said.

I couldn't help but shudder.

"I'll pull that up and make a note," Michael said. "What else?"

"Keys, cadaver—oh, then there's the . . ." Cat continued stalking around the kitchen, muttering under her breath.

Dune turned his attention to me. "I'll check Thomas and Dru's flight arrival time, too. I know you'll want to talk to them before you go, make sure they got to the island safely."

"Thanks, Dune." I closed my eyes and took several deep breaths. My thoughts kept straying back to Landers and what he was up to. Would any of us ever be safe again? If he were on a power trip of the magnitude everyone thought he was, what would be the retribution if we were successful in resurrecting Liam?

"Hold it. What about money?" When Kaleb spoke, I opened my eyes. "What's Dad supposed to live on for six months?"

Cat tapped her pencil on the notepad she was holding. "I can liquidate some assets, raise some cash, but we have to make sure we don't use any bills printed after the date he died."

"Yeah, I don't think being arrested for counterfeiting would be a good way to stay under the radar. I can go to the bank," Nate offered, putting the town map down on the counter. "Use my skills to sneak into the vault and get what we need. That way we won't have to explain our need for bills with specific dates."

"Nate," Cat scolded. "Liam would never approve of your stealing—"

"I know, I know." Nate held up his hands in mock surrender. "But do we have another option? It's not like we won't return the money."

She shook her head reluctantly. Nate took that as a yes and disappeared in the blink of an eye.

"Speedy," Michael said. The space on the kitchen table where his car keys had been was now empty. "He'd better not drive like he moves."

"Okay, what else?" Cat looked at the list in her hand. "I wish we could work out a place for Liam to hide, but I just don't see how."

"Stop worrying. He'll be alive." Michael sat down in one of the kitchen chairs before his eyes met mine. "That's all that matters."

"Wait." Cat's eyes lit up. "You can get it!"

"What are you talking about?" Michael asked.

"Liam's research. You can save it from going up in flames. It's a miracle," Cat said, clapping her hands together, her excitement visible. "All you have to do is get the disk. He only had one. It's in a clear case, and it always sat beside the mainframe computer in Liam's lab."

"Sure," I answered.

"Excellent." Cat snapped her fingers and pointed toward the living area. "You need coats. If I remember correctly, it snowed that weekend. Michael, come with me. Help me dig some up."

They left the room just as Dune shut the top of his computer.

"Thomas and Dru are in Charlotte. They're about to board their next plane, if you want to call them."

"Thanks." I stepped around the corner, pulled my cell out of my pocket, and sat down on the back stairs. Thomas answered before the first ring had finished.

After I hung up, I looked at the timetable in my hands and tried to wrap my brain around what was about to happen. I jumped when Kaleb stepped around the corner.

"I'm sorry."

"For what?" I asked, lowering the timetable.

"Not getting the files. What I said to you last night. Am I forgiven?"

I sighed. "Of course you are."

"You okay?" He lowered his body onto the step below me, then scooted down one more so that we were at eye level. "Tell me the truth."

"You know I'll tell you the truth. If I can be real with anyone, it's you, and not just because you have a built-in bull detector." I rested my chin in my hands. "The truth is, I don't know. I thought I'd have more time to prepare."

"Are you sure you want to do it?"

"What does your built-in bull detector tell you?"

"That you do."

I nodded.

"Well, since you're going anyway, the computer disk case Cat mentioned . . ."

"Yes?"

"The formula for my meds went up with the lab, too."

I looked at Kaleb, really looked. Tiny lines were etched in the skin beside his eyes; the creases on either side of his mouth were deeper than they'd been even two days ago. "You said your dad made some for you just before he died. How long have you been without it?"

"I've been tapering off for a while now. I ran out completely a few weeks ago. It only got bad today, with everything going on." The past few hours, all the emotions flying around—and Kaleb with no way to filter it all.

"Why didn't you tell anyone?"

"What could anyone do?" He shrugged.

"I'll get it. Where can I find it?"

"His bottom right desk drawer. It's in a hanging file folder with my name on it. Looks exactly like his research disk."

"Anything else you want me to get?"

"Just my dad."

I looked into his eyes and hated the rawness I saw there. I could only imagine what it cost him. "Is that why you could feel my emotions so clearly when we met? Because you didn't have a filter?"

"Yes. But—" He focused on the floor, and his long lashes cast a dark shadow on his cheekbones. There was no evidence of the playful, flirty Kaleb. "I'm pretty sure I would've connected with you anyway."

I didn't know the appropriate response to that statement. He seemed to have that affect on me. Fumbling around for words, I asked, "Um . . . hey, does everyone think that Landers is the one who killed your dad?"

"There weren't any other suspects," he answered, seeming grateful for the subject change. "The police questioned a few people, but they had no logical explanation for the fire, so ultimately they called it an accident."

"Was Landers questioned?"

"Briefly," Kaleb scoffed. "He had an iron-tight alibi."

"I cut my teeth on murder mysteries. Alibis can be faked."

"There was no way the authorities could have proved he did it. They don't even know about places like the Hourglass—how could we explain his motive?"

"I'm worried."

"I know," he said, not bothering to hide his grin.

I smacked his gargantuan bicep. "Don't tell me Michael won't try to get proof about your dad's murder when we go back."

"Okay," Kaleb said, raising his eyebrows. "I won't tell you that."

"But . . ." I motioned to the timetable on my lap. No room for error.

"He's not going to do anything to put you at risk. I'm not going to deny that if he gets the chance to find out who did it, he'll take it. But not if it puts you in danger." Kaleb took my hand, rubbing his thumb across my knuckles. "He's going to take care of you. That's what Michael does."

"I'm not worried about me."

"I am." He reached out with his free hand to tuck my hair behind my ear, and I froze. The tenderness in his touch threw me off. "I want you back in one piece."

I wondered what kind of emotion Kaleb felt coming from me now. Maybe he could help me identify it.

"Em?" Michael called out, breaking the tension. I let go of Kaleb's hand, jumped up, and almost tripped down the stairs. I pretended not to hear Kaleb laughing behind me.

"Hey," I said to Michael as I rounded the corner into the kitchen, sure my face was bright red. "Did you need me?"

"Can you come here a sec? I want to talk to you about something before we go."

"Sure." I followed him up the same—now empty—stairs I'd just been sitting on with Kaleb on rubbery legs. So many sources of anxiety were doing a number on my nervous system.

Michael went into his room, leaving the door open and sitting down on the edge of the bed. I leaned against his desk. I had no idea what else we could say to each other. I hoped he wasn't going to lecture me about Kaleb again. He looked down at his hands almost absentmindedly, clasping and unclasping them in his lap. "Are you scared?"

"A little."

A lot.

"Keeping you safe is as important to me as saving Liam. You know that, don't you?"

"I do. But I want us both kept safe. Listen," I said hesitantly, "I want you to promise me that you won't do anything stupid when we go back, like trying to find out who killed Liam. If we save him, it won't matter who did it."

"It will always matter who did it."

"I understand that, but we can deal with it when we're not in a life-or-death situation. Promise me."

"I won't try to find out who killed Liam."

"You didn't promise me you wouldn't do anything stupid."

He answered me with a tight smile. The weight of all the things that were unspoken between us pressed down on me. I couldn't make another move until I cleared one thing up.

"Michael—"

"Em, I—"

"You go first," I said. He had on a pale blue shirt, and the first few buttons were undone. A white T-shirt peeked out from underneath, and the collar was stretched just enough for me to see his collarbone. Something about it seemed so vulnerable.

"About last night," he said. "Grabbing you like that was wrong. What I said to you was wrong."

"No, it was right."

He stared at me in surprise.

I stared at his T-shirt collar. "I should probably thank you for not using the way I felt about you to sway my decision."

"The way you *felt*? You don't feel anything now?"

"It doesn't make a difference." I wondered if he could hear me over my erratic heartbeat. Did I look as anxious as I felt? "You've made your boundaries pretty clear. And then there's Ava."

"Ava?"

"I mean, because of your relationship."

He stood up and took a step toward me. "We don't have that kind of relationship. She might want one, but I don't."

I stared up at him, my heart bouncing off my ribs so hard I expected to go into cardiac arrest any second. "You don't? But you—she came to your room last night—"

"She's been playing that game ever since she moved in here. Trying to convince me she was the girl for me."

"Fun game." I was caught somewhere between relief and fury, thinking back on everything I'd seen. Realizing how much of my jealousy I'd projected onto the situation. Feeling like a total ass.

"She never won." He took one more step. "Never even got close. Ever since the day I got a voice mail and met up with a slightly older woman at Riverbend Park, the title of 'my girl' has been reserved."

"So you like older women?"

He lifted his hand and gave his bedroom door a solid push. A soft *snick* told me it had closed behind me.

"I like *you*. And I see now that I should have cleared that up a long time ago."

"This can't be a good idea," I whispered, not trusting my voice. Frozen. Afraid to touch him. Afraid not to.

Slowly, so slowly it made me ache, he placed one hand on the side of my neck, tracing the curve of my cheekbone with his thumb. I trembled. "I'm sorry. I want you to feel comfortable with me."

"I do."

"Then why are you shaking?"

Gathering all the bravado I had, I reached up to touch the center of his bottom lip. His eyes went dark with need. I moved to the slight cleft in his chin, wondering if the tiny prickles I felt came from his stubble or the ever-present electricity between us.

I got my answer when the lightbulb blew in his desk lamp.

"We do have one problem," he said, his voice deep, almost sleepy. "I still work for your brother."

"Just one problem?" I traced the line of his lower lip. I wanted to put my mouth there.

"At least. I'd hate to betray his trust. Wouldn't you?"

I pressed my palms against his chest, trying to still them, and wondered if my hands felt like charged up defibrillator paddles to him. "No."

For one second Michael hesitated. One crucial second when everything hung in the balance. Then he bent down, and my hands fisted in his T-shirt. He brushed his lips across mine.

Once.

I inhaled sharply.

Twice.

Nothing from me. Except maybe a whimper.

Three times.

"Michael?" His name came out in a whisper. I could tell by his breathing that his control was slipping. I stood on my tiptoes and reached up to tangle my hands in his hair. "You are *so* fired."

All the electrical tension that had been building between us exploded into heat the second his touch became more than whisper light. He took my face into his hands, using them to control the intensity and depth of our kiss, which quickly moved from sweet to reckless. It was the most lovely of assaults.

One second he was kissing me as if I was as essential to him as oxygen, and the next it was over. He stepped away, looking haunted.

"Did I do something wrong?" I touched my mouth, missing the heat of him.

"No." He shook his head and shoved his hands deep into the pockets of his jeans.

I didn't want his hands in his pockets. I wanted them on me. "Why did you—"

"Not because I wanted to stop kissing you." He looked at my lips. My pulse sped up, but my blood felt like lava moving through my veins. "Timing. My timing sucks."

Circumstances. Not because of me. I couldn't keep myself from grinning. "Would you like to try this again then, another time?"

"I'd very much like to try this again, another time." He grinned, but it carried a touch of sadness. "I'll give you a second to . . . uh . . . fix your hair."

"My hair?"

"I'll give you a second to fix my hair. I mean, I'll give you a second while I go fix my hair." He let out a sigh. "I mean, I'll see you downstairs."

He turned to walk out of the room, but unfortunately, he forgot to open the door first.

I managed to hold my laughter until he got it right.

I followed the smell of buttered popcorn to the kitchen. Peeking my head around the corner, I found everyone in various stages of preparation: Cat still making check marks; Dune clicking a mouse repeatedly; and Kaleb, watching it all, his face drawn. A flurry of popping sounds echoed off the walls as Nate leaned over the counter, eyeing the microwave like it was his job.

Maybe it was.

"I need a ring."

Michael almost dropped the bag of money he was counting when he heard my voice. He looked up at me, a ghost of a smile on his lips.

I shook off all thoughts of those lips and concentrated on the task at hand. "To travel. Duranium or whatever."

"Duronium," Cat corrected me.

"Yeah, that."

"I've got you covered." Kaleb fished in his pocket and pulled out a tiny ring, holding it between his thumb and forefinger. "I got it from the safe this morning."

"I can't take that," I protested. "It's your mom's. Isn't it?"

He reached out to catch my hand. "My mom isn't . . . in a position to save my dad. You are. She'd want you to have it. This way, it's like she's a part of it, even if she isn't here."

Michael watched us from the corner. After what had happened upstairs, I expected jealousy, or at least a hint of it, but there was nothing.

I took the ring, slipped it onto my index finger, and looked up at Kaleb. "Perfect."

"Perfect."

The moment was interrupted when the timer on the microwave beeped.

"Okay, Emerson." Cat bustled over and placed her hand on my back, ushering me to a seat at the table. "We're going to give you a crash course in traveling. You'll be with Michael, so you only need the basics, which is good. That's all we have time for."

"Do I need to take notes?" Nate placed the bowl of steaming popcorn on the table, and I grabbed a big handful. Comfort food. I stopped before tossing a piece into my mouth. "Can I eat this? Should I go in on an empty stomach?"

"It's not surgery, just time travel," Cat said.

"Just time travel," I muttered under my breath, and then reached out with the other hand for more popcorn.

"Look around. Notice anything different?" Cat asked.

I obeyed and almost sucked a corn kernel down my throat. After Dune whacked me on the back and stopped my coughing, I pointed to a shimmering square of light hanging in the atmosphere. It was as tall as the ceiling and at least ten feet wide.

"Holy . . . It's like a blanket made of water or something. And I can see it really, really clearly."

"That's one of the benefits of duronium. The way it interacts with your body chemistry helps you locate veils." Michael got a can of soda from the fridge, opened it, and slid it across the table toward me. "Veils guard the entrance to bridges, and they're kind of like a transition space or camo for travelers. Rips will stand out better for you now, too. When you're wearing duronium, they shimmer around the edges."

"Why didn't you tell me this stuff when you were explaining rips? That day at the coffeehouse?" I gave Michael a pouty face, as I popped open the can.

"Because I wasn't ready to explain time travel. And you weren't ready to hear it."

"True."

"You'll use this veil." Cat pointed to the one three feet away, sparkling like sunlight on the ocean. "Dune's research uncovered that this house was unoccupied at the time of Liam's death."

"I still don't understand how we get where we want to go."

Cat frowned. "You hold the date and exact time you want to travel to in your mind and step in. My exotic matter, your travel gene, and the duronium do the rest."

I recalled the night I'd asked Michael if it was that easy and he'd given me his standard "It's complicated" answer. "Really, Michael?"

"So you got that part right." He shrugged and a smile played at the corners of his mouth. "But you were wrong about the other part."

"What other part?"

"You don't have to click your heels together three times."

I launched the remaining popcorn in my hand toward his head.

"What about a time limit? Does time pass for you? Or us?"

Michael shook his dark hair, and popcorn fell to the table like giant buttery snowflakes. "It's a two-to-one ratio. For every two hours we spend in the past or the future, one hour goes by here. It's good because we can get more done when we're gone, and it's not as taxing on Cat. It's bad because we come back older than we would have been."

"I see." I kind of did, anyway. "What else?"

"Those are the basics," Cat said, dusting off her hands before wiping them on a paper towel. "Are you ready to go?"

"As ready as I'll ever be."

Suddenly I wished I hadn't eaten quite so much popcorn. I wasn't looking forward to tasting it twice.

Cat stood, purple fireball spinning.

Michael held a small duffel bag stuffed with money. The keys to his car were zipped into the pocket of my puffy jacket, and the keys to the science department were in his. The timetable was memorized but still in my right hand. My left hand held Michael's.

Kaleb, Dune, and Nate stood by, everyone's face tense. Kaleb's was so tight it physically hurt to look at him.

Cat flicked her wrist.

Michael stepped into the veil.

I followed.

"Focus on the date and time." Michael's voice echoed through the tunnel. The watery look of the veil extended as far as I could see, highlighted by a light sheen of silver. I could almost see through the fluid circular walls, as if I had a window to watch time move past. "Are you focusing?"

Snapping my head forward, I concentrated on the date and time where we wanted to land. "Yes."

"Good, because I'm useless right now. This is all you. The Emerson Show."

"Couldn't you come up with something better than that?"

"Focus, Em," Michael reminded me.

"Don't we need to walk, or something?"

"No. We stand still. Time flows around us."

I'd expected the bridge to be loud, like hurricane winds or a roaring river. Instead, it was achingly quiet. Occasionally, the muffled sound of a voice or music seeped through the undulating walls, but always briefly. I squeezed my eyes shut, and guessed we were getting closer to the end when the sounds became more concentrated.

"We're here," Michael said, grasping me gently by the shoulder. "You did it."

I opened my eyes. The veil shimmered in front of us, and I could see the room we'd just left, now empty and cloaked in darkness.

Chapter 42

*O*ur breath froze in the night air as we hurried through the cold, Michael holding my hand as we walked to the parking lot where his car was parked.

"I was out of town when Liam died. I'm glad I didn't drive," he said, holding our joined hands up to his lips and blowing his hot breath onto them as we approached his car. "Makes it easier to get to the Hourglass."

Easier.

"Where were you?" I asked.

"Florida. Spring break. Pretty sure the timing wasn't a coincidence."

Lights from distant neighborhoods twinkled on the horizon. No light shone from the windows of the campus buildings. The college was deserted and creepy with all the students gone. I walked a little closer to Michael.

"No wonder everybody heads to the beach instead of staying in the mountains over spring vacation. Why didn't we think of bringing a scraper?" He ran his hand across the layer of ice on the windshield before opening the car door for me. I put on my seat belt as he slid in and started the engine, jumping when alternative rock poured from the speakers.

He turned the radio down and scanned the parking lot to see if we had drawn attention to ourselves. It appeared as empty and desolate as it was two minutes ago. And as spooky.

Five minutes later Michael parked behind the science department.

"I'm going to go get John Doe. Sit tight." He opened his car door before I could protest.

I followed him to the back entrance. We hadn't talked about this part of the trip. "Hold on," I argued in a whisper. "There's no way you can get the body out of the building and into the car by yourself."

"Sure I can." He frowned at me as he sorted through the keys in his hand. "I know how freaked out you were when you heard about the cadaver. I'm not going to ask you to help me carry it."

"No, because you don't have to ask. We're a team, right?" I held up my hand for a fist bump.

"Em—"

"Right?" I said, knowing we didn't have time to fight about it. Michael knew it, too.

He gave me a fist bump back and we headed into the building.

Fifteen minutes after we retrieved the cadaver—Michael wrapped it up before I could see anything, and then assigned me the feet end to carry—he stopped the car in front of the gate to the Hourglass. It was closed.

"That gate's never closed. This means we're going to have to approach from a little farther away than I wanted." He pulled off onto the side of the road before killing the headlights and enveloping us in darkness. I started to open my car door, but he stopped me. "I want you to stay here."

My mouth dropped open. "What?"

"I think it would be a good idea if you stayed with the car."

I turned to face him, even though it was pitch-black. "You've lost your mind."

"I've been thinking about this. You did what I needed you to do by getting me back here. You could just wait, leave the car running—"

"Shut up. I'm serious, Michael." I would not back down. "Shut your mouth. Why do you keep leaving me out of the equation? If you think for one second I'm going to let you go to that lab by yourself, you're as crazy as I am. Sorry, as crazy as I thought I was. No way."

He tried again. "But—"

"No. You can't make me stay here. Do you want me to lie to you and tell you I will? Knowing I'll just follow you? All by myself? Alone and unprotected?"

He sighed in defeat. "Why won't you let me keep you safe?"

"I don't need a hero, Michael. I thought you recognized that I can handle myself."

"It's different this time. The stakes are life and death. I got you into this, and the least I can do is make sure you get out of it in one piece."

"I made the decision to help you all by myself. I know you have my back. And I have yours."

Michael reached out, wrapping his hand around the back of my neck and pulling me fiercely to his chest. "I'm scared to death. If I were by myself, I think I'd be fearless. But not with you beside me."

"Good. Because fearless is stupid."

"I'd retract that statement. You're one of the most fearless humans I've ever met."

I grunted. "Get out of the damn car."

We shut our doors quietly, and he tossed me the keys. I tucked them into my jacket pocket and zipped it up. The trees were covered in ice, making the grounds look like some kind of magical forest, entirely too enchanting to be the scene of a murder. I shuddered.

"Cold?" Michael whispered, wrapping his arm around my shoulders.

"No."

He gave me a little squeeze. "We'll go around back. I want to see which cars are in the parking lot."

"Why?"

"I just want to know if Landers is on site. I won't do anything about it."

Like I believed that. I looked at him, knowing my eyes were full of doubt.

"I'll *try* not to do anything?"

At least he was honest.

"What about John Doe?" I jerked my thumb in the direction of the trunk.

"The fire started around midnight. We'll have time to come back and get him. It's not a good idea to drag a dead guy across the lawn until we know what's going on anyway."

My nostrils flared. "Gross."

"Sorry." He stomped his feet and put his hands in his pockets. "We need to move."

Frozen grass crunched beneath our feet as we walked, the sound echoing into the clear night air. We crossed the stretch of lawn quickly, our footsteps quieting when we reached the cover of the trees and the pine needles beneath them. I watched Michael scan over the cars in the parking area, as if he were looking for one in particular.

"Any clues?" I asked.

"It's there."

We continued, practically retracing the steps I made when I visited the Hourglass the first time. After watching from the woods for a few moments, we scrambled across the lawn toward the house to press ourselves against the bricks.

Michael put his hand on my shoulder and whispered, "Last chance. Are you sure?"

I gave him an inappropriate finger gesture, and he swallowed a laugh.

We dropped to the ground, crawling along the side of the house and then scampering across the patio where Michael and Kaleb had talked about me. Steam rose from the pool, creating a mist above us.

Once we rounded the back corner of the house, I was in unfamiliar territory. It was darker than it had been the night when I spied on Kaleb and Michael, and the patio porch lights weren't on. The only light came from the pool.

I put my faith in Michael, dropping back to follow him as he darted from outbuilding to outbuilding. The terror that someone would see us—ruin our plan to save Liam or keep us from traveling back to the present—made my knees weak and my throat dry. By the time we reached the last outbuilding I was breathless, and not from running.

This building was the only one that showed any sign of occupation. It greatly resembled a horse barn and was stained what looked to be a dark red. A rooster weather vane creaked on the top, straining against the slight wind.

I didn't remember seeing it when I was here before. I realized I hadn't, because it hadn't been there.

The lab.

Chapter 43

I'm going in first," Michael whispered. "Liam doesn't know you, and I'm not taking any chances on freaking him out. Duck down by that tree to the left. The little building beside it is an old storage shed, but it's empty. No one ever goes in because the floor is rotted through, so no one will be inside to see you. You should be fine until I call for you. Can you do any nature sounds, birdcalls?"

"Birdcalls?"

He'd cracked from the pressure.

"In case you need me."

"The only extracurricular activities in the mental hospital involved stringing macaroni, and your average girl's boarding school is more interested in makeup application than hunting techniques," I whispered back. "Sorry."

"Okay, can you whistle?"

I nodded.

"Then if you need me, just whistle." He started for the lab.

"Michael," I whispered. He looked back at me. "Good luck."

Keeping my mind occupied took some creativity. After reciting the states and capitals, the Twenty-third Psalm, and all the teams in the American League, I'd started on the National League when I heard voices. Neither of them belonged to Michael.

I pressed my body up against the tree trunk. A man and a woman spoke softly, not quite in a whisper. I couldn't distinguish if I'd ever heard either of the voices.

"You said you wanted to be with me." The man's tone was suggestive, silky. "That you'd do whatever it took."

"I'll do anything . . . but this . . ." The woman's voice smacked of desperation. "I'm just not sure—"

She broke off. I couldn't see anything, but it sounded like some massive making out was going on. When the heavy breathing started, I began to get uncomfortable, but I was saved when the man started laughing. "Soon. Don't waste your energy."

"Why do you keep telling me no?" I heard something unzip and thought I might be sick.

More laughter from the man, and then more zipping. Judging from the woman's groan of frustration, I guessed he zipped her up. Hallelujah.

"There's a time and a place. And this is neither." His voice was harder now.

"I'm sorry." Her voice was shaking, and I could tell it wasn't from the cold. Whoever this guy was, he was a bully.

"You should be. But I forgive you. Do your job well, and maybe I'll reward you."

"Whatever you say, whatever you want," she said breathlessly. This chick needed a serious dose of self-confidence.

And a new boyfriend.

They walked away from the lab, deeper into the woods, leaves crunching beneath their feet. I stuck my head out slowly from behind the tree to try to catch a glimpse as they disappeared out of sight around the side of the empty storage building. Just then the door to the lab cracked, spilling light onto the ground, making each individual blade of frozen grass sparkle.

Michael called my name.

Hurrying toward him, I stepped through the doorway into the warm yellow light.

Chapter 44

Liam Ballard was ridiculously stereotypical. He really did have crazy Einstein hair, food on his shirt, and . . . a pocket protector. But if you looked past the outer trappings, it was easy to see that Kaleb didn't get all his good looks from his mother. Liam was big and muscular, with the body of an outdoorsman. I recognized him as the man surrounded by fishing gear in the picture in Michael's loft.

He extended his hand to shake mine and held on. I wasn't surprised when I felt a slight shot of electricity. Not the same kind of electricity I felt when I touched Michael, but definitely a connection. His smile was warm and welcoming, his eyes very kind. I understood why Michael looked at him as a surrogate father, and I wondered if he had room for another child in his life.

"Hello, Emerson," he said, his voice gruff.

"Hi, Lia—Doc— I really have no idea what to call you." I laughed.

"Liam is fine." He placed his other hand on top of mine, looking into my eyes intently. "Michael told me you're the reason he was able to travel back. Remarkable. Thank you for your willingness to help me and my family."

I was going to cry.

And then beg Liam to adopt me.

"However, once I get over the shock of your visit, I'm going to be very angry at both of you. How could you risk your lives this way, Michael?"

"I didn't have a choice."

"One always has a choice."

"Well, then, I chose to save you because you're like my father. And I wanted to." The words should have made Michael sound like a petulant child. Instead, he sounded like a broken man.

"You can't change the past just because of your loss, or grief." Liam exuded the kind of gentleness only the smallest or the biggest among us could manage. "Our gifts aren't meant to work that way."

"It's not just me. Kaleb and Grace . . . it's not right without you. Nothing is right."

A lump rose in my throat at the exposed emotion on Michael's face.

He continued, "Landers has the files, and no one knows what they contained or whose names were listed, except for you. I only know about Emerson because . . . that's a long story."

Liam looked at me. I shrugged. "Apparently I'm a rule breaker."

"The point is," Michael continued, "you're the only one who can stop him. And Em and I aren't breaking any rules by being here. The Novikov Principle applies."

Liam frowned. "Are you saying . . . I'm assuming there were remains. How are you—"

"I thought of that. We have a cadaver in the car; I need to go get it." Michael held out his hand, and I pulled the keys from my coat pocket and tossed them to him. "Can we talk after that?"

"Oh, I can quite assure you we'll be talking after that."

"What time is it?" Michael asked, in an attempt to defer Liam's wrath, I was sure.

Liam held up his watch, shaking it. The crystal was cracked down the middle. He pointed to a clock hanging above the door. Both hands pointed at eleven. "Do you need help?"

"We can't risk anyone seeing you. Em will stay here and get you briefed."

I frowned at him. "How are you going to get John Doe across the—"

"I'll drag him. There's a blanket in my trunk. We need to hurry, and Liam needs the rest of the details." I gasped when he grabbed my shoulders and kissed me hard on the mouth. "I'll be fine. Be right back."

The door slammed behind him and Liam looked at me. I was trying to figure out why Michael had left so quickly, and to interpret the kiss.

"Novikov Principle, hmm?"

I gave my head a shake so I could get with the program. "Right. All I know is that it works because it doesn't allow us to change the past, just 'affect it without producing any inconsistencies.' We replace you with the cadaver, and then you go into hiding, and the continuum isn't affected because everyone's timeline remains the same. Except for yours, I guess. But you didn't have one. Because you were dead." I winced and looked at him apologetically. "Sorry. Cat and Michael gave me the Cliffs-Notes version."

"How far back in time did you travel?" He lowered himself onto a stool beside a long worktable full of lab equipment. "How long have I been . . . gone?"

"Six months."

"A lot can happen in six months."

I rested my elbows on the table. "How much did Michael tell you?"

"Not enough. Too much. We spent most of our time talking about Grace."

"I'm sorry." I wanted to comfort him, but I didn't know how.

"So am I. And confused. Grace is very strong. I don't see my death sending her over the edge that way, making her that desperate. Considering how much she loves Kaleb, I know he would have been her first thought. Her every thought." He shook his head. "It doesn't make sense."

"I wish I had an explanation." We were quiet for a moment.

"Kaleb told me about you and your wife, about how amazing you were together. I've never heard anyone my age talk about their parents the way he talked about you two."

"We're a very happy family. Or rather, we were."

"Michael is positive you can get it all back. I'm sure he's right."

"Thank you, Emerson," he said kindly, but he looked like he was in pain. "Please, tell me about my son, what he's been up to. Michael tried to sugarcoat it."

"I don't think you have to worry. I get Kaleb. I understand where he's coming from. I lost my parents, too, and when you think you don't really have anyone left you . . . maybe you don't make the best choices."

"These choices—would you consider them to be irrevocable?"

"No, not all of them. They can remove tattoos."

"Tattoos?"

"Don't you think Michael should be back by now?" I asked. "John Doe—the cadaver—isn't that heavy."

He squinted, looking up at the clock, and I watched as fear marred his features.

I swung around.

Neither of the clock hands had moved since Michael left the lab.

Chapter 45

*Y*ou don't have *anything* in here that would tell us what time it is?" Scrounging around on his desktop, I tried to find something that would give me the correct time. "No cell phone? No watch besides the one on your arm?"

"I tend to lose things like cell phones and watches. And they're destroyed by time travel. I've been doing quite a bit of research lately." He opened a drawer in his desk, treating me to a view of at least half a dozen watches with cracked faces. "No good."

Research. A computer. A computer would have a clock. "Cat mentioned your mainframe. Where is it?"

"It's down at the moment. That's what I was working on when Michael showed up," he said, pointing to the corner. The mainframe didn't look like any other computer I'd ever seen. It had multiple screens, keyboards that displayed strange-looking symbols, and a central processing unit the size of a suitcase. Liam knelt down and started pushing buttons and wiggling cables.

A computer disk in a clear jewel case sat beside the largest monitor. The information Cat asked us to retrieve. It was slim enough for me to slip it into my inside jacket pocket. After that, I opened the bottom right desk drawer to grab the disk with the formula for Kaleb's meds. It was exactly where he said it would be. I tucked it into my pocket as well, keeping it on the inside, closest to my heart. I didn't think about what that meant.

Liam was still working on the CPU.

"I'm going to look outside, see if he's on his way back."

I opened the door. Nothing. The grounds were quiet, still sparkling in the moonlight. I stood on my tiptoes to look across the yard. Even though I was shivering in the cold, I wouldn't step into the warmth of the lab. I'd just decided to search for him when Michael stepped around the corner of the main house. Exhaling in relief, I waited until he was past the patio and then ran to help him.

"I got back as fast as I could. What's going on?" he asked as we approached the lab.

"It's the clock. It's broken. We don't know what time it is."

He uttered a curse under his breath as the door opened and Liam stepped out. Michael stopped him when he tried to take the cadaver. "No. Take Emerson and head for the car. I'll be there as soon as I set everything up. Just go!"

"I'm *not* leaving you here," I said.

"Go, Emerson," Michael insisted. He shoved the car keys at me. "Take these."

"Come with me." I accused him through my teeth as I grabbed them, "You promised we'd be safe."

"I promised you that *you* would be safe, and I don't want you anywhere near this lab. Go with Liam to the car." Michael leaned over to pick up the cadaver. My stomach rolled. "Please? Time is running out."

Liam took me by my upper arm, gently pulling me toward the house. "I'm sure Michael knows what he's doing. We're just holding him up."

"Go." Michael looked at me, pleading. "Stay safe."

He carried John Doe inside, and Liam and I hurried away across the grass. We were almost to the house when I heard a brief shout, followed by laughter.

Then the world exploded.

Chapter 46

When I opened my eyes, fire had completely engulfed the building. The steel beams that supported the roof curled in the heat of the flames. I lay on the ground, a few feet away from the lower patio. Liam was nowhere in sight.

I tried to sit up, but the ground slanted crazily. Hoping I didn't have a concussion, I attempted it again, more slowly this time. Looking in the direction of the burning building, I made out the shapes of two people standing in the distance. I shook my head, wondering if I had double vision. No, it was definitely two people. My pulse raced. Liam and Michael? As quickly as it had sprung to life, my heart stopped, dropping into my stomach. The figures weren't either of the men I wanted to see.

The two stood together, watching the fire blaze. Something

was off. They weren't racing around, shouting, or making any attempt to help. From their stances, they appeared to be enjoying themselves, as if standing around a bonfire instead of a burning building that might have people trapped inside.

Pushing myself up to my knees, I blinked and refocused on the faces that were lit by the blazing fire.

Nausea rose in my throat.

I knew the woman's face.

Her expression was more vulnerable than the one I was used to seeing. She chewed on a fingernail and kept looking up at the guy standing beside her.

I could only see the back of his head. I couldn't make out any details, just that he was tall and his shoulders were broad.

I heard sirens in the distance and pushed my spiraling emotions to the side. We were in danger of being caught on the property. I had to find Michael.

"Emerson. Emerson!"

Hope surfaced as a low voice called to me from the patio. I crept up the steps, trying to stay confined to the shadows. When I reached the top level, I looked for Michael but found Liam.

"Where is he?" I asked. "Liam, where is he?"

The sound of fire consuming the lab filled the silence between us. I looked up into his face, lit by the flames. His eyes relayed the truth he wouldn't speak.

"No." My knees gave out, and I slumped forward. Liam caught me under my arms and slowly lowered me to the ground. "He jumped out a window, something. He promised me before we came back that we'd be fine. He has to be safe."

"Sweet girl." Liam sat down on the ground beside me, his arm around my shoulders to keep me upright. "Once I knew you were breathing I scouted the front of the building. He couldn't have escaped through the back—that's where the explosion came from. Michael isn't there. I don't think he made it out."

My breath came in spasms, ripping through my lungs, a thousand knives in my throat. "He . . . he had to . . . if he died here, in the past . . . I would never have met him . . ."

"I wish that's the way it worked, but it isn't." Liam gently took both my hands in his.

"We have to find him. We have to take him back." I tried to pull my hands away, tried to stand, but Liam had the same massive strength his son did. Even my rage didn't sway his steady hold. "Please," I cried openly, begging, "let me go, please."

He whispered, "There's nothing to find, Emerson."

"No. No!" I insisted. "The police only found a few bones in the ruins of the lab. If the cadaver and Michael were both in the building, there would've been more."

"All of that could depend on where the fire started . . . how hot it grew. What kind of fire it was."

"What?" I didn't understand. I didn't want to. The sound of alarms grew closer, and Liam pushed himself into a crouch to peer over the retaining wall.

"We have to get out of here, get back through the bridge

before someone sees us. We can't afford to upset the continuum now."

"You're going back?"

"I can't let you go back alone."

"I'm not leaving." I ran my hands across the stone terrace seeking purchase, anything I could hold on to. My tears flowed so furiously they blinded me. "I'm not leaving without Michael."

"Emerson, we're about to be surrounded by firemen and policemen. We've got to get back to where the car is hidden before we're trapped."

"I can't leave without him, Liam. I can't."

"Sweetheart. He's already gone."

Chapter 47

All hell broke loose when we exited the bridge into the kitchen.

Cat gasped and turned unnaturally pale, covering her mouth with her hands. Dune and Kaleb seemed to freeze in place. Nate spoke first.

"Dr. Ballard? You're alive!" Nate rushed over to us to gape at Liam in disbelief, touching his arm tentatively.

"That's why I couldn't feel you," Kaleb said, staring at his father. "I really thought you were dead, because I couldn't feel you. But you weren't. You aren't. You just didn't exist." His face crumpled, and for a split second he looked exactly like a little boy. "Dad?"

Liam moved toward Kaleb and extended his arms. In two steps Kaleb was across the room, his father wrapping him in a hug.

I backed out of the room slowly. I didn't know where to go.

Cat followed, eyeing me cautiously. "Emerson?"

"Michael's gone." A full-body chill overtook me. "He was in the building when it . . ."

She looked away from me.

"Cat?" I'd thought I was too numb to feel anything, but her avoidance of my eyes ripped my heart to shreds. Every slash was a moment lost with Michael. *Cat?* Why don't you seem surprised? Talk to me."

She exhaled deeply. "The day after you, Kaleb, and Michael visited me at the college, he came back to see me by himself. He asked me to open a bridge to the future."

"No." The word was a plea. It couldn't be true.

"That's when he found out that you made it back." Now she met my eyes. "And that he didn't."

"No!" I wrapped my arms around my waist, holding myself together, my body warring against my emotions. "Please, please no."

"He wouldn't tell me what else he saw, just that he wasn't with you. I know he cared for you so much. I know he wanted you to be part of his future."

"Don't tell me that." I wanted it all to go away. Disappear like rips did when I popped them. "Why did we even go back if he was going to . . . Why?"

"I'm not sure, but I know Michael believed Liam had to be saved. I think he chose the greater good—what was best for *everyone* over what was best for him personally. There's a heavy responsibility that comes with your gift, and he always understood that."

"It's not a gift," I spat out. "It's a curse."

"Emerson!" Cat gasped, finally noticing my injuries. "You're bleeding!"

"It's fine," I insisted through chattering teeth.

"No, it's not. You're shaking, probably going into shock." She grabbed the blanket from the couch and tucked it around my shoulders. "We need to get you to the emergency room."

"No hospital. I can't. I don't want to." I looked up at her, my very life depending on her answer. "If he took precautions, if he somehow survived the fire and found a bridge, could he get back through without you and your exotic matter?"

Her face was full of pity. "Emerson—"

"Could he get back through?"

"It's a possibility." The look of pity didn't fade, and somewhere, deep down, I knew she was telling me what I wanted to hear.

I turned to stare at the grandfather clock in the corner. Half past midnight.

"I'm going to wait for him."

"At least sit down before you collapse." Cat helped me onto the couch, placing pillows behind my back. "Let me look at your cuts—"

"Don't touch me. Okay?" I forced myself to keep my voice steady, at a normal volume. "I'm fine."

"But—"

"Please!" I could feel myself edging toward hysteria with every second that passed. I needed her out. "I'm fine. Please leave me alone."

"I can't, you're hurt—"

"Cat?" I didn't want to break, and if she didn't leave me alone, didn't stop talking about Michael . . . I knew I might.

She left me.

I hoped and prayed that there was some possibility he'd survived. That by some miracle he could come back to me.

I sat in the dark, waiting. The grandfather clock in the entryway sounded the hour.

One.

I barely noticed when Nate and Dune headed up to bed. Dune started to say something, but stopped when he saw my face.

An hour passed; the clock sounded twice.

Cat came in to check on me but didn't speak. I ignored her, turning my body to face the clock, still as stone, watching the hands move. The house slowly went quiet, the only sounds the occasional creaks and pops common in older homes. I thought I heard Kaleb and Liam walk past, but I was too fixated on the time to pay close attention.

Dawn came. The sunrise brought no hope.

When the chimes sounded seven times, I stood, pushed the blanket to the floor, and walked up the stairs to Michael's bed. Alone.

He wasn't coming back.

Chapter 48

I knew who it was the second the door opened. He would be the only one who would come looking for me here, the only one who wouldn't be afraid to come in without knocking. He wouldn't ask for permission to enter because he knew I'd say no.

Kaleb wouldn't take no from me.

He crossed the room to the bed where I lay curled up in a ball, holding on to Michael's pillow and breathing in his scent. Kaleb reached out to touch me, but caught himself when he saw me flinch. I couldn't help it. The last time someone had touched me in this room, it had been Michael.

He dropped down into the desk chair.

"You should be with your father." My voice sounded raw, still full of smoke and tears.

"No, I should be with you. My father agrees."

I didn't have a comeback. I was too broken for a good one anyway.

"Em." He reached up to rub the back of his neck. I knew Kaleb could feel every single one of my horrible emotions. I started to tell him I had the formula for his meds in my pocket, but I realized he didn't need it now that his father was back.

Liam was alive.

Michael was dead.

Waves of sorrow crashed over me as Kaleb leaned forward in the chair, reaching out his hand. "This has to stop. Come here."

"Why?"

"Just . . . Just come over here."

I sat up on the edge of the bed to argue with him, my muscles aching and tense with anxiety. He caught me off guard, taking my hand and maneuvering me onto his lap.

"What are you doing?" Surely he wasn't making a move on me. A hysterical bubble of laughter threatened to escape from my throat. Everything that had happened in the past few hours was ridiculously surreal.

"Not what you think." He slid me away from his chest toward his knees so that I stayed on his lap, but barely. Leaning his head toward mine, he said, "Look at me. Emerson, look in my eyes."

I gave in.

The second I did, the pain began to disappear in a vacuum, both the physical and the emotional. A roaring sound filled my ears, and I couldn't see anything but the deep blue of Kaleb's eyes.

I unconsciously leaned in, pressing my face to his, our mouths so close we were breathing the same air.

The relief was enough to make oxygen bearable. I took the comfort from him for a moment before I realized what was happening. Once I did, I jerked away, pushing myself off his lap to land on the floor in front of him, my muscles bunching in spasms. The room went eerily silent.

"What did you just do?" I said, gasping for breath.

His eyes were full of agony, his voice bleak. He sounded like he was in physical pain. "Tried to help you. Taking some of your emotions."

"How long have you been able to do that?"

He shook his head. "As long as I can remember. Sometimes it doesn't work, though. It didn't with my mom, when I tried to help her. But I can help you."

I wanted to lean on him, find comfort in his embrace. Kaleb would do his dead level best to give me whatever I wanted. I knew it. All I had to do was ask.

The ache that had disappeared reformed in my chest and moved up to my throat. "I can't let you take on my hurt when you have more than enough of your own. The two of you fought like brothers. I know you loved each other like brothers, too."

Kaleb stood, and once again I was taken aback by the sheer size of him. "I know you did this—at least in part—for me. To keep me from going through everything you went through when you lost your parents. Now here you are, hurting more than you were before. I know, because I couldn't block out your emotions if I tried."

I bit down on my bottom lip. I would not cry. Crying could wait until I was alone. I *would not* cry. The tears formed and I fought not to blink, knowing if one tiny wet drop escaped, the battle would be over.

I lost.

My world, which I was struggling to hold up on my own, crashed down around me into so many pieces. I had to lean on a chair leg to keep myself upright. I watched my pain flash across Kaleb's face, finally hiding mine in my hands so I wouldn't have to see any more.

He dropped down beside me, pulling me into his arms and rocking me back and forth as I let the tears come, keeping my eyes closed, refusing to watch him share my grief. I remembered the way it felt to be in Michael's arms the night I told him about losing my parents. He'd rocked me to comfort me, too. The memory only made me cry harder. Kaleb stroked my hair and pressed his lips to my temple.

"It can't be true. Michael has to come back. This has to be a mistake." My tears had a mind of their own. No matter how hard I fought against them, they kept forming and slipping down my cheeks.

"I could make it better if you would just let me."

"I won't," I said. "Not that way. I'm not putting you through more pain just to spare myself."

"Even if I want to?" he asked softly.

I shook my head.

"He cared about you. It felt a lot like he loved you."

My sobs caught in my chest. "He never said it."

"That doesn't mean it wasn't true."

"Maybe."

"You've got to stay strong. We don't know what happened. What if he managed to survive it? You're a mess. Would you want him to see you like this?"

"I'm not a mess."

And he's not coming back.

Kaleb gazed down at me, cradled in his arms, tears and snot all over my face.

"I'm *not* a mess!" I jerked my sleeve down over my hand and wiped some of the moisture away. Struggling to sit up, I voiced the question I was most afraid of asking. "Do you feel him? His emotions?"

His answering smile held a world of sadness.

I buried my face in his chest and let go.

It took a while for me to stop weeping. When I finally ran out of tears, Kaleb stood and helped me to my feet. "Get cleaned up and then come downstairs. I'll have Cat bring you some clothes. You need to let her look at those cuts." He gestured to my hands and knees. I started to protest, but he interrupted. "Let her do it here, or I can take you to the hospital."

"I hate hospitals."

"I know."

"That's a dirty trick."

"I know that, too. Do it." He reached into his pocket before placing something in my hand and carefully curling my fingers around it.

When he left, I examined what he'd placed in my palm. It was his silver circle engraved with the word *hope*. I stared at it for a few moments before placing it in the exact center of Michael's bed.

I stripped off the jacket, hearing a clunk when it hit the ground. I picked it up and unzipped the pockets, finding the computer disks I'd retrieved as well as Michael's car keys. I squeezed the keys so hard the teeth hurt my fingers. Tears filling my eyes, I dropped them onto his nightstand. I left the computer disks where they were.

I walked blindly into the bathroom and turned the water to the hottest temperature I could stand. Before I stepped in, I stared at my reflection in the mirror.

My hair was gray instead of blonde, speckled with ashes, my face dark with soot and streaked with tearstains. The irises of my bloodshot eyes were bright green; they got that way when I'd been crying. My shoulder was already developing a deep purple bruise, and it hurt when I rolled it forward to stretch it. I looked down at my knees and the heels of my hands, both scabbed over.

As bad as I looked on the outside, the inside was much worse.

I stepped into the shower and stood under the spray until the hot water ran out.

Chapter 49

*W*earing only a towel, I cautiously opened the bathroom door to a fresh set of clothing on the bed, a soft pair of gray yoga pants I'd be able to roll up at the waist along with a white hoodie and tank top. There was a pair of thick blue fuzzy socks, even a package of new underwear. Bless Cat's heart and her wardrobe. I almost laughed at the underwear, but I couldn't quite bring myself to do it.

The time in the shower gave me more clarity about what I'd seen at the Hourglass. If what I believed to be true was in fact true, there were questions that needed to be answered.

And . . . Michael was gone. I had to make a choice. I could either break the same way I had when I lost my parents, or I could do whatever it took to find some kind of justice for him. I knew what would be easiest. I also knew what would be right.

I didn't know which choice would win.

I dressed and took the silver circle from the center of Michael's bed and tucked it into the pocket of the hoodie. Descending the stairs slowly, I winced each time my knees bent. One step at a time, one foot in front of the other, every forward motion another strain on the tightrope of my emotions. I passed by the common room, refusing to look at the couch or the clock, and stopped outside the kitchen.

Just function, Emerson. You can't drown in it yet. There are things that have to be done.

After a few deep breaths I opened the door and stuck my head in. It still smelled like popcorn.

"Hi." Cat was alone at the kitchen table. She stood, reaching out to help me into a chair. "Kaleb said you were going to let me look you over."

"The only thing that really hurts is my shoulder."

And my heart. But I doubted she could help me with that.

"Which one is it?" she asked.

"The right," I answered, counting it as a tiny victory when my lips didn't tremble.

She carefully pulled the hoodie to the side, making a pained face when she saw the bruise. "Liam said he threw you to the ground when the building blew up. Is that when this happened?"

Something she said sounded strange, distracting me from my pain. Both physical and emotional.

"Blew up." The building *had* blown up. Everything I'd read or heard indicated that there had been a fire, but never an explosion.

Cat seemed confused. "Am I wrong? Did I misunderstand Liam?"

I ignored her questions. "Where's Ava?"

"I don't know. No one's seen her."

"I saw her. In the past. She was standing with a man, watching the lab burn." Sorrow made my chest tight, and I checked my grief so I could continue coherently. "I thought I recognized him."

"What did he look like?"

"Tall. Broad shoulders. Light hair."

Cat's face remained immobile. "And you recognized him?"

"Yes." I didn't think she'd like it when I told her how. "I've met him."

"What?"

I crossed my arms on the table and laid my head down on top of them.

Everyone might think Landers had disappeared because he'd taken off with Liam's files. But he hadn't really.

He'd been living in my loft.

The late-morning air was crisp. Somewhere someone burned leaves. Kaleb and Liam sat in glider chairs in the backyard underneath an ancient oak tree. The overhanging branches dropped newly turned autumn leaves like rain. As they fell, the sun touched them from the east, setting them aglow.

It should have been a beautiful day.

"Liam." Cat approached them, her arms over her chest to brace herself against the chill in the air. Or maybe to protect herself from Liam's reaction. "I'm sorry to interrupt. We have to talk."

"It's fine, Cat." Something about his face was older than it had been yesterday. He pushed his foot against the ground, gliding back and forth in his chair. "Good morning, Emerson."

"Morning." I failed to see anything good about it.

Kaleb offered me his seat. I made a sound of protest, but he took me by the wrists anyway, avoiding my injured hands, and guided me into the chair.

Sparing Cat the difficulty of figuring out how to break the news, I said, "Jonathan Landers has been living in my bedroom."

No one spoke. Liam froze midglide. Kaleb swung his head around to stare at me.

"I didn't know it was him. He told me his name was Jack."

"Jack is his childhood nickname," Cat murmured.

"I made the connection last night, but it didn't sink in until this morning. I thought he was a ripple until I tried to pop him and he didn't disappear. He was . . . semisolid."

Liam leaned forward in his chair, placing his hands on his knees. His wedding band was encircled by infinity symbols. That must have been how he got through the bridge last night.

"When did you first see him?"

"The night the restaurant opened. A couple of weeks ago."

A lifetime ago.

"Living in your bedroom . . . was he there all the time? How did he appear to you?" Liam asked calmly.

"He'd be there, and then he'd be gone." My body felt heavy, weighted down by shame and sorrow. "Now I realize that there's probably a bridge in my room that I couldn't see before. I think he was traveling through it. Using the veil to disappear quickly."

"Did you ever see him when Michael was around?" Cat asked.

"No. But I did see him in Michael's loft once when I was in there alone. Jack claimed to be watching him. Michael's room is . . . was on the other side of the wall from mine." I focused on the ground, counting acorns. I wouldn't think about where he used to sleep. I wouldn't think about the pull I'd felt toward him, even through the concrete wall. "The veil must be divided by the two rooms."

Liam stroked his beard. I wondered if it was a nervous habit, the way Michael always twisted his thumb ring. The memory threatened to slice me open.

"But how?" Cat's skin had a pale gray sheen. "He doesn't carry the travel gene."

Liam stood up from the chair and began to pace. "There are rumors of ways to travel if you don't carry the specific gene, but they go against everything the Hourglass stands for—against the laws of nature and man. The cost would be dire."

"Landers doesn't care about any laws." A shower of leaves fell from the tree beside us when Kaleb plunged his fist into the bark. "He only cares about himself."

"What kind of cost?" I asked Liam. "Who would make him pay?"

He stopped pacing. "Among others, the universe itself."

"The ripples are changing. I started out seeing one person, now I'm seeing groups, snippets of scenery. I thought Jack was part of that, or something new that I didn't understand yet."

"You're seeing entire scenes?" The look of intensity on Liam's face made my heart constrict. "Multiple people?"

"What does it mean?" I asked tightly.

"I'm not sure," he answered. "But if ripples are growing, bleeding through the fabric of time, we have more to worry about than Jonathan Landers."

I didn't think I could handle worrying about more than Jonathan Landers.

Even with Liam alive and prepared to regain control at the Hourglass, Jack still had enough information to be dangerous. Information about me, my family. He had names and addresses of people with special abilities. Whether I was his intended target or not, I didn't doubt he would attempt to exploit every single person on the list.

"We need to find him." Kaleb kicked at the freshly fallen leaves that littered the ground. "We need to go to Em's loft and pull him out of the bridge."

"I don't think he's there anymore. He told me good-bye." I looked from Kaleb to his father. "Liam, you told Cat the lab exploded. One second it was there, the next second it was gone. Did you see who I saw, standing there watching it burn?"

Liam nodded. "I'd hoped to protect the identity of one of those people."

"One of those people?" Kaleb interrupted. "Landers had an accomplice?"

"I don't believe she knew what she was doing," Liam said quietly. "I believe she was used."

"She who?" Kaleb asked in a strained voice. No one spoke, letting him work it out for himself by process of elimination. He let out a string of curse words one didn't usually hear in everyday conversation, ending with a particularly venomous, "Bitch."

"Son—"

"Ava came here to hide her ability," Kaleb argued with his father. "That was shady enough. But you're actually going to defend her when she used it to *blow you up*?"

"She's a fire starter?" I asked, a picture of a tiny Drew Barrymore in my mind. Somehow the young blonde with the endearing lisp didn't mesh with Ava and her glamorous beauty. Kaleb had referenced the wrong Stephen King story for her nickname.

"Ava's gift is layered," Liam answered. "We think she can move things, push objects through time."

"You think? You mean you don't know?" I asked.

"Like Kaleb said, Ava came to the Hourglass to make her ability disappear. I never argued, only tried to make her life easier than it was at home. It seems Landers had a different idea. And a stronger influence."

"Where do we think Ava is now?" I asked.

Another shower of leaves fell from the tree as Kaleb made a sound of frustration and pain.

Landers had an accomplice, money, and a list of people with abilities.

"He told me he wanted to protect me. Protect my innocence. I almost bought it." Recoiling at the memory of the way he'd looked at me that day, I closed my eyes and tried to block out the image of his face. "I wonder if Ava did."

"He's a persuasive man," Liam said.

"He was stalking me. Now he and Ava are missing, and Michael is dead."

They wouldn't get away with it. I would do whatever it took to stop them. I'd let revenge keep me alive, and once that revenge was exacted . . . well, I'd reassess. My tenuous hold on sanity was slipping, and I doubted even Kaleb could help me once it did. I had to be alone, to think.

I left them all outside and climbed the stairs to Michael's room. A few seconds later, Cat stuck her head around the door-frame.

"Emerson, I—"

I held up one trembling finger, motioning for her to be quiet.

"Don't do this." She frowned, deep creases forming on her forehead. "You can't cut yourself off—it's not healthy."

"You have no idea." I laughed bitterly.

"Tell me what you're feeling. Talk to me." She looked so worried, almost like a mother concerned for her child. "Please."

The "please" got to me.

"I'm never going to see him again. There were so many things I didn't say, and after my parents . . . I swore I'd never leave anything unsaid. But I did. Now he's gone."

Could we have had the same kind of lifetime connection Grace and Liam did? I'd never know. I'd wonder about the possibility for as long as I lived.

Cat moved toward me slowly with her hand outstretched, as if she was approaching the scene of an accident.

She kind of was.

"Don't touch me." I scrambled farther back on the bed, out of her reach, pulling my knees up to my chest and wrapping my arms around my legs. I rocked back and forth. "Did you know there are seven stages of grief?"

I said the words so conversationally that I must have sounded manic. Cat stepped back and silently lowered herself into the desk chair.

"I learned all about it in counseling. Seven stages. And guess what? Four of them suck. Where's the balance? Why not eight stages of grief? Give me some kind of benchmark for my suffering; let me know I'm halfway there." A dry laugh escaped, and I paused to regain control. I needed to be in control.

I focused on a cobweb in the corner by the ceiling, a tiny remnant of forgotten life stirring in a wayward breeze. "But there are just seven. I should be able to talk myself through the first few— shock and denial, pain and guilt. I already have experience, so it'll be easier, right? I can tell myself all the right things, remind myself of the coping mechanisms."

Resisting the urge to stand and tear the fragile cobweb to the ground, I hugged my knees more tightly to my chest. "I . . . got stuck in those stages when I lost my parents. For months. I almost disappeared."

Cat's frown had only deepened since she sat down. It didn't go with the rest of her face.

"When I came to him from the future, why didn't I tell him to get out of the building before it exploded?" I couldn't understand why I'd keep knowledge like that to myself now or ever. "How could I let him die that way? How could he choose to die that way?"

"You couldn't have said anything—there are rules, especially if you remain connected to the Hourglass in the future." She was trying to comfort me, but her explanation only made me angry.

"Who makes these rules?"

"You'll find out soon enough." She stood, speaking matter-of-factly. "I expect after today they'll be paying a visit."

I stared at her blankly. "What are you talking about?"

"What if I told you," Cat said, leaning over to look deep into my eyes, "that you could change things?"

I looked back, afraid to believe but desperate to do so.

"The fact is that I'm already in enough trouble." She paused, pressing her lips together, and I could almost see the gears clanking in her brain. "If Landers is missing . . . and we can gain access to the Hourglass . . . there's a bridge there. I could put you through."

"Put me through?"

"So you could change things?" The question was leading.

Save Michael. She was talking about saving Michael. I sat up on my knees. "Yes. Oh yes, please—"

"Wait." She held up one finger. "It's not that simple. Once the powers that be show up, you could be stripped of the choice to ever use your ability again."

"I don't care." There was no rule I wouldn't break or consequence I wouldn't accept if I could bring Michael back. I scooted to the edge of the bed. Hope rose like the sun in my chest, warm, full of possibility. "When can I go?"

She checked her watch as she stood up. "Give me thirty minutes. I have a feeling Liam and everyone else will be going to your place to see if they can find any sign of Landers. I'll tell them you want to stay here, and that I'm going to stay with you. And Emerson?"

"Yes?"

"You can't tell anyone. Liam never breaks the rules. I'm actually shocked he came back with you. What we're about to do is dangerous and very, very wrong." Her mouth was set in a harsh line. "Do you understand?"

"I understand."

Chapter 50

*T*he cicadas sang cheerfully as we drove through the dusky twilight on the way to the Hourglass. It made what I was about to do feel even more surreal, as if I should be catching lightning bugs in a jar and playing flashlight tag instead of resurrecting the dead.

Cat maneuvered her car up the long drive skillfully, keeping a close eye on the rearview mirror. Satisfied that no one had followed us, she pulled over, parking close to a willow tree. The low-hanging branches partially obscured the car.

"We're going to go straight to Liam's old office inside the house. Follow me, and act like you're supposed to be here, no matter who we see or what they say."

"Got it."

"When I open the bridge, you need to focus on when you and Michael went into the lab together. And you have to be careful not to be seen by anyone—I mean *anyone*, Emerson. No matter how tempted you are to call out to Michael, you can't do it until *after* you and Liam have left the lab. You'll have seconds before the explosion."

I looked down at my clothing and hoped it would be enough to persuade him it was a "different" me. We'd cleaned up the warm coat I wore to travel back to save Liam as best as we could, and I'd added a bright green scarf. I had my hair long and loose instead of pulled back in a ponytail. I'd also tucked Kaleb's silver circle into my pocket as a good-luck charm.

"You have to convince him to cooperate. If he refuses, if something happens to you . . ."

She didn't have to complete the sentence. If anything happened to me, no one would be coming back to save us.

"You keep saying 'if.' It's not doing a lot for my confidence."

She grasped my forearm and squeezed. "You need to understand what kind of risk you're taking. Do you?"

I nodded.

I followed her to the house, trying not to look terrified. Cat didn't knock or use a key, just opened the front door and walked in. I caught a quick impression of open spaces and warm colors as she pulled me into a dark room.

She gestured through the doorway. "The hallway leads you to a sitting room. In that room is a set of French doors that exit onto the patio. The patio has a stone wall that you can use as a shield. Once you hit the grass you'll have to make a run for it to avoid being seen."

"What do I do if—"

The question was interrupted by the sound of a door opening and closing. Cat grabbed me, pushing me down behind the desk. Muffled voices filled the air, and then disappeared.

"If you're going to go, the time is now." She lifted her hands and the sphere appeared. Her face glowed in its eerie light. "Are you ready?"

I stood and stepped into the veil.

Chapter 51

The long tube of light was illuminated in the same soft shades of water and silver as the night before. It felt different without Michael by my side, less thrilling, more terrifying. I twisted the ring and concentrated on the date of Liam's death, holding the scene of Michael and me crossing the grass to the lab in my mind. Thoughts of the things we'd said, the things we hadn't said, kept trying to intrude. I forced myself to focus. I could almost imagine Michael's voice in my ear, encouraging me to do the same.

Soon I could hear the unfiltered sounds and see the shimmer that signified the end of my journey. When everything went quiet again, I stayed inside the bridge, scoping out the room, making sure I was alone. All I could see was a faint hint of light shining from an illuminated bookshelf.

It appeared to hold a collection of hourglasses, from the most archaic designs to the most futuristic. I hadn't noticed them when I'd been standing in the room with Cat.

I stepped through the veil and tiptoed to the doorway of Liam's office, peeking my head out just like I had fifteen minutes ago, but in a completely different time. The house felt as empty as it had then. It was now cloaked in a darkness so deep I cursed myself for having not brought a flashlight. I tiptoed toward the French doors that led out to the patio and pushed down carefully on the curved door handles.

Locked.

And then, behind me, the unmistakable sound of footsteps.

Panic clawed its way up my chest. I stopped the scream bubbling in my throat and looked over my shoulder.

I was alone.

Turning my attention back to the doors, I felt for a push button. There was only a deadbolt—the kind that had to be unlocked with a key.

"Okay, think, think, think." I searched for a hook on the wall or a side table, hoping I'd miraculously find what I was looking for. No luck. A memory tugged at me, and I lifted my eyes, catching a glimpse of something sitting on top of the doorframe.

A key.

Exactly where my parents used to store the bathroom key in case I locked myself in when I was little. I stretched as high as I could and cursed under my breath. Too short. I didn't dare jump—if I missed more than once, made too much racket, I might not have time to get outside.

Grateful my vision had adjusted to the dim light, I looked around the room. A plush velvet ottoman sat in front of an armchair fifteen feet away from me. I hurried over to it, praying it was on wheels. Finally, success.

Rolling the ottoman over to the door, I climbed up precariously and knocked the key to the ground. It pinged when it hit the hardwood floor. Not bothering to return either of the items to their proper places, I slipped the key into the lock.

The cold air outside made my eyes water. Lights were on in the lab, and no one occupied the frozen expanse of yard. I crossed my fingers, snuck down the patio steps, and took off running.

I reached the tree line that bordered the woods fairly quickly. I wished I could see something, someone to let me know I'd come out of the bridge in the right time period.

Wish granted.

I scrambled for quick refuge, sliding inside the abandoned building with the rotting floor that Michael had once told me to avoid. Even though the door barely hung from the hinges, I pushed it closed with a soft scuffing sound—the smell of molding leaves and gasoline permeating my nostrils. The floor looked to be in good enough shape. Even if it wasn't, it didn't matter.

I had no other alternatives at the moment.

Landers and Ava were already in the woods, walking straight toward me.

I opened the door half an inch, leaving just enough space so I could see outside.

"I'm sorry."

"You should be. But I forgive you. Do your job well, and maybe I'll reward you."

"Whatever you say, whatever you want."

If possible, the conversation was even more desperate the second time around. At least now I knew that Michael and Liam were in the lab, and that I was merely a few feet away, hiding behind a tree, listening to the same conversation.

That was weird.

I leaned as close to the door as I dared, peering through the crack with one eye.

Jack stood, starkly handsome against the winter landscape, carrying the cool assurance that he was justified in what he was about to allow. It made me hate him even more.

"How long do you think we have before they come looking for us?" Something about Ava's voice was different now, maybe because they were closer to me this time. Or maybe because she sounded scared.

"They won't come looking. There will be no evidence this was caused by a time-related ability." He threw off her worry as if it were meaningless—he was right to do so. According to Kaleb, no traditional authority even knew anything like the Hourglass existed. "Stop being so concerned with the repercussions. You act like policing me is your job."

I tried to catch a glimpse of Ava's face as they walked past the building and into the woods, but all I saw was the flash of a long necklace and a blue coat. Then they were gone.

A rectangle of golden light formed on the frozen grass.

Michael—alive, whole, breathing—leaving the lab to retrieve John Doe from his car.

I watched him hurry to the side of the house, keeping him in my sight line until he disappeared.

This was the worst part, knowing what was about to happen and being forced to wait. I tried to use the time wisely, testing the floor gingerly with my foot. Michael and I needed a quick shelter after I pulled him from the building to avoid the blast.

The wooden planks were stronger around the perimeter of the room, and as I scanned it to find the best place for us to hide, the unthinkable happened.

The logs that made up the interior walls morphed from blank, decrepit slats to ripples filled with life. In the light from a kerosene lantern, the images came faster and faster, a crazy quilt appearing on a rack beside a woodburning stove, a young girl— her dark skin shining like ebony—singing to a carved wooden doll, a young mother rocking a baby in the corner.

"No, no, no." I closed my eyes tightly and opened them again. The images were still there, now with more details filled in. The room had completely transformed. I thought about Liam's words, that ripples were bleeding through the fabric of time. I'd gone from seeing individual people to a jazz trio to a horse-drawn carriage, and now the inside of a whole cabin with occupants intact. How far could the color run—how wide would the ripples spread?

I looked out the window, now hung with homespun curtains. Outside, other tiny cabins formed a kind of semicircle around an open area.

There was no lab in sight.

Do I pop the little girl or her mother and the newborn?

Because one of them had to go. Everything needed to disappear, and quick. I needed to see the present time out of the window, not an entire scene from the past.

The little girl was closest, so she was the winner. Or the loser, depending. I reached out and tapped her gingerly on the shoulder, rather than lunging into her as if my arm was a rapier and she was the target.

The dissolve was different than anything I'd ever experienced.

Instead of an instant pop and poof from the little girl, the fade started at the top of the scene and ran down like rivulets of rain on glass.

Something was very, very wrong, but I didn't have time to think about it. Like a screen wipe in a movie, the lab reappeared, filling in from the top to the bottom. Michael was walking toward the door—dragging John Doe.

I had maybe a minute. I ran, giving no thought to possible exposure. Jack and Ava were secured somewhere in the woods, preparing to do serious damage, and now Liam, Michael, and I were busy arguing in the doorway to the lab. When I reached the side of the building, I pressed my body against it, squeezing my eyes closed. I wasn't sure if I was supposed to see myself.

I wasn't sure I wanted to.

"I'm not leaving you here."

"Go, Emerson. Take these."

"Come with me. You promised we'd be safe."

I sounded desperate. In that moment I realized that somehow I'd known Michael wasn't going to make it out of that building alive. But that was then.

I wouldn't let history repeat itself.

"I promised you that you would be safe, and I don't want you anywhere near this lab. Go with Liam to the car. Please? Time is running out."

"I'm sure Michael knows what he's doing. We're just holding him up."

"Go. Stay safe. I'll get to you when I can."

The second I was positive the pathway to the front door was clear, I stepped away from the side of the building and into the lab.

Michael stood frozen; his shoulders slumped forward, defeated. His fingers gripped the body as if it was a lifeline.

"Michael!"

He looked up, and his eyes widened, filling with fear. Shaking his head violently, he said, "Why are you here? Get out, Em, run!"

"No." Grabbing Michael's wrist, I kicked at John Doe as hard as I could, and the body fell to the ground. It landed with a thud, one arm escaping from the plastic it was wrapped in. The sight turned my stomach. "We both run."

Still holding tight to Michael, I dragged him outside and hauled ass, my feet pounding against the frozen ground. I heard Michael's heavy breathing behind me as he followed me through the woods and into the tiny shack.

Two seconds after the door shut behind us, the lab burst into flames.

Chapter 52

*W*hat did you do? Emerson, what have you done?"

"I saved your life."

"The rules—"

"Don't say anything about rules, or you'll be dead in the future because *I* killed you. No one else is following them besides you, and I'll be damned if some misguided sense of honor makes you do something stupid right now." My heart was so conflicted. Part of me wanted to throw my arms around him and never let go. The other part wanted to rage at him for knowing that he was going to die and choosing to do so instead of stopping it.

"Why did you come back to get me?"

Rage took a clear lead. "Did you even think, for one second, about what losing you would do to me? To your mom and sister? To Kaleb? To all the people who care about you?"

"It was *all* I could think about."

"Then why did you do it?"

"I didn't have a choice. It was the way things were supposed to happen. Once I knew that you would make it back safely—" He stopped. "I had to believe you'd be okay with my choice, eventually. And you were."

"Was I?"

He stared up at the ceiling. "When I saw you, you were being taken care of. You were . . . loved."

"Who was *taking care* of me?"

He met my eyes. "Kaleb."

I shook my head.

"So I knew you had a future. I had to let go of the fact that I wasn't part of it."

"Maybe I don't want a future without you in it." I licked my lips and tried to push down my nerves. How screwed up was I? The prospect of a conversation about my feelings was more terrifying than the drama going down outside the door. "Did you think of that?"

"My death was staring me in the face. I shouldn't have been able to think of anything, but there you were, at the top of the list."

I wondered how I ranked so high.

Another explosion rattled the windows, causing us both to jump.

"We should get out of here," he said, gesturing toward the door.

"We can't yet. There's too much going on outside. We have to wait until some of the traffic clears out. So since we have some time to kill"—I paused, grimacing at my word choice—"I have some things I have to tell you before we go back. So much has happened in the last twenty-four hours."

"You came back to get me that fast?"

"Trust me, it didn't feel fast. I don't know whether to start with the bad news or the bad news," I sighed. "Okay, first. You were right about Jonathan Landers being the murderer."

"I knew it."

"That's not the worst part. He's been living in my loft since the day I met you. Yours, too."

Michael's face registered confusion. "I don't understand."

"No one else does either. Somehow he managed to travel and he's been frequenting the bridge that spans our rooms. I thought he was a rip. I tried to touch him to make him go away and ended up with a handful of glow-in-the-dark goo."

His upper lip curled. "Why didn't I see him?"

"I guess because he didn't want you to. He must have manipulated the bridge and used it to hide."

Michael jerked his head in the direction of the window, where Jack could clearly be seen directing a fire truck across the lawn.

"Why didn't you tell me about him?"

My body went hot with shame. That was a tougher question to answer.

How could I tell Michael that I'd wanted to keep Jack to myself, along with his flattery and attention? I'd thought of him as some kind of guardian angel, and he was nothing of the sort. He was a killer, and he'd been in my home. He'd watched me sleep. I'd been stupid enough to listen when he claimed he wanted to protect me.

"I didn't think it was a big deal at first. And then—then it started feeling like a lie. Like something I should keep secret. I should've known then that it was wrong."

His expression turned pensive. "We both have regrets about things we didn't tell each other."

"In your room, after we kissed . . ." I trailed off. "You said you wanted to kiss me again. But you knew you weren't going to come back. Was it just a kiss good-bye?"

"What kind of kiss do you think it was?"

I knew I'd probably be angry later for letting him off the hook so quickly, but my sorrow turned into some kind of giddy relief that started in my toes and jumped directly to my mouth. Uncontrollable and impulsive.

"I hope it was a kiss good-bye. If so, I think a kiss hello is in order." I fiddled with the knot in my scarf, tightening it, then loosening it. "I mean, I did bring you back from the dead. Basically."

Michael stared at me for a moment before stepping forward to take my face in his hands. The buzz from his touch almost knocked me off my feet.

"It was a kiss good-bye. I didn't think I'd ever see you again, and I didn't want to die without knowing what kissing you felt like." He groaned. "It all sounds so dramatic."

"It was." I remembered the rending of my heart when I thought I'd lost him. "It was terrible."

"I'm sorry."

"I've not forgiven you." I could feel my legs shaking, hear the tears in my voice. "I don't know how long it's going to take me to forgive you, or if I ever will, but I'm so happy that you're here right now."

"Emerson—"

"I don't know what any of this means, but I know that when I thought you were gone, I couldn't breathe. It felt like half of me was missing." I kept babbling, my edit button not only broken, but completely obliterated. "I'm seventeen. Who feels like this at seventeen?"

"Em—"

"And as far as Ava is concerned, or Kaleb, I don't want anyone in the space between us. I—"

"Emerson!" His voice carried urgency.

"What?"

"Please stop talking." He lowered his lips, stopping just before he reached mine. "I can't kiss you when you're talking."

The joy that rushed through my veins eclipsed the pain of almost losing him. I gave one second of thought to the Emerson outside on the grass, the one who was waking up to grief and loss.

Then I let it go, sinking into the kiss, into his body, now whole and perfect and right in front of me.

We knelt, the door cracked open enough for us to see everything taking place in the yard. The flames were almost out. Vehicles were backing up, making slick, muddy tire treads in the grass. The fire chief was directing the traffic jam. Soot and ash covered his face, and his breath crystallized in the night air as he huffed out orders.

"All we have to do is make it to Liam's office," I said. "Cat's keeping the bridge open."

"Let me go first."

I raised one eyebrow.

"I know you can take care of yourself. And me." He looked outside, leaning to the left and right, watching Landers through an inch of space. "This is a precaution. I know the house and the people who could be in it. You don't."

"Point taken."

I stared at the curve of his lips, not thinking about the bridge or the things we'd have to deal with on the other side of it. Just Michael, how grateful I was that he was alive, how much I wanted to touch him. How much I wanted him to touch me.

He kept his eyes on the activity outside. "Emerson. You can't look at me like that. Not right now."

"How do you know how I'm looking at you?"

"I can feel it." He smiled. I couldn't see it, but I could hear it in his voice. He hooked one arm around my neck and gently pulled me to his side. "Hold it. You only told me one piece of bad news.

What else is there, besides the fact that Jonathan Landers has been stalking you?"

"The ripples, they're changing. We both saw the jazz trio at the opening of the Phone Company, but I've seen other things since. The worst happened here, right before I came to save you. This whole room transformed. I looked out the window and saw a scene from at least a hundred and fifty years ago."

"What?" he breathed out.

"I can't explain it. It was like I'd traveled back in time."

"More like *time* traveled to *you*." He paused, thinking. "Rips have been more detailed for me lately, but nothing that intricate. Did you tell Liam?"

I nodded. "He's worried."

"That's saying something. Did he have any explanations?"

"No."

He let go of me and pulled the door open another half inch. "Looks like all the key players are talking to the fire chief."

"We can't go yet," I protested. The crowd might be thinning out, but the grounds still looked too full to navigate without being noticed.

"We can't leave Cat holding the wormhole open for much longer. She's on enemy territory if the people at the Hourglass are still loyal to Landers."

"Just a few more minutes."

"Just a few." He rose and pulled me to my feet.

"Since we're waiting . . ." I grabbed the collar of his jacket, stood on my tiptoes, and pressed my lips to his. His skin was cool at first, but heat flared the second we touched. It warmed me to the tips of my toes and fingers, and I'd have bet cold, hard cash my hair was standing on end, light shooting from each individual strand. I didn't want to open my eyes to check.

He pulled me closer, trailing his mouth along the line of my jaw and down my neck. I held on to his jacket more tightly, pulling him even closer.

"I'm ready to get out of here," he murmured in my ear. "Get you somewhere I can kiss you properly."

"This isn't properly?" I was shaking again. What was it about this boy that made me shake? "If not, can I *handle* properly?"

"I'll do my best to make sure you can." He kissed his way across my cheekbone to my lips, his hands sliding under my jacket, his fingers burning against the cotton of my T-shirt. I couldn't help thinking about how his hands would feel on my bare skin. "Or that you can't handle it. Whatever you want."

I wanted to be alone with him. Really alone. "Maybe we should take this back to my place."

He lifted his head to look at me, a strange expression on his face. I let out a nervous giggle. "That sounded better in my head."

"It sounded pretty damn good out of it."

We reached the house without incident. It almost went too smoothly.

"Did I say thank you?" Michael asked as we ducked into Liam's office. "If not, thank you." He raised our joined hands to his lips and kissed the inside of my wrist.

"I can't remember." I couldn't remember anything. Hello, erogenous zone. "And you're welcome."

He just grinned.

Still holding hands, we stepped into the veil.

I focused on returning to Liam's office. The silver swirls consumed me again, and all I could hear was the occasional ghostly voice or strain of music.

When we reached the veil, Michael whispered, "Stay in the bridge." I'll come back to get you when I'm sure we're in the clear."

"Hurry."

He gave my hand a squeeze and disappeared.

I remained in the bridge alone, focusing on standing still instead of moving forward or backward. It felt so different from traveling. It was as if I was being pushed and pulled, and my life depended on maintaining the balance. The waterlike silver swirls seemed to move clockwise and counterclockwise at the same time. Faces, complete with moving mouths and blinking eyes, faded in and out of focus.

I didn't like it.

Where was Michael?

The longer I waited, the more oppressive it became, and the closer the faces pushed against the surface of the bridge. I could see details now, eyelashes, eyebrows, dimples, and whiskers. The faces pressed against the barrier in waves, and even though I couldn't hear them, it looked like their mouths were forming my name in silent screams of warning.

I closed my eyes. Even after a full three minutes of waiting, I could still see the imprints of their faces on my eyelids.

I had to get out.

I stepped from the bridge through the veil and opened my eyes.

To see Cat.

She was pointing a gun at Michael.

Chapter 53

"What's going on?"

A one-handed shove hit me from behind. Michael caught me in his arms.

I regained my balance and looked up into the face of Jack Landers.

Keeping the gun trained on us, Cat made a beeline to Jack, her eyes blazing. My mouth dropped open as I watched her wrap her body around his and kiss him with more tongue than I ever wanted to see again in my entire life.

Not that I thought I'd be alive much longer.

"Cat?" Michael pulled me behind his back to shield me. If being pushed by Jack had thrown me off balance, Cat's betrayal had me reeling. "What are you doing?"

She touched Jack's face with reverence, focusing solely on him. "I thought you were dead."

"I almost was. The formula kept me alive." Jack took her hand and pressed her fingers to his lips. "I ran out on my last trip back. I thought I was going to be stuck in there forever."

"That's why I came. I hoped you could piggyback on Emerson's gene and exit when she came back through, especially with my exotic matter holding the bridge open. It worked."

Landers's voice was reverent. "Thank you."

"Cat?" Michael said again, pleading.

She ignored him.

"But why? Why did you travel if I wasn't here to help you?" Cat's voice broke and she rested her forehead against Landers's. "You need the formula in your system, and you need me for optimal results. Where did you need to go so badly that you'd risk your life?"

"It doesn't matter. I'm here now."

"Cat," Michael persisted, interrupting them. "*What* is going on?"

"Damn it, Michael. Shut up."

When she turned around, we both took a step back. Her usually serene face was twisted into a venomous expression of loathing. "The Boy Scout routine is old."

"I can't believe what I'm seeing. Are you really *with* him?" Michael asked, his voice thick with anger.

"I realize you have the whole young, idealistic thing going on, but surely you can catch up." She snaked her arm around Jack's waist, leaning her head against his shoulder.

He was looking at me, and his eyes no longer lacked pigment. They were bright blue. And terrifying.

There was a moment of complete silence before Michael spoke again. "Why?"

"Because Jack and I could do more together than we could apart. Because sitting on the sidelines for all those years made me sick." She stopped, looking up at Jack. When she noticed his focus was on me, she cleared her throat and her fingers gripped the gun more tightly. I wrapped my hands around Michael's arm.

"You didn't sit on the sidelines," Michael argued. "You're an integral part of what we do. We can't travel without you."

"You *couldn't* travel without me," she corrected. "Liam hit a scientific jackpot. He created molecularly complete exotic matter—in an ingestible formula. Unfortunately, the exact formula went up in smoke with him when he died."

Michael's muscles grew tense under my fingers. "That's the reason you let us go back to save him. Because you wanted the formula."

"When you discovered that you weren't going to make it back from your little rescue mission, I thought I'd gotten rid of two problems I never expected Liam to come through that bridge with Emerson."

"How could you do this?" Michael whispered. "Liam and Kaleb love you. You're family to them."

"No. Not family. Not even a poor distant relation."

"That's not true." He took a step toward her. "Liam *trusted* you—"

Cat pointed the pistol at Michael's head and cocked the hammer. The bullet slid into the chamber, the sound echoing off the office walls.

"Liam sampled my DNA to get that formula. He didn't even know what he'd discovered, but he still wouldn't give me a copy." No hint of guilt for committing murder touched Cat's eyes or tainted her voice. "So I used it against him. A misunderstanding kept me from retrieving the research before we killed him. As we all know, exotic matter can be quite destructive when it moves as fast as Ava can throw it."

"Ava?" Michael said.

"The fire that incinerated the lab wasn't *normal*, Michael." Cat scoffed. "I really have to question how normal you are, as hard as we pushed Ava to distract you. Seduce you. Poor, poor rejected girl."

"But why?" I asked, looking at each of them, my stomach turning as I thought of how Cat and Landers had manipulated Ava. I wondered if any of us really knew her at all. "Why did you do it?"

Jack answered, "I wanted the ability to time travel. There was no 'recipe' for the formula, but there was a full bottle of pills. Cat was willing to experiment."

Michael shook his head in disgust. "You're both insane."

Jack was quiet for a moment, his eyes calculating. "Are we really? Don't we all have things we'd like to change in our pasts? Wrongs to right? Why wouldn't one change devastating experiences, horrible history, if one had the choice? You know how that feels, don't you, Emerson?"

I couldn't speak. He'd hit too close to home.

The blue of Jack's eyes had faded a bit, and it seemed as if his hair was no longer just blonde, but somewhat gray at the temples. "I always thought I could appeal to Grace to travel back and change things for me, if the opportunity presented itself. Kaleb dealt with so much; surely she would be sympathetic, understand my plight."

"But she didn't," Michael said.

"She argued. Then she connected me to Liam's death. I had to take action."

My face went numb as I struggled against the nausea rising in my throat. "It was you. She didn't try to commit suicide, or Kaleb would have felt it coming. He felt nothing. You tried to kill her."

"I did not," he protested politely. "I simply used my ability."

"Your ability?" Michael asked. "Do you even have one?"

Jack laughed, a doubled-over, out-loud belly laugh. "Not an ability you've ever seen me use. Or rather, not one that you remember. I've not *been allowed* to use it since an unfortunate choice many moons ago. But I carry the same time-related ability gene as the two of you. Just not the travel gene."

"Which one do you carry?" I asked, hating the weakness I heard when my voice shook. "What can you do?"

His answering smile was wide, and the creases in his face were deeper than I remembered.

"I can steal time."

Chapter 54

"How?" Michael asked. "How do you 'steal' time?"

"By stealing memories."

"I don't understand."

"It was so easy to take Grace on a walk down memory lane. As she thought them, I took them, but only the ones keeping her alive. When she had nothing left to live for, there was a handful of prescription sleeping pills *right there.*" He laughed. "It's been rather easy to keep her incapacitated. Such a waste of ability to end her life."

"You stole Grace's good memories. Did you steal Ava's memories, too?" Michael pointed at Landers. "Her blackouts. You were responsible for those."

"Yes." He looked pleased, as if his star pupil had solved a particularly difficult problem. "I stole Grace's memories, and Ava's memories. And yours, Emerson."

My nausea turned to cold dread and coated my throat.

"Mine? What do my memories have to do with this?"

"Everything, really. Grace was out of commission. I needed someone else who could travel to the past. My search for information led me to the files. The files led me to you."

I looked up at him in disbelief. I didn't speak. I couldn't.

"My love, you were quite a different girl when I first found you. You mainly existed to drool and breathe, and you relived each moment of those terrible experiences every night in your dreams." His expression took on a gracious quality, as if he was ready to accept praise. Or worship. "I took the memories of what really happened and I kept them as collateral."

"I don't—what do you mean, what *really* happened?"

"Not only were you on the shuttle bus that killed your parents and all those other people; you were the sole survivor of the accident."

The room seemed to tilt, and the dread in my throat slid down to my gut.

"The grief and the guilt, your multitude of serious physical injuries—it almost ruined you." Jack shook his head. "You never fully recovered."

"No, that's not true." I backed up, hitting the edge of Liam's desk.

"You were institutionalized for a while, and then you went to live with your brother and sister-in-law. They felt guilty, you see. It put quite a damper on their lives." He looked down at me with false pity. "Such a waste for everyone involved. I knew I could change it, so I did. I found you, and I took all those terrible memories. You weren't lucid enough for anyone to notice, and I knew they'd come in handy.

"Then I changed your history. Thanks to that one bottle of pills, Cat and her exotic matter, and a couple of other key elements, I traveled back in time. I ran into you in the hotel lobby, stopped you from getting on the bus. Then I raced up the mountain to make sure it went off the road in just the right place. It needed to be submerged in the lake to slow any rescue efforts. Everyone had to perish." He said the words so casually, dismissing countless human lives. "I knew I was taking a chance, but I believed if I spared you the trauma of your physical injuries and the memory of the accident—and it was truly horrific—you'd recover from that black dog of depression that claimed you so fully."

Michael's breathing sped up. But I couldn't look at him. My eyes were glued to Jack.

"Then I made sure to guide your path through the next few years. I even created a scholarship to your boarding school for someone with your specific needs when life in Ivy Springs became too difficult. When you'd recovered to my satisfaction, the scholarship went away." He beamed and clapped his hands together like a child. I could almost smell the madness. "You came back. To think that thanks to Cat, I did all that work, changed all those years, in just one day."

"No, no, no, no." Black spots formed in front of my eyes as my lungs threatened to explode with the effort of holding back sobs. "You're saying . . . *my parents are dead because of you.*"

"Not at all. I'm saying you are alive—truly alive—because of me. You aren't looking at this logically. Fate claimed your parents, not me. You lived because I chose for you to live. I simply intervened in your circumstances. I saved you." He took a step toward me, reaching out. "This ties us together."

"I'm not tied to you. My whole life is a *lie* because of you."

"But Emerson, love—"

"Stop calling me that." A moan started in my throat, low but persistent. I clamped my hand over my mouth.

"I was so very close to convincing you to trust me. Then I could have shared our history with you under much different circumstances. But I was traveling too often, using too much of the compound too fast. I ran out before I got what I wanted. I ended up stuck in the bridge."

Cat finally spoke up, her voice wrecked with anger. "That's what did it? That's why you ended up stuck in that hole? Making sure some little girl's life was . . . sunshine and kittens, just so you could convince her to do what you wanted?"

"I'd hardly say her life was sunshine and kittens—"

"But taking the risk was needless. You don't need her. I have information about another alternative," Cat said pointedly. "I was planning to tell you yesterday, until Kaleb burst through the door and told us you were missing. Until I thought you were dead."

He stared at Cat for a long moment. I noticed that he no

longer stood straight, but slightly hunched over, as if he needed support. "Another alternative?"

She nodded, and the satisfaction on his face chilled me to my soul.

"The question-and-answer session is over." Cat kept the muzzle of the gun pointed at Michael and me. "You said you brought the computer disk back. Where is it?"

"I'm not sure," I hedged. "A lot has happened since—"

"Don't play with me."

Cat took aim and pulled the trigger.

The glass doors to Liam's bookcase exploded into shards as Michael turned to shield me. I wrapped my arms around his waist and braced for another shot, wishing my body were big enough to protect him instead of the other way around.

When the gun remained silent, I opened my eyes to assess the damage. I had to choke back a sob. The side of Michael's neck was covered in tiny lacerations, blood dotting his skin.

"Surely you understand the gravity of the situation," Cat said over the sound of the last pieces of tinkling glass hitting the floor. "I *want* the computer disk with the exotic matter formula and I want it now. Where is it?"

"Catherine. Be patient," Jack said casually, as if he were discussing dinner plans. A beatific smile spread across his face like slow poison. "I'm sure I can convince Emerson to divulge that particular information."

"How do you plan on doing that?" Cat demanded.

"Making Emerson whole again made life better for all of us. She knows that. Which is why she'll cooperate now that she has a chance to do so." Jack spoke to Cat, but his eyes were on me. His answer almost sounded sensual as it slipped off his tongue. "If she doesn't, I could always give her the pain back."

I swallowed convulsively as the bile rose in my throat. He was talking about his collateral.

Michael reached out for my hand.

"No." I struggled not to sound like I was pleading when I really just wanted to drop to my knees and beg. "I didn't ask you to do what you did. You can't make me help you . . . because of some . . . sick and twisted idea about what I owe you."

Jack's answering smile broadcast his tolerance, as if I were merely misbehaving instead of telling him no. "I did what I did because it was necessary. Consequences be damned."

"Consequences," Michael said under his breath. "All this traveling you've been doing—changing things. It's had an effect, hasn't it? The space-time con—"

"Is fine. We're talking about the formula now." Jack's voice was dismissive. He stepped away from Cat, moving closer to me. "Are there memories you can't live without, Emerson? Those of your parents, healthy and alive? Of who you are at all? Or do you want me to return some of the more . . . unpleasant ones? The time in the hospital? The agony, the grief? Did you really believe it was simply mind-numbing?"

The thought of more pain than I'd experienced already was

almost too much to take. Then Michael squeezed my hand, reminding me that if pain came, I wouldn't have to deal with it alone.

"It doesn't matter what you say." I took a deep breath and looked Jack dead in the eye. "I won't give you the computer disk. I can't hand you the power to hurt anyone else."

As quickly as a lightning strike, Jack was beside me.

Michael tried to step between us, and Cat shoved the gun under his chin. He let go of my hand as he prepared to strike, his intent to fight for control clear. I cried out.

"Michael, don't." Tears escaped to journey down my cheeks. I looked into his eyes, begging. "I need you on the other side of this."

If I survive it.

He stopped cold. The pain began.

I held Michael's face in my mind's eye as my ears filled with the same rush of air that overtook me when Kaleb tried to take my pain. This time the sound pushed its way into my brain. I cried out, my body sliding to the ground in bone-crushing agony as memories flooded my mind.

The slow slide of the shuttle bus, wrapping itself around a tree. Fire, calls for help, the smell of burning flesh and the metallic tinge of blood in my mouth. I knew I was screaming; I could hear myself. I couldn't stop.

The visions kept coming. Squeaky metal wheels on a hospital distribution cart, bringing endless trays of food that went back untouched. My arms, looking as if someone had draped skin over my bones. My body, insignificant under the covers, as if it belonged to a small child.

Thomas, heartbreak written all over his face.

The rushing sound slowed, and I curled up into a ball. Freezing, I shoved my hands into the pocket of my jacket to wrap it around me. I heard Michael begging quietly, the sound more painful than if he'd been screaming directly in my ear. Bits and pieces, pictures of my life, kept coming at me. I had no hope of deflecting them.

Two caskets. A long black hearse. An endless array of pills, the clinical smell of a hospital. Staring at the same spot on the ceiling for days on end. Dru crying. Shock treatment. The feeling of hundreds of tiny needles grafting skin onto my back as the medication haze failed to cover the pain. Staring into the face of a counselor as he talked to me about survivor's guilt. My screaming morphed into helpless whimpers.

"Stop." Michael's voice grew louder. "I'll give you whatever you want. Please don't do this to her. Please."

The pictures disappeared. Except for the pounding in my head, the room went quiet.

Before the memories could take root, Jack's face loomed over me, his expression charitable. I closed my eyes to block him out. The sound of air rushing past my eardrums returned, this time in a vacuum. I could feel the memories slipping away again, leaving nothing but static. I lay there shaking, my muscles as fatigued as if I'd been running for days.

"See, love," I heard Jack say in a tender voice. "I can give. Or I can take away. The choice is yours." His next words were a whisper. "Don't *ever* forget what you owe me."

My cheek lay flat against the wooden floor, tears the only thing between. My head felt too heavy to lift, my eyes too tired to keep open. Jack's invasion of my mind left me wrecked in a ball on the ground. Broken.

"Now," Cat said. "Tell us where the computer disk is."

I shifted slightly and something dug into my ribs.

Cat wanted the disk. And I had it.

"No." I pushed myself into a sitting position as my strength returned in a hopeful rush.

"Emerson, tell them," Michael pleaded. "Tell them where it is. Don't let him hurt you again."

"I say we kill you both where you stand," Cat offered, all the ugliness in her soul manifested in her face. "We can find it without you. There can't be too many places to look."

I found it almost impossible to think over the pounding in my head. "If I tell you . . . where it is . . . what's going to keep you from killing me?"

Cat raised her eyebrows and turned to Jack, now standing beside her.

"Why would I throw away a useful tool, even if there are other options?" Jack said, fingering the chain of the pocket watch. His hair seemed silver in the moonlight shining in through the window. "She's learned her lesson. If we need her again, I'm quite sure she'll comply."

Cat shook her head. "But—"

"Enough." It was one word, but it had the effect of one thousand. Cat might be in control of the gun, but Jack was clearly the one who controlled the partnership. "We have things to do. We don't need any more complications in the way."

He turned away from her and put his hand on the back of the love seat. It appeared he was using it to hold himself upright.

"Emerson. Where is it?"

I worried my bottom lip against my teeth, hesitating, even though my mind was already made up. The adoration that had taken up residence on Jack's face gave me pause.

"Understand. I'm not doing this for you," I said in the strongest voice I could muster as I stood up. "I'm doing this for me."

He smiled.

I zipped and unzipped my jacket nervously. "What are you going to do with it?"

Cat started laughing. Jack silenced her with a glance.

"I have plans."

Drawing down my zipper and sliding my hand into my inside pocket, I pulled out the computer disk. I held it up, praying it was the right one.

"Right here, the whole time?" Jack asked, now resting most of his weight on the back of the love seat.

I nodded.

"How clever. Bring it here, Emerson." Like a good little girl. He raised his hand, palm out.

My pulse jumped as I moved toward him, fully aware that the disk might not be the only thing he had plans for. I held the plastic jewel case so tightly it bit into my flesh.

Jack's eyes were a gray-blue now. Colder than they'd been before. Staring straight into my soul.

He took my hand in his and slid the computer disk case from my grip.

"I'll be seeing you soon." Now that I was close to him I saw that his hair had gone almost completely white. He took a step forward and faltered. Cat rushed to his side, pulled his arm over her shoulder, and helped him toward the door.

Without another word, they were gone.

The second the front door closed, Michael rushed toward me and wrapped me in his arms.

"I thought he was going to take you with him." He covered my face with kisses. "I was more terrified of that than I was when Cat pushed that gun against my throat. Are you okay?"

I couldn't remember what Jack had shown me.

I buried my head in Michael's chest and nodded. Holding on. Just holding on.

"Michael, you've got to get to a hospital. Those cuts—"

"They're fine." He held me tighter. "They're small, already stopped bleeding. But we do need to get out of here. We need to tell Liam that Jack's out of the bridge—that he's got the computer disk with the formula."

"He doesn't."

"What?"

I pulled away to look up at him, shaking with triumph.

"If I did it right, they don't have the formula for exotic matter. They have the formula for Kaleb's emotion control meds."

Chapter 55

*T*he second Thomas laid eyes on me, he grounded me indefinitely.

That's not true, exactly. He hugged me first. But the grounding occurred shortly thereafter.

The couch became my new base of operations. I still wore Grace's duronium ring, and I could see the veil to the bridge too clearly to be comfortable in my room. Forget sleeping in it. I'd also shoved a bookcase in front of the door and forbidden anyone else to go in. Thomas didn't say a word.

But he did start perusing local real estate listings.

The nightmares started on the sixth day of my sentence.

Flames. Bright and hot, licking around me, as I lay powerless, forced to watch. My parents with their eyes open. Unblinking, cold and dead.

That night I woke up screaming. Thomas came to my bedside and sat with me, holding my hand until I calmed down. But I didn't go back to sleep.

The next day I watched a marathon of animated movies, craving a fix of fairy-tale endings. Characters in Disney films mostly started out just like me—orphaned, defeated, alone—and they all triumphed in the end.

Unfortunately, I dozed off sometime shortly after Ariel's misidentification of a fork.

This time I dreamed more than images. I smelled burning flesh, the sickly sweetness of a mass of flowers covering two caskets, the sharpness of hospital disinfectants. I felt shock treatments traveling through my nervous system to my brain, a jolt as a hotel shuttle bus wrapped around a tree. I heard the whine of metal as it broke away and slid down the side of the snow-covered mountain.

I didn't remember any of these things actually happening to me, but I knew in my gut that they did.

I drank two pots of coffee that night.

When Dru woke up the next morning and caught me trying to stay awake by rocking back and forth in a chair and reciting "Casey at the Bat" from memory—backward—she put her foot down. I could hear her arguing with Thomas in their bedroom.

"You can't isolate her right now, Thomas. She might have given us the basics of what happened, but she didn't tell us all of it. She's hiding something. At least let her call Lily. Even prisoners—"

"Prisoners are in prison because they've made poor choices. I'm proud of her for saving Liam Ballard, but damn. Was it really worth it if *that* is what she's turned into?" He lowered his voice, but I'd stopped rocking and had tiptoed over to press my ear against their bedroom door. "I can't watch her be reduced to a . . . shell of herself. We just got her back."

"Then let her make contact with someone," Dru pleaded. "Someone she feels comfortable talking to about whatever it was that happened to her."

He was quiet for a few seconds. "Do you really think that will help?"

"It's worth a try." More silence. "I have Michael's number on my phone. I could call and ask him to come over."

Talking to Lily would have been spectacular—I'd only been able to make contact to tell her I wouldn't be at work—but talking to Michael would be heaven.

Thomas and Dru hadn't allowed me to see or talk to him since the day he'd picked up his stuff from the loft and returned his key to Dru. Even then I'd gotten only a quick hug and a kiss on the forehead, and enough conversation to learn that all interested parties were now back at the Hourglass, trying to figure out how to start over.

Even Ava.

My heart leapt at the thought of seeing him now. So did my feet. Thomas entered the living room to find me curled up in a blanket and absently singing the ABCs.

I'd do whatever it took to talk to Michael. If that included serving up some extra crazy with a side of sauce, so be it.

"Babe?" he called over his shoulder to Dru, watching me with wide eyes as I kept singing, twirling my hair around my finger. "You might want to hurry."

The nanosecond Michael's black convertible turned the corner, I launched myself off the front steps. Before he had it in park, I'd opened the door and jumped across the seat into his arms.

I never thought I could be reassured by someone's presence, simply by knowing and being known. When I looked into Michael's eyes, I centered. He cupped my face in his hands and lifted my mouth to meet his. The kiss consumed every breath, every thought, burning my raging fear down to a smoldering ember.

He moved his lips to the space just under my ear, and his mouth formed the shape of a smile against my skin. "I missed you."

I almost laughed when I realized the needle for the parking meter at the curb was spinning around like a rotary fan set on high. "I missed you, too. But my reprieve is only for two hours."

"I'll take every second of it I can get." He sat up and wrapped me in his arms, cradling my head against his shoulder. "I broke at least ten traffic laws on the way over."

"I can't stop worrying about what's going on, how everyone

is dealing with the fallout. Any word on Cat or Jack?" Saying his name made my chest hurt.

"No. Dune hacked into their e-mails and bank statements. Jack made a huge cash withdrawal in New York City. He purchased two plane tickets to Heathrow with a credit card, but the trail went cold after that. Liam has feelers out, but they haven't been seen."

Jack and Cat, somewhere in the wind. The knowledge hit my subconscious and started brewing up new nightmares.

"What about the Ballards?"

"Liam only comes out of his office to spend time with Kaleb. And to sit with Grace." A wrinkle formed between his eyebrows.

I reached up to smooth it away. "No change?"

He shook his head. "We all hoped bringing her home—letting her hear Liam's voice—would change things. I don't know how he's doing it. I can't imagine how I would deal if it was you. If that isn't enough for him to worry about, it seems the Hourglass is going to be held responsible for Jack and Cat's actions."

"By who?"

"The infamous powers that be."

"Cat mentioned those." I put my arms on top of his and tucked them more firmly around me. "But why? None of that was Liam's fault. He wasn't even *alive*."

"I don't know all the details, but things are pretty bad." Michael held me tighter. "Liam looks like he hasn't slept since the night we rescued him, and Kaleb is actually behaving."

"How is Kaleb?" It felt strange to ask, but I wanted to know. Needed to know.

"He's having a hard time. Doesn't understand why he couldn't feel what Cat and Jack were up to."

I tilted my chin to look up at him. "How's Ava?"

"Managing. Dune found e-mails and texts between Jack and Cat that confirmed what Liam suspected. They used Ava, in terrible ways, the worst of which was forcing her to do things against her will with lies and threats, and then taking the memory of them." Michael's mouth straightened into a thin, angry line. "She had no idea she was the one who blew up the lab."

My stomach turned. I wondered what Ava's dreams looked like.

"What about you, Em?" he asked, reaching up to stroke my cheek with the back of his hand. "We didn't get a two-hour pass to talk about everyone else. Dru told me you aren't sleeping. Why?"

"Well." I stared at the dashboard and reminded myself that I *wanted* to talk to him about what was happening. "When I sleep, I dream."

"About Jack?"

"About all the things he showed me." Tortured me with. "I think my realities are bleeding into each other, Michael. Half the time I don't know which one is real."

"Give me details."

"Sometimes I dream about things that I'm sure happened, but that I don't exactly remember. They're so real—I can smell things. Feel them. They have to be from the reality he showed me." As if he left traces of them to spread like slow poison.

"Do the memories ever come back when you're awake?"

"No."

"Good." Michael nodded, but the worry in his eyes didn't fade.

"Except for one—from a recurring nightmare. It's about Jack, and in it he whispers over and over that . . . that I owe him."

"You don't owe him *anything.*"

"Don't I?" I pushed away from him and sat up. "As sick and wrong as Jack is, if he hadn't interfered in my life, I wouldn't have a life."

"That's not—"

"What if he can find another way to manipulate our circumstances? He's got Liam's files—what if he finds a traveler who has no idea what he or she can do? Someone he and Cat can manipulate." I tried to control my anxiety, but now that I was voicing all the things that had haunted me silently, I couldn't stop. "We don't know what he's done to the continuum. We don't know what he's changed, or who he's changed. We're all balloons balanced on the point of a needle. There will be consequences for what I did—giving him the wrong formula. He'll be back."

"You saw what kind of shape he was in physically. He could be dead by now," Michael argued. "He can't hurt you anymore."

"You know that's not true. He's already done so much damage. Ava, Grace . . ." I finally confessed the thing that had been pressing down on me. "Michael, what if he finds a way to give those terrible memories back to me—and not just in my dreams—and then doesn't take them away?"

"Em—"

"And you . . . us. I know you'd stay with someone you were committed to no matter what the cost. Even if that person was—"

I stopped before the word came out.

Michael's face, so full of compassion, hardened. "Why won't you say it?"

"You don't like it when I refer to myself as crazy." I closed my eyes.

"Because you aren't crazy. After everything you've learned about yourself, I can't believe you almost said that."

I slumped back against the passenger-side door. "But you don't know what it was like, even after Jack changed my true reality into one that was slightly better. How bad things were . . . how sick I was. What if I end up with memories of both?"

"It wouldn't change how I feel. Damn it, look at me." He wrapped his hands around my upper arms and pulled me toward him. My eyes flew open. "I love you—broken in pieces, whole, however. No matter what the future brings. No matter what was in the past."

"I'm scared. I don't want to be, but I am."

"That's okay."

"Is it? Aren't I supposed to be brave, fearless? Isn't that what the world expects?" I didn't feel like a superhero or the star of an action movie. I felt out of balance and terrified.

"Screw what the world expects. Think about all the things you've faced. You cracked, but you didn't break. You're still standing. I'd call that fearless. You've already conquered so much."

"That all depends on which reality you're referencing. The original or the Jack Landers version?" I asked wryly. "Because there's a difference that involves lucidity and basic human functioning."

"Pick one." Michael dropped his forehead to touch mine and lowered his voice. "No matter what your reality looks like, you're the girl I'm in love with today, and the same girl I'll be in love with tomorrow and all the days after that. Not just because of who you *are*, but because of who you *were*."

The tears I'd been holding back finally escaped.

"It's all part of your story, Em. And I want to be a part of your story, too."

I felt it then, the stirring of hope.

"It's okay to be afraid, but you don't have to give in. You have what it takes to fight it."

"You sure about that?"

"Yes." He pointed at my heart. "It's right here. And right here," he continued, touching my temple. "And you have backup when you need it."

He was right.

I had the determination to conquer my fears.

I had the Hourglass, everyone connected to it—Kaleb, Liam, Nate, Dune—people who understood my life and my abilities.

I had Lily, who had stuck by me through everything . . . I had friends.

I had Thomas and Dru, a niece or nephew on the way . . . I had family.

I had Michael, who wanted to be part of my story . . . I had love.

It didn't matter what Landers had done in the past, and in that moment it didn't matter what he could do in the future. It didn't matter who I had been or what I would become.

I had everything I needed.

Chapter 56

We sat together in a wrought-iron chair on the patio, wrapped in each other's arms, watching the sun set behind the redbrick buildings of the town square. The clock in the tower chimed eight times, echoing through the chill in the early autumn air. The sound equaled comfort.

"Before I forget, I wanted to give you this." He leaned back to pull something out of his jeans pocket. "Hold out your hand, please. Oh, and close your eyes."

I obeyed. He slid Grace's ring off my finger, only to replace it with another. This one felt heavier and had a slightly wider band.

"Open."

I opened my eyes to a shiny duronium ring with a row of interconnected, hand-carved infinity symbols encircling the band.

"Michael, it's beautiful. I love it." I placed my hands on his cheeks and the replica gas lamps flickered above us. I whispered my next words—savoring the first time I said them out loud. "And I love you."

"Remember the night we sat here, and I fed you all the clues the future Em had given me to convince you I was legit? The bluegrass, the belly ring—"

"The designated hitter?"

"Yes." He grinned.

"Hmph."

"What else did I tell you?"

"That you had a teddy bear named Rupert."

He rolled his eyes. "About you, and the first time I saw you."

Answering made me feel shy, but I did it anyway.

"That I said I would take your breath away the first time you saw me." I was still holding his face, and he reached up to put his hands over mine.

"You did it then. And you just did it again."

His kiss was sweet, soft, and easy at first. I felt urgency stir just under the surface, but I refused to let the desire to hurry things interfere in the moment. I wanted to savor every single one.

We had all the time in the world.

My brother's voice floated down from the open window. "Emerson!"

Well, as soon as my grounding was over, we had all the time in the world.

"Be right up!"

I stole one more kiss before walking Michael to his car. After I watched him drive away, I approached the steps that led up to the front door, my fingertips on my mouth, lost in my thoughts of him.

I looked up just in time to avoid running into the hoopskirted Scarlett O'Hara wannabe with the silk parasol.

I guess I could have gone through her.

But this time I went around.

Acknowledgments

I was just telling Ethan (known as The Husband) the other day that my mind is so full of stories I can't even remember what's on the takeout menu from the Chinese place. If I've forgotten to thank you, it's not you, it's me. Probably.

Thanks to:

My agent, Holly Root. The words *molten lava holy cats* changed the game. You changed my life. I am forever grateful.

My editor, Regina Griffin. I will always remember our first phone call, when I realized you loved my people like I did, and that we were completely on the same page when it came to this story. I am beyond lucky to have you—I am blessed.

Everyone at Egmont USA. Alison Weiss, Katie Halata,

Nico Medina, Mary Albi, Elizabeth Law, Greg Ferguson, Rob Guzman, and Doug Pocock. I am the luckiest girl in the world to have you as my publishers. Your passion for excellent stories and for your authors sets you apart. Thank you.

My copy editor, Nora Reichard. I feel like I should offer an apology for all my mistakes instead of a thank-you for your meticulous work. (Thanks also for the "LOL"s in the comments. Those were my favorite.)

I don't think I'll ever stop looking at the *Hourglass* cover, and it's all due to designer Alison Chamberlain, and master of perfection, Greg Ferguson. (I was going to add that I make out with the cover daily, but that would be inappropriate.)

There are sales reps, co-agents, and editors out there who I'll never meet. Thank you for your work, and for believing in *Hourglass.* Thank you to everyone at Waxman Literary, especially Lindsey Kennedy, for being so sweet when I call, and for helping me navigate all the crazy forms!

There are readers, and there are readers who are cheerleaders and friends. C.J. Redwine, Kimberly Pauley, M.G. Buehrlen, and Bente Gallagher were some of the first, and some of the best. Special thanks to C.J. for not running when I chased her down the hall that Sunday to ask if she was really a writer, and for the Ninja Root recommendation.

Katie Bartow, Sophie Riggsby, Saundra Mitchell, and Jen Lamoureux. Your e-mails and friendships keep me going. *gives you all a BinBons clone* *and a hug*

Rachel Hawkins and Victoria Schwab. What would I do without you two? I don't even.

Beth Revis. You're kind of a big deal. And not just to me.

Jessica Katina, LeeAnne Blair, and Amelia Moore. You know me, and yet you still love me. How blessed am I? (And the smile in my author photo is thanks to these three.)

If I listed the reasons to thank the following people, we'd be here until the sequel comes out. But I owe bushels to Sally Peterson, Sam Pullara, Leigh Menninger, Kate Hart, Shannon Messenger, Lori Joffs, Coryell Opdahl, Tammy Jones, Jen Corum, Jen Root, Jen Phillips, Jody Boyer, Chad and Meghan Stout, Tracy Carter, Laine and Brian Bennett, Karen Gudgen, Jessica Sendewicz, and Dian Belbeck.

There are a few teachers who always believed, even when I didn't. Dr. Sandra Ballard, I hope you enjoy your namesakes. Mrs. Peggy Crabtree, you endured me twice with a smile on your face. Or was that a grimace? Coach Aubrey, O captain! My captain! Mrs. GeeGee Hillman, you saw something in an eight-year-old girl she couldn't see in herself. Your little turtle finally crossed the finish line.

Keith and Deborrah McEntire. This book wouldn't exist if it weren't for you and your grandchildren-herding skills. Thank you for giving me your boy, and loving my boys. Also, to Elton and Mandy McEntire, for being the best uncle and aunt ever.

Wayne and Martha Simmons. Thank you for making Trixie Belden books my reward for learning my multiplication tables (even though I can't go higher than times three to this day without help), for taking me to the bookstore every Friday night, for letting me have my way with my imagination, and most of all for loving me.

Andrew and Charlie. I love you to the depths of my very soul. All the book deals in the world wouldn't be worth it if I couldn't share them with my boys.

Finally, Ethan. What a journey, and how happy I am to have made it with you. I love you, Mackydoodle. (Shut up. You know I had to say it.)